核心 素養
108課綱

Grimm Brothers Fairy Tales
Reading & Listening Training Book

英文閱讀聽力
素養訓練課

格|林|童|話

U0069965

• 原著 Brothers Grimm　　• 英譯 Margaret Hunt　　• 改寫 Richard Luhrs

108 課綱閱讀聽力素養培植書　　以名著閱讀法及聽重點的聽力訓練策略
用英文故事打造聽讀的素養力！

108課綱閱讀聽力素養培植書！
以名著閱讀法及聽重點的聽力訓練策略
用英文故事打造聽讀的素養力！

閱讀英文故事能培養108課綱強調的閱讀理解能力，在讀故事書時，會反覆演練「理解內容、統整前後文推理、反思評價提出概念」的過程。讀懂故事能**深化閱讀素養力**，也可以**培養更寬廣的思辨分析力與想像力**，更能鍛鍊學習腦！

透過本書精心設計閱讀訓練法中最有效的「**名著閱讀法**」學習策略，循序漸進地掌握閱讀故事的重點，幫助讀者培養閱讀原文書的實力，體驗不用頻查字典就能品味原文小說的感動，實戰練習累積閱讀素養。「**聽重點**」的聽力策略，幫助讀者體驗不用字字聽懂，就能輕鬆聆聽童話名著的樂趣。

《格林童話》是格林兄弟完成的世界經典童話，並譯成一百多種語言出版各地，至今風靡全球。本書選取的英文版本，為瑪格麗特‧杭特（Margaret Hunt）於1884年完成的英譯作品。由於完成年代距今已久，部分用法及用字較艱難，本書特以**全民英檢中級程度字彙**加以改寫故事，並列出其中**使用頻率較高的字彙**，不僅幫助讀者學習經典名著，沉浸於閱讀的樂趣，更能藉由搭配精心設計的練習，同步加深字彙記憶，培養閱讀與聽力的能力。

1 本書精選 **8 篇童話故事**，如〈睡美人〉、〈小紅帽〉、〈青蛙王子〉等膾炙人口大作，帶你品味文學芬芳，提升閱讀素養；搭配彩繪插圖，逗趣生動，增添學習樂趣。

2 本書以每篇故事所**使用的字數**區分難易度，共分 **Step 1** 以及 **Step 2** 兩個學習階段，帶領讀者由淺入深漸進學習。

3 本書共有兩大部分，精心設計各種實用學習幫手，讓你更有效率、更輕鬆地學會閱讀原文書：

> **課本 Main Book** 全英語呈現，藉由學習彩圖字彙、單字英英註釋、課文英文釋義及文法解析等設計，不需字典也能讀懂。

> **聽力訓練書 Training Book** 重點字彙複習，以**聽重點**的聽力策略，引導你無礙聽懂文學名著。

4 讀完一段課文後，隨即有Stop & Think測驗掌握**推論及細節的能力**，以及有Check Up練習各種**常見的閱讀測驗題型**，如字彙選填、是非題及配合題等6種題型變化，不僅驗收閱讀理解成效，也為日後參加英語檢定作準備。

強力推薦給這些人！

- 準備大考學測的學生。
- 想在多益、托福等各種英文考試中得高分。
- 想上全英語教學或雙語教學課程。
- 想把英語根基扎得又深又牢。
- 想順暢閱讀《時代》雜誌推薦小説原著。
- 正準備出國留學的人。

關於格林兄弟的童話世界

　　格林兄弟為十八世紀德國語言學家，哥哥雅各・格林（Jacob Ludwig Carl Grimm, 1785–1863）和弟弟威廉・格林（Wilhelm Carl Grimm, 1786–1859）先後出生於德國萊茵河畔的哈瑙（Hanau），父親為律師，母親為家庭主婦，家中共有九個兄弟姊妹。兩兄弟先後進入馬爾堡大學攻讀法律，之後都擔任過卡色勒圖書館館員、哥廷根大學教授和普魯士皇家科學院院士。而就在他們擔任圖書館館員期間，開始了民間故事的蒐羅。

　　他們認為，童話是一種古老的信仰，為了保存民間文學，他們耗費數十年時間，哥哥負責蒐集各地流傳的故事，弟弟則透過優美的文筆，加以潤飾改寫，以符合當時的語言習慣，可以説是口傳文學彙整的先驅。

　　由於故事來自民間，兩兄弟又堅持忠於「口述文學」，因此早期的格林童話不乏各種寫實的社會現象，內容較為殘酷，並定名為《獻給孩子和家庭的童話》。爾後歷經多次改版，才成為今日我們所熟悉的《格林童話》，為銷售量僅次於聖經的德文作品，與《安徒生童話》、《一千零一夜》並列世界童話三大寶庫。

　　除了在民間文學的保存上具有卓越貢獻之外，兩兄弟本身就是語言學家，也曾攻讀法律，因此在法律、歷史等領域，亦成績斐然。先後出版過《德國文法》、《德國英雄神話》、《德國語言史》等作品，更著手進行《德國大辭典》的編纂計畫，雖未能於有生之時完成，然而兄弟倆對當代及後世的貢獻，已足夠兩人名留青史。

本書分兩大部分，第一部分為全英文的課本，第二部分為訓練書，訓練書是為培養
「聽重點、解全文」的聽力能力而編寫的。

Main Text

Stop & Think

Key Words

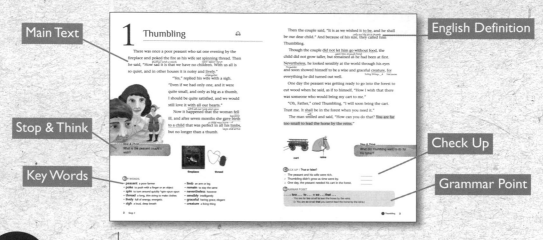

English Definition

Check Up

Grammar Point

Main Book 課本 | 分兩個學習階段（2 Steps），共 8 篇故事。

1 讀課文（Main Text）

首先，只看全英文的課文，不懂的單字、片語或用語，可以透過以下精心設計的
學習幫手了解字義，因此不需字典也能讀懂課文：

● **字彙搭配彩圖呈現**，圖像學習超easy。
● 簡明易解的**英英重要單字注釋**（Key Words），快速擴充字彙量。
● **課文中附註英文釋義**（English Definition）、同義字或反義字，搭配上下文，
　熟練字彙運用。
● **文法解析**（Grammar Point）學習常見句型。

2 試做練習題（Stop & Think / Check Up）

讀完課文後，立即透過綜合測驗題型，檢核文章理解程度及字彙能力。

Stop & Think　引導式問題，**訓練你抓出文章主旨**（details）、**推論文章含意**
　　　　　　　（make inference），以及**培養獨立思考的能力。**

Check Up　6 種英語檢定常見題型，包含**選擇題、字彙選填、是非題及配合題**等，
　　　　　　為參加考試作準備。

Training Book 訓練書

訓練書以配合題 （Vocabulary Practice: Match.）複習字彙，再以聽力填空題（Listen and Fill in the Blanks）引導學生聽關鍵字或片語，聽解原文，同時強化記憶單字發音，提升整體聽力能力。書末附有課本的正確答案和翻譯。

1 Vocabulary Practice: Match.
● for reviewing Key Words

2 Listen and Fill in the Blanks
● to guide readers to listen to Key Words

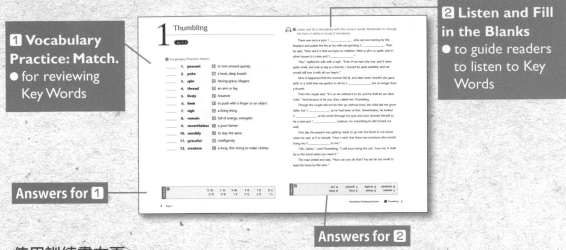

Answers for 1

Answers for 2

3 使用訓練書左頁

首先做**字彙配合題**（Vocabulary Practice: Match.），替字彙選出正確的英英解釋，複習故事中的關鍵字，奠定聽解原文的基礎。

4 聽MP3使用訓練書右頁

播放MP3，先不要看原文，輕鬆聆聽，遇填空處，再仔細聽，寫下聽到的字彙或片語，不確定時可以反覆播放，再閱讀上下文確定答案。

5 再次聽MP3朗讀並複誦

一面看一面讀出聲音，可以記得更牢。本書課文皆由英語母語人士以正確、清晰的發音朗讀。聽課文時，要注意聽母語人士的發音、語調及連音等。最好自己在課文上把語調和連音標示出來，然後大聲地跟著MP3朗誦，盡量跟上英語母語人士的速度。

6 不聽MP3，自己朗讀課文

接著，不聽MP3，自己唸課文，並盡量唸得與母語人士一樣。若有發音或語調不順的地方，就再聽一次MP3，反覆練習。

7 重新閱讀英文課文

現在再回來看課本，再讀一次英文課文，如果讀得很順，練習題也都答對，訓練就成功了。

★ 正確答案請見訓練書書末的〈Answers〉。

Table of Contents

MAIN BOOK

Step 1

1 Thumbling

There was once a poor peasant who sat one evening by the fireplace and poked the fire as his wife sat spinning thread. Then
pushed with a stick   *spin–spun–spun*
he said, "How sad it is that we have no children. With us all is so quiet, and in other houses it is noisy and lively."
energetic

"Yes," replied his wife with a sigh.

"Even if we had only one, and it were quite small, and only as big as a thumb, I should be quite satisfied, and we would still love it with all our hearts."
with all our love and care

Now it happened that the woman fell ill, and after seven months she gave birth
became
to a child that was perfect in all his limbs,
a child was born
but no longer than a thumb.
legs and arms

Stop & Think
What is the peasant couple's wish?

fireplace   thread

KEY WORDS

- **peasant** a poor farmer
- **poke** to push with a finger or an object
- **spin** to turn around quickly *spin–spun–spun
- **thread** a long, thin string to make clothes
- **lively** full of energy; energetic
- **sigh** a loud, deep breath

- **limb** an arm or leg
- **remain** to stay the same
- **nevertheless** however
- **sensibly** intelligently
- **graceful** having grace; elegant
- **creature** a living thing

Then the couple said, "It is as we wished it to be, and he shall be our dear child." And because of his size, they called him Thumbling.

only as big as a thumb

Though the couple did not let him go without food, the child did not grow taller, but remained as he had been at first. Nevertheless, he looked sensibly at the world through his eyes and soon showed himself to be a wise and graceful creature, for everything he did turned out well.

gave him enough food

However

living thing *because*

One day the peasant was getting ready to go into the forest to cut wood when he said, as if to himself, "How I wish that there was someone who would bring my cart to me."

"Oh, Father," cried Thumbling, "I will soon bring the cart. Trust me. It shall be in the forest when you need it."

will

The man smiled and said, "How can you do that? You are far too small to lead the horse by the reins."

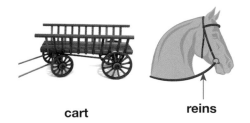

cart   reins

Stop & Think

What did Thumbling want to do for his father?

CHECK UP | **True or false?**

1 The peasant and his wife were rich.   _____
2 Thumbling didn't grow as time went by.   _____
3 One day, the peasant needed his cart in the forest.   _____

GRAMMAR POINT

> • **too . . . to . . . = so . . . that . . .**
>   • You are far **too** small **to** lead the horse by the reins.
>   (= You are **so** small **that** you cannot lead the horse by the reins.)

"That's not important, Father. If my mother will just harness the horse, I shall sit in the horse's ear and tell him where he must go."

"Well," answered the man, "let's give it a try."
let's try it.

When the time came, the mother attached the horse to the
harnessed
cart and placed Thumbling in his ear, and then the little child
put
cried, "Giddy-up! Giddy-up!"
shouted   (a command used to get a horse to start moving or go faster)

Then the horse went quite properly as if with his master, and the cart went the right way into the forest. It happened that just as the horse was turning a corner and the little one was crying, "Giddy-up," two strange men came towards him.

"My word," said one of them. "What is this?"
My God

"There is a cart coming, and a driver is calling to the horse, but still he cannot be seen. That can't be right," said the other. "We will follow the cart and see where it stops."

Stop & Think
How did Thumbling bring
the cart to his father?

master

KEY WORDS

- **harness** to tie an animal to a vehicle
- **attach** to connect one thing to another
- **place** to put
- **properly** correctly
- **turn a corner** to change direction at a corner

- **exactly** right
- **get hold of** to grab
- **amazement** a great surprise
- **aside** to one side
- **exhibit** to show; to display

The cart, however, drove right into the forest and exactly to the place where the wood had been cut. When Thumbling saw his father, he cried to him, "Do you see, Father? Here I am with the cart. Now take me down."

The father got hold _(bring)_ of the horse with his left hand and with the right took his little son _(grabbed)_ out of the ear. Thumbling sat down quite happily on a straw, but when the two strange men saw him, they did not know what to say in their amazement. _(surprise)_ Then one of them took the other aside and said, "Listen. The little fellow would make us rich if we exhibited him in _(showed)_ a large town for money. We will buy him."

Stop & Think
Why did the two strange men want to buy Thumbling?

straw

CHECK UP | Finish the sentences.

1 The cart drove right
2 The mother attached the horse
3 The strange men wanted to exhibit Thumbling

a. in a large town.
b. to the cart.
c. into the forest.

GRAMMAR POINT

- **tell someone / see wh- S (subject) + V (verb)**
  - I shall sit in the horse's ear and **tell him where he must go.**
  - We will follow the cart and **see where it stops**.
- **"-ing" form (present participle)**
  - There is a cart **coming**.

They went to the peasant and said, "Sell us the little man. He shall be well treated with us."

We will be nice to Thumbling.

"No," replied the father. "He is the apple of my eye, and all the money in the world cannot buy him from me."

Thumbling is my dear child

Thumbling, however, when he heard the men's idea, crept up the folds of his father's coat, placed himself on his shoulder, and whispered in his ear, "Father, do give me away. I will soon come back again."

creep–crept–crept

Then the father sold him to the two men for a large sum of money.

amount

"Where will you sit?" the man asked Thumbling.

"Oh, just set me on the edge of your hat, and then I can walk back and forth and look at the country and still not fall down."

placed

They did as he wished, and when Thumbling had said goodbye to his father, they went away with him.

Stop & Think

Do you think it was right for the peasant to sell Thumbling?

fold

whisper

KEY WORDS

- **creep** to move slowly and carefully
  *creep–crept–crept
- **whisper** to speak quietly with one's breath, not the voice
- **sum** amount
- **back and forth** repeatedly from one side to the other
- **necessary** needing to be done
- **good manners** good behavior; politeness

- **take . . . off** ≠ put . . . on
- **slip into** to go quickly into a space
- **stick** to push something in
  *stick-stuck-stuck
- **no use** useless; in vain
- **crawl** to move slowly on the ground with your hands and knees
- **frustration** a disappointed feeling

They walked until it was dark, and then the little fellow said, "Do take me down. It is necessary."

"Just stay up there," said the man on whose hat Thumbling sat. "I don't care. The birds sometimes drop things on me."
drop bird shit

"No," said Thumbling. "I know good manners. Take me down quickly."
politeness

The man took his hat off and put the little fellow on the ground by the side of the road. Thumbling jumped and crept around a little on the ground, and then he suddenly slipped into a mousehole which he had been looking for.
slid
"Good evening, gentlemen. Just go home without me," he shouted to the men and laughed.

walking stick

They ran to the mousehole and stuck their walking sticks into it, but it was no use. Thumbling crawled still
stick-stuck-stuck
useless
farther in, and as it soon became quite dark, they had to
further
go home with their frustration and
disappointment
their empty pockets.

crawl

Stop & Think
Did Thumbling really want to use the toilet?

CHECK UP | **Choose the right words.**

1 Thumbling _____ a mousehole. (crept up | slipped into)
2 Thumbling's father sold him for a large _____ of money. (sum | manner)
3 The two men went home with their _____ and empty pockets. (edge| frustration)

GRAMMAR POINT

> **V (verb) + O (object) (imperative sentence)**
> • **Sell us** the little man. • Do **give me** away.   * "Do" adds emphasis.
>   • Do **take me** down.

04

When Thumbling saw that they were gone, he crawled back out of the underground tunnel. "It is so dangerous to walk on the ground in the dark," he said, "and how easily a neck or a leg can be broken." Fortunately he soon stumbled against an empty

hit his foot and walked awkwardly

snail shell. "Thank God," he said, "that I can spend the night in

sleep overnight safely

safety." And he got inside it.

Not long afterwards, as he was just falling asleep, he heard

later

two men go by, and one of them was saying, "How shall we get hold of the rich pastor's silver and gold?"

steal

"I could tell you that," cried Thumbling, interrupting them.

"What was that?" said one of the thieves in fright. "I heard

fear

someone speaking."

They stood still listening, and Thumbling spoke again. "Take

not moving

me with you, and I'll help you."

Stop & Think

Look at "the rich pastor's silver and gold." Is a "pastor" a place, person, or thing?

(K)EY WORDS

- **underground** below the surface of the earth
- **fortunately** luckily
- **stumble** to walk awkwardly
- **shell** the hard, outer part that protects an animal, egg, or seed
- **safety** ≠ danger

- **interrupt** to speak when someone else is already speaking
- **fright** fear
- **hand out** to give
- **might** power; strength
- **alarmed** worried

8   *Step 1*

"But where are you?"

"Just look on the ground and see where my voice is coming from," he replied.

imp

There the thieves finally found him and lifted him up.

≠ put him down

"You little imp, how will you help us?" they asked.

"Listen," he said. "I will creep into the pastor's room through the iron bars and will hand out to you whatever

give   anything

you want to have."

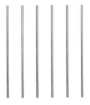

iron bars

"Come on, then," they said, "and we will see what you can do."

When they got to the pastor's house, Thumbling crept into the room, but instantly cried out with all his might,

immediately   strength

"Do you want to have everything that is here?"

hand out

The thieves were alarmed and said, "Please speak softly,

worried   ≠ loudly

so as not to wake anyone up."

in order not to

Thumbling, however, behaved as if he had not understood this and cried again, "What do you want? Do you want to have everything that is here?"

CHECK UP | Answer the questions.

1 Where did Thumbling sleep after he crawled out of the mousehole?
   a. In the pastor's house.   b. In a tunnel.   c. In a snail shell.
2 When did Thumbling creep into the pastor's house?
   a. In the morning.   b. At noon.   c. At night.

GRAMMAR POINT

• it . . . to + V (preparatory "it")
   • It is so dangerous to walk on the ground in the dark.

The maid, who slept in the next room, heard this, sat up in bed, and listened. The thieves had run some distance away in their fright, but at last they felt braver and thought, "The little rascal wants to make fun of us." They came back and whispered to him, "Be serious, and hand something out to us."

naughty child *insult* *spoke quietly*

Then Thumbling again cried as loudly as he could, "I really will give you everything; just put your hands in." The maid, who was listening, heard this quite clearly, jumped out of bed, and rushed to the door. The thieves took off and ran as if a wild animal were behind them, but as the maid could not see anything, she went to light a candle.

moved quickly *left*

light–lit–lit

When she came back with it, Thumbling, unseen, went to the granary. The maid, after she had examined every corner and found nothing, lay down in her bed again and believed that,

who could not be seen

Stop & Think
Look at "went to the granary."
Is a "granary" a place, person, or thing?

maid   **wild animals**

KEY WORDS

- **maid** a female servant
- **rascal** a naughty child or young man
- **take off** to leave
- **light** to start a fire *light-lit-lit
- **examine** to check
- **intend to** to plan to do something
- **arise** to get up *arise-arose-arisen
- **grab** to get hold of
- **precisely** exactly
- **soundly** (sleep) deeply
- **be aware of** to know; to realize
- **awake** to wake up (≠ fall asleep)

after all, she had only been dreaming with open eyes and ears.

Thumbling had climbed up into the hay and found a beautiful place to sleep. There he intended to rest until daylight
planned
and then go home again to his parents.

But that was not what happened.

Truly, there is much worry and pain in this world. When the
Really
day began, the maid arose from her bed to feed the cows. Her
arise–arose–arisen
first walk was into the barn, where she grabbed an armful of hay,
the amount of hay that fits in one's arm
and precisely that very one in which poor Thumbling was lying
exactly
asleep. He, however, was sleeping so soundly that he was aware
of nothing and did not awake until he was in the mouth of a
wake up
cow, who had picked him up with the hay.
≠ put him down

barn

hay

Stop & Think
Did the maid find Thumbling in the barn?

CHECK UP | Fill in the blanks with the correct words.

> thieves   rascal   light   soundly

1 The little _____ wants to make fun of us.
2 Thumbling was sleeping so _____ in the barn.
3 The _____ had run some distance away in their fright.
4 The maid went to _____ a candle.

GRAMMAR POINT

> **had + p.p. (past perfect: earlier past)**
>   • Thumbling **had climbed** up into the hay and found a beautiful place to sleep.

"Oh, no!" he cried. "How have I got into the wool-cleaning mill?"

But he soon discovered where he was. Then he had to take care not to let himself
watch out
get between the cow's teeth and be torn
tear–tore–torn
apart, but he was therefore forced to slip
move
down into the stomach with the hay.

"In this little room there are no windows," he said, "and no sun shines in, nor will a candle be lit." His surroundings were especially unpleasing to him, and the worst was that more and
≠ satisfying
more hay was always coming in through the door, and the space growing smaller and smaller. At last, in his anguish, he cried
becoming   *pain; worry*
as loudly as he could, "Bring me no more fodder! Bring me no more fodder!"
food for animals

Stop & Think
Was Thumbling in a real room?

tear apart

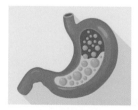
stomach

fodder

KEY WORDS

- **mill** a factory that makes cloth or flour
- **discover** to realize; to find out
- **tear apart** to break something violently into small pieces * tear-tore-torn
- **be forced to** to do against one's will
- **surroundings** the place around you
- **unpleasing** ≠ satisfying

- **realize** to understand
- **terrified** extremely afraid; frightened
- **stool** a seat without a back
- **spill** to drop or pour liquid suddenly
- **evil** extremely bad; cruel
- **spirit** ghost

The maid was just then milking the cow, and when she
getting milk from a cow
heard someone speaking and saw no one and realized that
it was the same voice that she had heard in the night. She
was so terrified that she slipped off her stool and spilled
frightened   *fell*
the milk.

stool

She ran quickly to her master and said, "Oh heavens,
My goodness
Pastor, the cow has been speaking."

"You are mad," replied the pastor, but he went himself

cowshed

to the cowshed to see what was there. He had just set his
a building where cows are kept   *put*
foot inside, however, when Thumbling again cried, "Bring
me no more fodder! Bring me no more fodder!"

Then the pastor himself was alarmed, thinking that an

spirit

evil spirit had gone into the cow, and ordered her to be
an evil spirit had controlled the cow
killed. She was killed, but her stomach, with Thumbling
inside, was thrown on the dunghill.
animal waste

dunghill

Stop & Think
Why was the cow killed?

CHECK UP | True or false?

1 Thumbling was finally safe. _____
2 The pastor thought that an evil spirit had gone into the maid. _____
3 The maid felt terrified in the barn. _____

GRAMMAR POINT

> **S (subject) + V (verb) . . . , nor Modal + S (subject)**
> • No **sun shines** in, **nor will a candle** be lit.

Thumbling had great difficulty in working his way out. He
finding his way out
succeeded in getting some room, but just as he was going to
space
thrust his head outside, a new misfortune occurred. A hungry
thrust–thrust–thrust   *terrible event*   *happened*
wolf ran up and swallowed the whole stomach at one gulp.
                                                 ≠ eat slowly

Thumbling did not lose courage. "Perhaps," he thought, "the
wolf will listen to what I have got to say." And he called to the
wolf from out of his belly, "Dear wolf, I know of a magnificent
feast for you."
excellent meal

"Where is it to be had?" said the wolf.
      Where can I eat it?
"In such and such a house. You must creep into it through
      some; ≠ specific
the kitchen sink, and you will find cakes, bacon, and sausages,
and as much of them as you can eat." And he described to the
wolf exactly his father's house.

| gulp | belly | bacon | sausages |

Stop & Think

What did Thumbling say to
make the wolf bring him home?

KEY WORDS

- **difficulty** a difficult thing or time; hardship
- **thrust** to push forward *thrust–thrust–thrust
- **misfortune** a terrible event
- **swallow** to make food go down your throat
- **at one gulp** ≠ eat slowly
- **magnificent** excellent; wonderful

- **squeeze in** to try to get into a small place
- **content** the feeling of satisfaction
- **violent** loud and unpleasant (≠ soft)
- **rage** to show great anger
- **likewise** in the same way
- **strength** power and energy

The wolf did not need to be told this twice. He squeezed himself in at night through the sink, and ate to his heart's content [to his satisfaction] in the pantry. When he had eaten his fill [he had eaten as much as he could], he wanted to go out again, but he had become so big that he could not go out the same way. Thumbling had expected this, and now he [predicted] began to make a violent noise in the wolf's body and raged and [showed anger] screamed as loudly as he could.

"Will you be quiet?" said the wolf. "You will wake up the people."

"What do I care?" replied the little fellow. "You have eaten your fill, and I will celebrate likewise." And he began once more [in the same way] to scream with all his strength.

squeeze in

Stop & Think

Look at "in the pantry." Is a "pantry" a person, place, or thing?

CHECK UP | Put the events in order by marking them 1, 2, 3, and 4.

_____ The wolf ate the cow's stomach at one gulp.
_____ Thumbling told the wolf about a feast.
_____ Thumbling was going to thrust his head outside.
_____ The wolf ate to his heart's content.

GRAMMAR POINT

— **need to / begin to**
- The wolf did not **need to** be told this twice.
- He **began to** make a violent noise in the wolf's body.
- And he **began** once more **to** scream with all his strength.

At last his father and mother were aroused by the noise,
woken up
ran to the kitchen, and looked in through the opening in the
door. When they saw that a wolf was inside, they ran away. The
husband fetched his axe, and the wife fetched the scythe. "Stay
got and brought back
behind," said the man when they entered the room. "When I
have hit him with the axe, if he is not killed by it, you must cut
him down and chop his body into pieces."

Then Thumbling heard his parents' voices and cried, "Dear
Father, I am here. I am in the wolf's
body."

The father, full of joy, said,
"Thank God, our dear child
has found us again." And he
told the woman to take away
her scythe, so that Thumbling
would not be hurt by it. After
that he raised his arm and
lifted
struck the wolf so powerfully on his
hit

Stop & Think
Why did the peasant tell his
wife to take away her scythe?

scythe

axe

scissors

KEY WORDS

- **fetch** to get something and bring it back
- **chop** to cut into pieces
- **sorrow** sadness
- **go through** to experience
- **for one's sake** for one's good or benefit

- **breathe** to take air into your body
- **riches** money; wealth
- **embrace** to hug
- **spoil** to damage
- **journey** a long trip

head that he fell down dead, and then the peasant and his wife got knives and scissors to cut the wolf's body open and bring the little fellow out.

"Ah," said the father, "what sorrow we have gone through for your sake."

We have experienced much sadness because of you.

"Yes, Father, I have traveled the world a great deal. Thank heaven, I breathe fresh air again."

a lot

"Where have you been, then?"

"Ah, Father, I have been in a mouse's hole, in a cow's stomach, and then in a wolf's belly. Now I will stay with you."

"And we will not sell you again, not for all the riches in the world," his parents said, and they embraced and kissed

wealth

hugged

their dear Thumbling. Then they gave him something to eat and drink and had some new clothes made for him, for his old ones had been spoiled on his journey.

damaged

Stop & Think

Did Thumbling's father regret selling Thumbling?

CHECK UP | **Choose the right words.**

1 The peasant _____ his axe. (chopped | fetched)
2 Thumbling's parents had gone through _____ . (sorrow | riches)
3 Thumbling's clothes had been _____. (spoiled | raised)

GRAMMAR POINT

so that . . . / so . . . that . . .
- And he told the woman to take away her scythe, **so that** Thumbling would not be hurt by it.
- He raised his arm and struck the wolf **so** powerfully on his head **that** he fell down dead.

2 Little Red Riding Hood

Once upon a time, there was a dear little girl who was loved by everyone who looked at her, but most of all by her grandmother, and there was nothing that the grandmother would not have given the child. *her grandmother gave her everything she could to the child* Once she gave the girl a little hood of red velvet, which suited her so well that she would *looked so good on her* never wear anything else. So she was always called Little Red Riding Hood.

One day her mother said to her, "Come, Little Red Riding Hood. Here is a piece of cake and a bottle of wine. Take them to your grandmother. She is ill and weak, and they will do her good. *be good for her health* Set out before it gets hot, and while you are going, walk nicely *Start your journey* and quietly and do not run off the path, or you may fall and *leave the road* break the bottle, and then your grandmother will get nothing. And when you go into her room, don't forget to say good morning, and don't look into every corner before you do it." *greet your grandmother before you do anything else*

Stop & Think
When did Little Red Riding Hood set out for her grandmother's house?

hood

velvet

KEY WORDS

- **suit one well** (clothes) to look good on one
- **do one good** to be good for one's health; to benefit one
- **set out** to start a journey *set-set-set
- **run off** to leave (≠ stay)

- **look into** to check; to investigate
- **give one's word** to promise
- **to one's** to one's house
- **be to** should; must

"I will take great care," said Little Red Riding Hood to her
I will be careful.
mother, and gave her word on it.
promised;≠ broke her word
  The grandmother lived out in the woods, about two miles from

the village, and just as Little Red Riding Hood entered the woods,

a wolf met her. She did not know what an evil creature he was,
living thing
and was not at all afraid of him.

"Good day, Little Red Riding Hood,"

said the wolf.

"Thank you kindly, wolf."

"Where are you going so early?"

"To my grandmother's."
To my grandmother's house.
"What have you got in your apron?"

"Cake and wine. Yesterday was baking

day, so my poor sick grandmother is to
should
have something good to make her

stronger."

apron

Stop & Think
What might the wolf do when he
finds out where the grandmother
lives?

CHECK UP | **Finish the sentences.**

1 The grandmother lived out
2 The grandmother gave the little girl
3 The mother gave the little girl
4 Little Red Riding Hood kept the wine and cake

a. wine and cake.
b. in her apron.
c. a little hood of red velvet.
d. in the woods.

GRAMMAR POINT

> • **(reason) . . . , so . . . (result)**
>   • Yesterday was baking day, **so** my poor sick grandmother is to have something good to
>   make her stronger.

"Where does your grandmother live?"

"A good mile farther on in the woods. Her house
At least a mile
stands under the three large oak trees, and the nut

trees are just below. You surely must know it," replied
certainly
Little Red Riding Hood.

oak tree

The wolf thought to himself, "What a tender young

creature, and what a nice fat mouthful! She will be
What a delicious, juicy meal for me!
better to eat than the old woman. I must act cleverly,

so as to catch both." So he walked for a short time by
in order to
the side of Little Red Riding Hood, and then he said,

nut tree

"See, Little Red Riding Hood, how pretty the flowers

are about here! Why do you not look around? I believe,
around
too, that you do not hear how sweetly the little birds

are singing. You walk seriously along as if you were

going to school, while everything else out here in the

woods is merry."

Stop & Think

Why did the wolf want Little Red
Riding Hood to look around?

mouthful

KEY WORDS

- **tender** easy to eat and cut (≠ tough)
- **so as to** in order to
- **merry** causing joy and happiness; pleasant
- **Suppose . . . ?** What if . . . ?
- **a bunch of** a group of things

- **please** to make one happy
- **get (to)** to arrive
- **whenever** every time something happens
- **meanwhile** while something else is happening
- **straight** right away; immediately

Little Red Riding Hood raised her eyes, and when she saw the sunlight dancing here and there through the trees and pretty flowers growing everywhere, she thought, "Suppose I take Grandmother a fresh bunch of flowers? That would please her, too. It is so early in the day that I shall still get there in time." And so she ran from the path into the woods to look for flowers. And whenever she had picked one, she imagined that she saw a still prettier one farther on, and ran after it, and so went deeper and deeper into the woods.

shining
What if *bring*
make her happy
I will arrive there early enough.
every time
thought

Meanwhile, the wolf ran straight to the grandmother's house and knocked at the door.

While Little Red Riding Hood was picking flowers *immediately*

"Who is there?"

"Little Red Riding Hood," replied the wolf. "I am bringing cake and wine. Open the door."

"Lift the latch," called out the grandmother. "I am too weak to get up."

latch

Stop & Think

Did Little Red Riding Hood run off the path?

CHECK UP | **True or false?**

1 The wolf pretended to be Little Red Riding Hood.   _____
2 The grandmother got up and opened the door.   _____
3 Little Red Riding Hood went straight to her grandmother's house.   _____

GRAMMAR POINT

What . . . ! / How . . . ! (exclamation)
- **What** a tender young **creature**!
- **What** a nice fat **mouthful**!
- **How pretty** the flowers are about here!

The wolf lifted the latch, the door flew open, and without
saying a word he went straight to the grandmother's bed and ate

opened quickly

her. Then he put on her clothes, dressed himself in her cap, laid
himself on the bed, and closed the curtains.

Little Red Riding Hood, however, had been running about
picking flowers, and when she had gathered so many that she

running around

could carry no more, she remembered her grandmother and
continued on the way to her house.

She was surprised to find the cottage door standing open,
and when she went into the room she had such a strange feeling
that she said to herself, "Oh dear, how uncomfortable I feel
today, and at other times I like being with Grandmother."

I usually like being with Grandmother, but I feel something is wrong today.

Stop & Think

How did Little Red Riding Hood
feel when she went into the
room?

cottage

curtain

 WORDS

- **run about** to run around
- **gather** to collect
- **cottage** a small house in the country
- **uncomfortable** ≠ comfortable
- **receive** to get
- **reply** an answer

She called out "Good morning," but received no answer. So she went to the bed and opened the curtains. There lay her grandmother with her cap pulled far over her face, looking very strange.

covering her face

"Oh, Grandmother," she said, "what big ears you have."

"The better to hear you with, my child," was the reply.

answer

"But Grandmother, what big eyes you have," she said.

"The better to see you with, my dear."

"But Grandmother, what large hands you have."

"The better to hug you with."

"Oh, but Grandmother, what a terribly big mouth you have."

"The better to eat you with."

Stop & Think
What weird things did Little Red Riding Hood notice when she saw her grandmother?

CHECK UP | Fill in the blanks with the correct words.

> received   cottage   curtains   gathered

1 Little Red Riding Hood had _____ so many flowers that she could carry no more.
2 The wolf closed the _____.
3 She was surprised to find the _____ door standing open.
4 When Little Red Riding Hood called out "Good morning," she _____ no answer.

GRAMMAR POINT

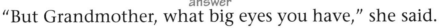

• **find + O (object) + V-ing**
  • She was surprised to **find the cottage door standing** open.

And as soon as the wolf had said this, with one bound he was
jump
out of the bed and swallowed up Little Red Riding Hood.

When the wolf had satisfied his hunger, he lay down again in
eaten to his heart's content
the bed, fell asleep and began to snore very loudly. A hunter was
just then passing the house, and thought to himself, "How the
old woman is snoring! I must see if she wants anything."

So he went into the room, and when he came to the bed,
he saw that the wolf was lying in it. "Do I find
you here, you old criminal?" he said. "I have
(The wolf had been doing bad things for a long time.)
searched for you for a long time."
looked for
Then, just as he was going to
fire at the wolf, he realized that
shoot
the wolf might have eaten the
grandmother and that she might
still be saved, so he did not fire,
but took a pair of scissors and
began to cut open the stomach
of the sleeping wolf. When he
had made two snips, he saw the
two small cuts with scissors
little red hood shining.

Stop & Think

Why didn't the hunter fire
at the wolf?

KEY WORDS

- **bound** a quick, long jump
- **snore** to breathe loudly during sleep
- **criminal** one who seriously breaks the law
- **search for** to look for
- **fire at** to shoot
- **pop out** to come out suddenly

- **frightened** scared
- **barely** almost not at all; hardly
- **collapse** to fall down suddenly
- **at once** right away; immediately
- **delighted** very happy; very pleased

Then he made two more snips, and the little girl popped out, crying, "Ah, how frightened I have been. How dark it was inside the wolf." And after that the old grandmother also came out alive, but barely able to
hardly
breathe. Little Red Riding Hood, however, quickly fetched
got and brought back
some great stones with which they filled the wolf's belly,
put the stones in the wolf's belly
and when he awoke he wanted to run away, but the stones were so heavy that he collapsed at once and fell
immediately
dead.

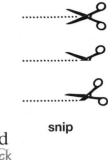

snip

pop out

Then all three were delighted. The hunter cut off the
very happy
wolf's skin and went home with it. The grandmother ate the cake, drank the wine which Little Red Riding Hood had brought, and felt better. But Little Red Riding Hood thought to herself, "As long as I live, I will never again
For the rest of my life
leave the path by myself to run into the woods when my
run off
mother has told me not to do so."

Stop & Think
What did Little Red Riding Hood learn after this terrible event?

CHECK UP | Answer the questions.

1 How did the hunter save Little Red Riding Hood and her grandmother?
   a. With a gun.   b. With a pair of scissors.   c. With stones.
2 Why did the hunter stop at the grandmother's house?
   a. He heard her snoring.   b. He saw her killing the wolf.   c. He wanted to rest.

GRAMMAR POINT

as soon as (the moment)
   • And **as soon as** the wolf had said this, with one bound he was out of the bed and swallowed up Little Red Riding Hood.

It is also said that once when Little Red Riding Hood was
one time
again taking cakes to her old grandmother, another wolf spoke
to her, and tried to lure her away from the path. Little Red
persuade her to leave the path
Riding Hood, however, was careful, went straight forward on
her way, and told her grandmother that she had met the wolf
and that he had said good morning to her, but with such an evil
his eyes looked evil
look in his eyes that she was certain he would have eaten her up
if they had not been on a public road.

"Well," said the grandmother, "we will shut the door, and he
may not come in."

Soon afterwards the wolf knocked and cried, "Open the door,
Grandmother! I am Little Red Riding Hood, and I am bringing
you some cakes." But they did not speak or open the door.
The wolf crept two or three times around the house and at last
jumped onto the roof, planning to wait until Little Red Riding
Hood went home in the evening and then to sneak after her
and eat her in the darkness. But the grandmother knew what he
after the sun had set
was thinking.

Stop & Think

What did Little Red Riding Hood
do when she met another wolf?

KEY WORDS

- **lure** to persuade one to do something wrong
- **onto** = on to
- **sneak (in)** to go in secretly
- **pail** a bucket
- **sniff** to smell quickly

- **stretch** to pull one's body to full length
- **keep one's balance** ≠ fall down
- **drown** to die under water
- **harm** to hurt someone

In front of the house was a great stone trough, so she said to the child, "Take the pail, my dear. I made some sausages yesterday, so carry the water in which I boiled them to the trough." Little Red Riding Hood carried water until the great trough was quite full. Then the smell of the sausages reached the wolf,

the wolf smelled the sausages

and he sniffed, looked down, and at last stretched out his neck so far that he could no longer keep his balance and

he fell down

began to slip, and slid down from the roof straight into

directly

the great trough, and he drowned.

couldn't breathe in the water and died

But Little Red Riding Hood went happily home, and no one ever did anything to harm her again.

trough

pail

Stop & Think
Where did the second wolf die?

CHECK UP | Put the events in order by marking them 1, 2, 3, and 4.

_____ Little Red Riding Hood carried water until the great trough was quite full.
_____ The wolf slid down from the roof straight into the great trough, and he drowned.
_____ Little Red Riding Hood told her grandmother that she had met the wolf.
_____ The wolf tried to lure Little Red Riding Hood away from the path.

GRAMMAR POINT

• **If + had + p.p. . . . , . . . would + have + p.p. (unreal past condition)**
  • He **would have eaten** her up if they **had not been** on a public road.
    (= If they **had not been** on a public road, he **would have eaten** her up.)

3 The Golden Goose

There was a man who had three sons, the youngest of whom, called Dummling, was despised, mocked, and sneered at on
≠ respected   *made fun of*   *looked down on*
every occasion.

One day the man's eldest son wanted to go into the forest to cut wood, and before he went, his mother gave him a beautiful sweet cake and a bottle of wine so that he would not suffer from hunger or thirst.

When he entered the forest, he met a little grey-haired old man who wished him good day and said, "Do give me a piece of cake out of your pocket, and let me have a mouthful of your
the amount of wine that fits into one's mouth
wine. I am so hungry and thirsty." But the clever son answered, "If I give you my cake and wine, I shall have none for myself. Go away." And he left the little man standing there and went on.

Stop & Think
How was Dummling treated on every occasion?

grey-haired

 WORDS

- **despise** to look down on (≠ respect)
- **mock** to make fun of
- **sneer at** to smile or speak in an unkind way
- **occasion** a time when something happens
- **suffer from** to feel pain in one's body or mind

- **thirst** the feeling of needing to drink water
- **stroke** a hit or strike at something
- **bandage** to cover a wound with a bandage
- **be one's doing** be one's fault or responsibility
- **as well** too
- **punishment** the act of punishing

But when he began to chop down a tree, it was not long before he made a bad <u>stroke</u>, and the axe cut him on the arm, *cut*
so that he had to go home and <u>have it bandaged up</u>. And this *have his arm covered with a bandage*
was the little grey man's doing. *And the little man had caused the injury.*

After this the second son went into the forest, and his mother gave him, like the eldest, a cake and a bottle of wine. The little old grey man met him as well, and asked him for a piece of cake and a drink of wine. But the second son too said, <u>sensibly</u> *very sensibly*
enough, "What I give you will be taken away from myself. Go *If I give you the cake, I will have no cake to eat.*
away." And he left the little man standing there and went on.

His punishment, however, was not *The second son received his punishment right away.*
<u>delayed</u>. When he had made a few cuts at the tree, he struck himself in the leg, so that he had to be carried home.

Stop & Think
Why did the grey-haired old man punish the eldest and second sons?

bandage

CHECK UP | True or false?

1 Dummling was respected on every occasion. _____
2 The eldest son had to have his leg bandaged up. _____
3 The punishment of the second son was not delayed. _____

GRAMMAR POINT

leave someone doing something
- And he **left the little man standing** there and went on.

ashes

ash cakes

Then Dummling said, "Father, do let me go and cut wood." The father answered, "Your brothers have hurt themselves doing it. Don't try it, because you do not understand anything about it." But Dummling begged so long that at last his father said, "Just go, then; you will get wiser by hurting yourself." His mother gave him a cake made with water and baked in the ashes, and with it a bottle of sour beer.

Your brothers have hurt themselves by trying to cut wood.

for such a long time

you will learn a lesson

When Dummling came into the forest, the little old grey man met him, greeted him, and said, "Give me a piece of your cake and a drink out of your bottle. I am so hungry and thirsty."

Dummling answered, "I have only ash cake and sour beer. If that pleases you, we will sit down and eat." So they sat down, and when Dummling pulled out his ash cake,

a cake baked in ashes

Stop & Think
Did Dummling get the same cake and wine as his brothers had gotten?

 WORDS

- **beg** to ask strongly for something
- **ash** soft grey powder from burned things
- **have a good heart** to be a good person
- **feather** the thing that cover a bird's body
- **pure** not mixed with something else
- **inn** a place to stay overnight; a small hotel

it was a fine sweet cake, and the sour beer had become

The little grey-haired old man magically changed the cake and wine.

good wine. So they ate and drank, and after that

the little man said, "Since you have a good

Because you are a kind person,

heart and are willing to share what you

have, I will give you good luck. There

stands an old tree; cut it down, and you

will find something in its roots." Then the

little man left him.

Dummling went and cut down the

tree, and when it fell there was a goose

sitting in the roots with feathers of pure

gold. He lifted her up, took her with

feathers made from pure gold

him, and went to an inn where he

thought he would stay for the night.

The owner had three daughters, who

saw the goose and were curious to

know what such a wonderful bird could be, and

each wanted to have one of its golden feathers.

Stop & Think

Why did the old grey-haired man give Dummling the goose?

feathers

CHECK UP | Finish the sentences.

1 Dummling's mother gave him
2 The old grey man gave Dummling
3 The daughters wanted to have

a. one of the goose's golden feathers.
b. ash cake and sour beer.
c. good luck.

GRAMMAR POINT

- **Since (reason) . . . ,**
  - **Since** you have a good heart and are willing to share what you have, I will give you good luck.
    (= Because you have a good heart and are willing to share what you have, I will give you good luck.)

The eldest daughter thought, "I shall soon find an opportunity to pull out a feather." And as soon as Dummling had gone out, she grabbed the goose by the wing, but her fingers and hand remained stuck to it.

she could not pull her fingers or hand away from the wing

The second came soon afterwards, thinking only of how she might get a feather for herself, but as soon as she had touched her sister, she was stuck too.

At last the third daughter came with the same idea, and the others screamed out, "Keep away, for goodness' sake,

(a phrase used to express surprise)

keep away!" But she did not understand why she should keep away. "The others are there," she thought, "so I may as well be there too,"

should for the same reason

and she ran to them, but as soon as she had touched her sister, she remained stuck to her. So they all had to spend

Stop & Think

What happened when the eldest daughter grabbed the goose by the wing?

KEY WORDS

- **stuck** unable to separate; fixed
- **scream** to shout very loudly with emotion
- **hang on to** to hold tightly

- **wherever** to or in any place
- **shame** the feeling of embarrassment or guilt
- **good-for-nothing** lazy and useless

the night with the goose.

The next morning Dummling took the goose under his arm and left, without worrying about the three girls who were hanging on to it. They had to run after him again and again, now left, now right, wherever his legs took him.
<u>any place he went</u>

In the middle of the fields the parson met them, and when he saw them he said, "Shame on you, you good-for-nothing girls. <u>You should feel embarrassed</u> <u>you girls are lazy and useless</u> Why are you running across the fields after this young man? Is that polite?" At the same time he grabbed the youngest by (In old times, it was polite for women to keep their distance from men.) the hand to pull her away, but as soon as he touched her, he too became stuck, and was himself forced to run behind them.

field

parson

Stop & Think

How many people were running after Dummling and his goose?

CHECK UP | **Answer the questions.**

1 Why did the daughters want to touch the goose?
   a. To mock Dummling.   b. To take care of it.   c. To get its feathers.
2 Who did the three daughters meet in the middle of the fields?
   a. The owner of the inn.   b. The grey-haired old man.   c. The parson.

GRAMMAR POINT

> **without + V-ing**
> • The next morning Dummling took the goose under his arm and left, **without worrying** about the three girls who were hanging on to it.

🎧 **17**

Before long the bell-ringer came by and saw his master, the
In a short time
parson, running behind the three girls. He was shocked at this

and called out, "Hi, Parson! Where are you going so quickly? Do

not forget that we have a christening today." Running after the
(the ceremony in which a parson officially gives a child a name)
parson, he took him by the sleeve, and was stuck to it. While
grabbed the parson's sleeve
the five were running in this way one behind the other, two

workmen came with their hoes from the fields, and the parson

called out to them and begged that they would set him and the

bell-ringer free. But they had just touched the bell-ringer when
separate them from each other
they were stuck fast, and now there were seven people running

behind Dummling and the goose.

bell-ringer   **sleeve**   **hoe**

Stop & Think

How did the bell-ringer feel
when he saw the five people
running?

KEY WORDS

- **sleeve** part of a shirt that covers one's arm
- **workman** a worker who does physical work;
  a laborer
- **set one free** to help one let go; to allow
  one to be free
- **whoever** anyone
- **follower** a person who follows
- **son-in-law** the husband of one's daughter
- **make excuses** to offer reasons

Soon afterwards Dummling came to a city, where the king had a daughter who was so serious that no one could make her laugh. So he had ordered that whoever could make her laugh should marry her. When Dummling heard this, he went with his goose and all her followers before the king's daughter, and as soon as she saw the seven people running on and on, one behind the other, she began to laugh quite loudly, and as if she would never stop.

≠ stopping

Dummling immediately asked to have her for his wife, but the king did not like this son-in-law, and made all sorts of excuses and said Dummling must first show him a man who could drink a cellarful of wine.

asked to marry her

gave all kinds of reasons to stop Dummling from marrying the princess

all the wine kept in a cellar

Stop & Think
Why did the princess finally laugh?

CHECK UP | **Choose the right words.**

1 The parson asked the _____ for help. (bell-ringer | workmen)
2 The king did not like this _____. (son-in-law | follower)
3 The workmen did not _____ the people _____. (set; free | make; excuses)

GRAMMAR POINT

who (relative pronoun)
• The king had a daughter **who** was so serious that no one could make her laugh.
• Dummling must first show him a man **who** could drink a cellarful of wine.

Dummling thought of the little grey man, who could certainly help him, so he went into the forest, and in the same place where he had cut down the tree, he saw a man sitting who had a very sad face. Dummling asked the man what he was so unhappy about, and he answered, "I have such a great thirst and cannot quench it. Cold water I cannot stand; a barrel of wine I have just emptied, but that to me is like a drop on a hot stone."

accept; put up with

finished drinking (a German proverb meaning "not enough to make a difference")

"There I can help you," said Dummling. "Just come with me, and you shall be satisfied."

He led him into the king's cellar, and the man bent over the huge barrels and drank and drank till his groin hurt. Before the day was over, he had emptied all the barrels.

cellar

barrel

Stop & Think
Do you think the little old grey-haired man helped Dummling?

KEY WORDS

- **quench** to satisfy one's thirst
- **cellar** a room under a house used to store things
- **barrel** a large container
- **groin** the area where your legs meet

- **bride** a woman who is getting married
- **furious** very angry; very mad
- **condition** something which must be done
- **strap** a belt

Then Dummling asked once more for his bride, but the king was furious that such an ugly fellow, whom everyone called Dummling, should take away his daughter, and so he set a new condition: Dummling must first find a man who could eat a
(the king did so again to stop Dummling from marrying his daughter)
whole mountain of bread.

Dummling did not think long, but went straight into the
for a long time
forest, where in the same place there sat a man who was tying up his body with a strap, making an awful face, and saying,
looking sad
"I have eaten a whole ovenful of rolls, but what good is that
(a whole ovenful of rolls still couldn't reduce his hunger)
when one has such a hunger as I? My stomach remains empty, and I must tie myself up if I am not to die of hunger."
or I would die because of hunger
At this Dummling was glad and said, "Get up and come with
Stand up
me, and you shall eat yourself full."
eat so much that you will feel full

Stop & Think
What must Dummling do to marry the princess this time?

strap

roll

CHECK UP | Fill in the blanks with the correct words.

cellar   strap   furious   quench

1 The man wanted to _____ his thirst.
2 Dummling led the man into the king's _____.
3 The king was _____ that Dummling should take away his daughter.
4 The man was tying up his body with a _____.

GRAMMAR POINT

have / has + p.p. (present perfect: recent past event)
• I **have eaten** a whole ovenful of rolls.

He led him to the king's palace, where all the flour in the whole kingdom was collected, and from it he ordered a huge mountain of bread to be baked. The man from the forest stood before it, began to eat, and by the end of one day the whole mountain had vanished.

Then Dummling for the third time asked for his bride, but the king again looked for a *tried to find a way to keep the princess from marrying Dummling* way out and ordered a ship which could *ordered Dummling to find a special ship* sail on land and on water. "As soon as you come sailing back in it," he *you come back in this special ship* said, "you shall have my daughter for your wife."

Dummling went straight into the forest, and there sat the little grey man to whom he had given his cake. When he heard what Dummling wanted, he said, "Since you have given me food to eat and wine to drink, I will give you the ship, and I

Stop & Think
How long did it take the man to finish eating the huge mountain of bread?

K EY WORDS

- **palace** the official home of a king and queen; a castle
- **vanish** to disappear
- **prevent . . . from . . .** to stop . . . from . . .
- **inherit** to receive money or property from someone after he or she has died

do all this because you once were kind to me."

you had a good heart

Then he gave him a ship which could sail on land and
water, and when the king saw that, he could no longer prevent

not ... anymore

Dummling from having his daughter. The wedding was

marrying

celebrated, and after the king's death, Dummling inherited his

received

kingdom and lived for a long time happily with his wife.

Stop & Think

Do you think Dummling was really a
stupid man? Why or why not?

CHECK UP | Put the events in order by marking them 1, 2, 3, and 4.

_____ Dummling inherited the king's kingdom.
_____ The king ordered a ship which could sail on land and on water.
_____ Dummling led the man to the king's palace.
_____ All the flour in the whole kingdom was collected.

GRAMMAR POINT

• **auxiliary verb (be verb) + p.p. (passive voice)**
  • All the flour in the whole kingdom **was collected**.
  • The wedding **was celebrated**.

4 Hansel and Gretel

Beside a great forest lived a poor wood-cutter with his wife and his two children. The boy was called Hansel and the girl Gretel.

He had little to eat, and once when there was great hunger throughout the land, he could no longer earn even his daily bread. Now when he thought about this at night in his bed and tossed about in his anxiety, he groaned and said to his wife,

couldn't sleep because he was worried

"What will happen to us? How are we going to feed our poor children when we no longer have anything even for ourselves?"

"I'll tell you what, husband," answered the woman. "Early

(an idiom used to suggest a plan)

tomorrow morning we will take the children out into the forest to where it is the thickest. There we will light a fire for them and

where there are the most trees

give each of them one more piece of bread, and then we will go to our work and leave them alone. They will not find their way home again, and we shall be rid of them."

Stop & Think

Why couldn't the wood-cutter sleep at night?

wood-cutter

KEY WORDS

- **toss** to turn one's body from side to side
- **anxiety** a feeling of worry; concern
- **groan** to make a deep sound showing pain or worry
- **be (get) rid of** to throw away; to desert
- **trim** to cut something carefully

- **coffin** a long box in which a dead body is buried
- **all the same** nevertheless
- **unable** ≠ able
- **stepmother** one's father's wife, who is not one's real mother
- **upset** to make one feel worried

"No, wife," said the man, "I will not do that. How could I stand to leave my children alone in the forest? The wild animals would soon come and tear them to pieces."

tolerate

kill and eat them

"Oh, you fool!" she said. "Then we must all four die of hunger, and you may as well trim the boards for our coffins." And she gave him no peace until he agreed.

prepare to die

kept bothering him

"But I feel very sorry for the poor children, all the same," said the man.

nevertheless

The two children had also been unable to sleep because of hunger and had heard what their stepmother had said to their father. Gretel wept bitter tears and said to Hansel, "Now all is over for us."

We are dead.

"Be quiet, Gretel," said Hansel. "Do not upset yourself, and I will soon find a way to help us."

calm down

Stop & Think

What did the stepmother plan to do to Hansel and Gretel?

CHECK UP | **Fill in the blanks with the correct words.**

upset   stepmother   unable   tossed

1 The wood-cutter _____ about in his anxiety.
2 "Do not _____ yourself," said Hansel to Gretel.
3 The two children had also been _____ to sleep.
4 The _____ gave her husband no peace until he agreed.

GRAMMAR POINT

- **no longer (= not . . . anymore)**
  - He could **no longer** earn even his daily bread.
    (= He could **not** earn even his daily bread **anymore**.)
  - We **no longer** have anything even for ourselves.
    (= We do **not** have anything even for ourselves **anymore**.)

And when the old folks had fallen asleep, he got up, put on
his little coat, opened the door downstairs, and crept outside.

their parents

The moon shone brightly, and the white pebbles which lay
in front of the house glittered like real silver pennies. Hansel
stooped down and stuffed the little pocket of his coat with as
many as he could fit in. Then he went back and said to Gretel,
"Be comforted, dear little sister, and sleep in peace. God will not
abandon us." And he lay down again in his bed.

put

Don't worry

When day dawned, but before the sun had risen, the woman
came and awoke the two children, saying, "Get up, you lazy
little ones. We are going into the forest to gather wood." She
gave each a little piece of bread and said, "There is something
for your dinner, but do not eat it up before then, for you will get
nothing else."

because

Stop & Think
What did Hansel put in his
pocket?

pebbles

glitter

silver
pennies

KEY WORDS

- **folks** people
- **glitter** to shine brightly
- **penny** a small one-cent coin
- **stoop** to bend one's body downward
- **stuff** to put something into a small space

- **comfort** to make one feel less worried or upset
- **abandon** to desert
- **chimney** a pipe that allows smoke to pass out of a building up into the air
- **constantly** all the time

Gretel put the bread under her apron, as Hansel had the pebbles in his pocket. Then they all set out together on the way to the forest.
started the journey
When they had walked for a short time, Hansel stood still, looked back at the house, and then did so again and
not moving
again. His father said, "Hansel, what are you looking at there and staying behind for? Pay attention, and do not forget how to use your legs."
don't forget how to walk

"Ah, Father," said Hansel, "I am looking at my little white cat, which is sitting up on the roof and wants to say goodbye to me."

The wife said, "Fool, that is not your little cat. That is the morning sun which is shining on the chimney."

Hansel, however, had not been looking back at his cat, but had been constantly throwing the white pebbles from his pocket onto the road.

chimney

Stop & Think
Why did Hansel keep throwing the white pebbles onto the road?

CHECK UP | **True or false?**

1 Hansel had the pebbles in his pocket.   _____
2 Gretel crept outside after her parents had fallen asleep.   _____
3 Hansel had been looking back at his cat.   _____

GRAMMAR POINT

as (= because)
* Gretel put the bread under her apron, **as** Hansel had the pebbles in his pocket.
  (= Gretel put the bread under her apron **because** Hansel had the pebbles in his pocket.)

When they had reached the middle of the forest, the father
said, "Now, children, pile up some wood, and I will light a fire
gotten to
so that you will not be cold." Hansel and Gretel gathered twigs
and branches together, as high as a little hill. The wood was lit,
and then the flames were burning very high.

The woman said, "Now, children, lie down by the fire and
rest. We will go into the forest and cut some wood. When we
have finished, we will come back and take you home."

Hansel and Gretel sat by the fire, and when noon came, each
arrived
ate a little piece of bread, and as they heard the strokes of the
the sound of the axe cutting wood
axe, they believed that their father was near. It was not the axe,
however, but a branch which he had tied to a dying tree, and
which the wind was blowing backwards and forwards.
the branch

Stop & Think
Where did the children sit down
and rest?

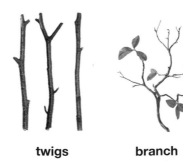

twigs   branch

KEY WORDS

- **pile up** to put things in a pile
- **flame** fire
- **fatigue** tiredness
- **brand-new** completely new

And as they had been sitting such a long time, their eyes closed with fatigue and they fell fast asleep. When at last they

they closed their eyes because they were tired

awoke, it was already dark night. Gretel began to cry and said, "How are we to get out of the forest now?"

But Hansel comforted her and said, "Just wait a little until

made her feel less worried

the moon has risen, and then we will soon find the way." And when the full moon had risen, Hansel took his little sister by the hand and followed the pebbles which shone like brand-new

≠ old

silver pieces and showed them the way.

They walked the whole night long and by dawn had come once more to their father's house. They knocked at the door, and when the woman opened it and saw that it was Hansel and Gretel, she said, "You naughty children, why did you sleep so long in the forest? We thought you were never coming back at all."

(Their stepmother pretended to care about the children, but she really didn't.)

Stop & Think

When did Hansel take his little sister by the hand and follow the pebbles?

CHECK UP | True or false?

1. The children's parents came back and took them home. _____
2. The children had been sitting for a long time. _____
3. The children knocked at their father's door at noon. _____

GRAMMAR POINT

as adjective as + N (noun)
- Hansel and Gretel gathered twigs and branches together, **as high as a little hill.**

The father, however, rejoiced, for it had broken his heart to
↳ felt joy
leave them behind alone.
    abandon them

Not long afterwards, there was once more great hunger
throughout the land, and the children heard their mother
saying at night to their father, "Everything is eaten again; we
have one half loaf of bread left, and that is all. The children
must go. We will take them farther into the woods, so that
they will not find their way out again. There is no other way of
saving ourselves."

The man felt guilty, and he thought, "It would be better for
you to share your last mouthful with your children."
                        last bit of food
The woman, however, would listen to nothing that he had
to say, but scolded and reproached him. He who says this must
        talked angrily to and blamed
likewise say that, and as he had surrendered the first time, he
One who says this must in the same way say that
had to do so a second time too.
        agreeing to abandon his children

Stop & Think
How did the wood-cutter
feel when he saw that the
children had come back?

break one's heart   scold

KEY WORDS

- **rejoice** to show or feel joy
- **break one's heart** to make one feel very sad
- **guilty** feeling shame
- **scold** to talk angrily about someone's behavior
- **reproach** to blame someone for something
- **surrender** to give up
- **crumble** to break into small pieces

The children, however, were still awake and had heard the conversation. When the old folks were asleep, Hansel again got up and wanted to go out to pick up pebbles as he had done before, but the woman had locked the door, and he could not get out. Nevertheless, he comforted his little sister and said, "Do not cry, Gretel. Go to sleep quietly, and the good God will help us."

Early in the morning the woman came and took the children out of their beds. Their piece of bread was given to them, but it was even smaller than it had been the time before. On the way into the forest Hansel crumbled his in his pocket, often stood still, and threw the crumbs on the ground.

broke his bread into crumbs

Stop & Think
What did Hansel use to mark the way home this time?

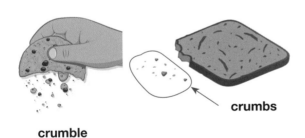

crumbs

crumble

CHECK UP | **Choose the right words.**

1 The stepmother _____ and reproached the wood-cutter. (crumbled | scolded)
2 Hansel _____ his bread in his pocket. (reproached | crumbled)
3 The wood-cutter _____ when his wife said, "The children must go." (guilty | rejoiced)

GRAMMAR POINT

- **-er + than . . . (comparative)**
  - The bread was even **smaller than** it had been the time before.

"Hansel, why do you stop and look around?" said the father. "Go on."

"I am looking back at my little pigeon which is sitting on the roof and wants to say goodbye to me," answered Hansel.

"Fool," said the woman, "that is not your little pigeon; that is the morning sun that is shining on the chimney." Hansel, however, little by little, threw all his crumbs on the path.

≠ quickly

The woman led the children still deeper into the forest, where they had never in their lives been before. Then a great fire was again made, and the mother said, "Just sit there, you children, and when you are tired, you may sleep a little. We are going into the forest to cut wood, and in the evening when we are done, we will come and take you home."

Stop & Think
Why did Hansel keep stopping and looking around?

pigeon

make a fire

 WORDS

- **pigeon** a grey bird with short legs
- **little by little** slowly over a period of time; bit by bit
- **done** finished (≠ unfinished)
- **scatter** to throw things in different directions

When it was noon, Gretel shared her piece of bread with Hansel, who had scattered his along the way. Then they fell asleep and evening passed, *time went by* but no one came for the poor children. They did not awake until it was dark night, and Hansel comforted his little sister and said, "Just wait, Gretel, until the moon rises, and then we shall see the crumbs of bread which I have thrown about. They will show us our way home again."

When the moon came, they set out, but they found no crumbs, for the many thousands of birds which fly about *around* in the woods and fields had picked them all up. Hansel *eaten them all* said to Gretel, "We shall soon find the way." But they did not find it.

> **Stop & Think**
> When did the children awake?

CHECK UP | **Answer the questions.**

1 What did Hansel have in his pocket the second time he left home?
   a. Pebbles.   b. Bread.   c. A pigeon.
2 Why couldn't the children find their way home this time?
   a. They fell asleep.   b. The moon rose.   c. The birds had eaten the crumbs.

GRAMMAR POINT

> • **not . . . until . . .**
>   • They did **not** awake **until** it was dark night.

25

They walked the whole night and all the next day too from morning till evening, but they did not get out of the forest. They were very hungry, for they had nothing to eat but two or three berries which grew on the ground. And as they were so
except

exhausted that their legs could carry them no longer, they lay
tired   *they couldn't walk anymore*

down beneath a tree and fell asleep.
under

It was now three mornings since they had left their father's house. They began to walk again, but they always went deeper into the forest. If help did not come soon, they would surely die of hunger and exhaustion.

When it was midday, they saw a beautiful snow-white bird sitting on a branch, which sang so delightfully that they stood
joyfully

still and listened to it. And when its song was over, it spread its wings and flew away before them, and they followed it until they reached a little house, on the roof of which it settled.
rested

Stop & Think
Look at "on the roof of which it settled." What does "it" refer to?

berries

KEY WORDS

- **exhausted** very tired
- **beneath** under
- **exhaustion** the feeling of being exhausted
- **midday** noon
- **delightfully** joyfully; pleasingly
- **settle** to sit or rest in a comfortable position
- **approach** to move toward

- **be built of** to be made of certain materials
- **work on** to start doing something
- **lean** to move one's upper body backwards or forwards
- **nibble** to take a small bite of food
- **gnaw** to bite something hard repeatedly

And when they approached the little house they saw that it was built of bread and covered with cakes, and that the windows were made of clear sugar.

"We will go to work on that," said Hansel, "and have a good meal. I will eat a bit of the roof, and you, Gretel, can eat some of the window. It will taste sweet."

<u>start eating</u>

Hansel reached up and broke off a little of the roof to see how it tasted, and Gretel leaned against the window and nibbled at the panes. Then a soft voice cried from the living room, "Nibble, nibble, gnaw; who is nibbling at my little house?"

<u>pulled off</u>

<u>took small bites</u>

<u>called out</u>

<u>I hear someone nibbling and gnawing</u>

panes

lean

Stop & Think

What were the windows of the little house made of?

CHECK UP | Fill in the blanks with the correct words.

> approached   settled   exhausted   nibbled

1 The children were so _____ that their legs could carry them no longer.
2 Gretel leaned against the window and _____ at the panes.
3 The snow-white bird _____ on the roof of a little house.
4 The children _____ the little house.

GRAMMAR POINT

nothing . . . but
- They had **nothing** to eat **but** two or three berries which grew on the ground.

26

The children answered, "The wind, the wind, the heaven-born wind," and went on eating without worrying. Hansel, who

(The children said it was the sound of wind that came from heaven.)

liked the taste of the roof, tore down a great piece of it, and Gretel pushed out the whole of one round windowpane, sat down, and enjoyed herself with it. Suddenly the door opened

ate the windowpane

and an ancient woman, who supported herself on crutches, came creeping out. Hansel and Gretel were so terribly frightened that they dropped what they had in their hands. The old woman, however, nodded her head and said, "Oh, you dear children, who has brought you here? Do come in, and stay with me. No harm shall come to you."

You will not be hurt.

She took them both by the hand and led them into her little house. Then good food was set before them: milk and pancakes

placed

with sugar, apples, and nuts. Afterwards, two pretty little beds

---

Stop & Think

How did Hansel and Gretel feel when they saw the ancient woman?

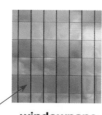  

| windowpane | crutch | nuts |

KEY WORDS

- **heaven** where God lives; paradise
- **crutch** a stick that helps people walk
- **harm** injury; damage
- **pretend** to behave as if something were real when it's not
- **in reality** in fact
- **witch** an evil woman who can do magic

- **keen** very strong (ability to see, smell, or hear)
- **human being** a person
- **hatred** the feeling of hate (≠ love)
- **mockingly** with unkind laughter
- **escape** to run away from

were covered with clean white sheets, and Hansel and Gretel lay down in them and thought they were in heaven.

felt as if they were in heaven

The old woman had only pretended to be so kind. She was in reality an evil witch, who waited for children to pass and

in fact

had only built the little house of bread in order to lure them

attract

there. When she caught a child, she killed, cooked, and ate it, and that was a feast day for her. Witches have red eyes and cannot see far, but they have a keen sense of smell like animals

the ability to smell as well as animals

and are aware when human beings come near. When Hansel and Gretel came into her neighborhood, she laughed with hatred and

≠ love

said mockingly, "I have them;

laughing in an unkind way

they shall not escape me."

Stop & Think
Why did the witch lure children to her house?

CHECK UP | Choose the right words.

1 The ancient woman supported herself on _____. (heaven | crutches)
2 The witch said, "They shall not _____ me." (pretend | escape)
3 The witch said, "No _____ shall come to you." (hatred | harm)

GRAMMAR POINT

> **pretend to**
> • The old woman had only **pretended to** be so kind.

27

Early in the morning before the children were awake, she was already up, and when she saw both of them sleeping *out of bed* and looking so pretty, with their round and rosy cheeks, she whispered to herself, "That will be a tasty mouthful." *as pink as a rose*

Then she seized Hansel with her wrinkled hand, carried him into a little stable, and locked him in behind an iron door. All his screaming could not help him. Then she went to Gretel, shook her till she awoke, and cried, "Get up, lazy thing, fetch *shouted* some water, and cook something good for your brother. He is in the stable outside and is to be made fat. When he is fat, I will *will be fed until he becomes fat* eat him."

Gretel began to weep bitterly, but it was all in vain, for she *weep-wept-wept* *↑ sadly* *≠ successful* was forced to do what the wicked witch commanded. And now the best food was cooked for poor Hansel, but Gretel got nothing but crab shells. Every morning the woman crept to *only* the little stable and cried, "Hansel, stick out your finger so that *put your finger through the door*

Stop & Think

What sort of food did Gretel eat at the witch's house?

wrinkled hand   **stable**   **crab shell**

KEY WORDS

- **cheek** the soft part of face below the eye
- **tasty** delicious
- **seize** to grab suddenly
- **wrinkled** having lines and folds
- **stable** a place where horses are kept
- **weep** to cry *weep–wept–wept

- **in vain** no use (≠ successful)
- **wicked** evil (≠ kind)
- **astonished** very surprised
- **impatient** ≠ patient
- **lament** to express how sad one is
- **beast** a large and dangerous animal

I may feel if you will soon be fat." Hansel, however, always stretched out a little bone to her, and the old woman, who had weak eyes, could not see it, thought it was Hansel's finger, and was astonished that there was no way of making him fat.

stuck out

very surprised

When four weeks had gone by and Hansel still remained thin, she became impatient and would not wait any longer. "Now, then, Gretel," she cried to the girl, "move yourself, and bring some water. Let Hansel be fat or thin, tomorrow I will kill him and cook him."

No matter whether Hansel is fat or thin

Ah, how the poor little sister did lament when she had to fetch the water, and how her tears did flow down her cheeks. "Dear God, do help us," she cried. "If the wild beasts in the forest had eaten us, we would at least have died together."

("did" adds emphasis)

(She wished wild animals had eaten her and Hansel; in this way they would at least have been together.)

Stop & Think

What did Hansel do to make the witch think that he was still thin?

CHECK UP | Finish the sentences.

1. The witch carried Hansel
2. Gretel got nothing but
3. Hansel stretched out
4. Hansel was locked in

a. behind an iron door.
b. a little bone.
c. into a little stable.
d. crab shells.

GRAMMAR POINT

- **there be no way of V-ing**
  - There **was no way of making** him fat.

"Just keep quiet," said the old woman. "Your noise won't help you at all." *[crying]*

Early in the morning Gretel had to go out, hang up the pot of water and light the fire. "We will bake first," said the old woman. "I have already heated the oven and rolled the dough."

She pushed poor Gretel out to the oven, from which flames *[made it into a bread shape]* were already darting. "Creep in," said the witch, "and see if it is properly heated, so that we can put the bread in." Once Gretel was inside, the old woman planned to shut the oven and let her *[As soon as]* bake in it, and then she would eat her, too.

But Gretel saw what she had in mind and said, "I do not *[knew what she was thinking]* know how to do it. How do I get in?"

"Silly goose," said the old woman. "The door is big enough. *[Stupid girl]* Just look; I can get in myself." And she crept up and stuck her head into the oven.

Stop & Think
What will Gretel probably do after the witch gets into the oven?

roll the dough

KEY WORDS

- **dough** thick flour ready to be baked into bread
- **dart** to move suddenly and quickly
- **bolt** to lock by sliding a bolt
- **miserably** unhappily and painfully

- **spring** to jump suddenly
  *spring–sprang–sprung
- **chest** a large box to put things in
- **pearl** a kind of jewel
- **jewel** a precious stone

Then Gretel gave her a push that drove her far into it, shut the iron door, and bolted it.

made her go

bolt

"Oh!" Then she began to scream quite horribly, but Gretel ran away, and the evil witch was miserably burned to death.

≠ happily

Gretel, however, ran like lightning to Hansel, opened his little stable and cried, "Hansel, we are saved. The old witch is dead."

Then Hansel sprang like a bird from its cage when the door was opened. How they did rejoice and hug each other and dance about and kiss each other. As they no longer had any need to fear the witch, they went into her house, and in every corner there stood chests full of pearls and jewels.

jumped *spring-sprang-sprung*

they didn't need to

jewels

pearl

Stop & Think
What did the children find in the house?

CHECK UP | Put the events in order by marking them 1, 2, 3, and 4.

_____ The witch crept up and stuck her head into the oven.
_____ Hansel sprang like a bird from its cage.
_____ Gretel gave the witch a push that drove her far into the oven.
_____ The witch had already heated the oven and rolled the dough.

GRAMMAR POINT

● **plan to**
• The old woman **planned to** shut the oven and **(to)** let her bake in it.

"These are far better than pebbles," said Hansel, and he stuffed into his pockets whatever could be put in. Gretel said, "I, too, will take something home with me," and filled her apron full.

<u>put</u>

"But now we must go," said Hansel, "so that we may get out of the witch's forest."

When they had walked for two hours, they came to a great stream. "We cannot cross," said Hansel. "I see no boards and no bridge."

<u>river</u>

long, flat pieces of wood

"And there is also no ferry," answered Gretel, "but a white duck is swimming there. If I ask her, she will help us over." Then she cried, "Little duck, little duck, do you see? Hansel and Gretel are waiting for you. There's neither a board nor a bridge in sight. Take us across on your back so white."

boat

within the area one can see

The duck came to them, and Hansel seated himself on its back and told his sister to sit by him. "No," replied Gretel, "that will be too heavy for the little duck. She shall take us across, one after the other."

Stop & Think
How did the children cross the stream?

stream

ferry

 KEY WORDS

- **ferry** a boat or ship which carries people from one place to another
- **seat oneself** to sit down
- **familiar** knowing something or someone because you've seen it, him or her before

- **handful** the amount of something that fills one's hand
- **tale** a story
- **fur** the soft thick hair that covers the bodies of animals such as bears

The good little duck did so, and once they were safely across and had walked for a short time, the forest seemed to become more and more familiar to them, and after a while they saw their father's house far in the distance.
far away

Then they began to run, rushed into the living room, and threw their arms around their father's neck. The man had not had
hugged their father's neck
one happy hour since he had left the children in the forest. The woman, however, was dead. Gretel emptied her apron until pearls and precious stones ran about the room, and Hansel threw one handful after another out of his pocket to add to them. Then all sorrow was at an end, and they lived together in perfect happiness.
all sadness was gone

My tale is done. There runs a mouse, and whoever catches it
(The storyteller has finished telling the story.)
may make himself a big fur cap out of it.
by using the mouse's fur

Stop & Think
How did the father feel after he left his children in the forest?

CHECK UP | Answer the questions.

1 What did Gretel and Hansel carry home with them?
   a. A white duck.   b. Pebbles.   c. Pearls and jewels.
2 What had happened to their stepmother?
   a. She had died.   b. She had gotten lost.   c. She had run about the room.

GRAMMAR POINT

neither . . . nor . . .
• There's **neither** a board **nor** a bridge in sight.

Step 2

5 Rumpelstiltskin

30

Once there was a miller who was poor, but who had a beautiful daughter. One day he had to go and speak to the king, and in order to make himself appear important, he said to the king, "I have a daughter who can spin straw into gold."

seem

The king said to the miller, "That is a skill which pleases me well. If your daughter is as clever as you say, bring her tomorrow to my palace, and I will see what she can do."

makes me happy

And when the girl was brought to the king, he took her into a room which was quite full of straw, gave her a spinning wheel and a reel, and said, "Now get to work, and if by early tomorrow morning you have not spun this straw into gold, you must die."

if she can really spin straw into gold

led her to

Stop & Think

What special skill did the miller say his daughter had?

spinning wheel   reel

KEY WORDS

- **miller** a person who owns or works in a factory that makes flour
- **spin . . . into . . .** to produce something by spinning
- **reel** a round object onto which thread can be rolled
- **have no idea** not to know

Then he himself locked up the room and left her in it alone. So there sat the poor miller's daughter. She did not know what to do, and she had no idea how straw could be spun into gold. She grew more and more frightened until at last she began to weep.

didn't know *became* *cry*

But all at once the door opened, and in came a little man who said,

immediately

"Good evening, Miss miller. Why are you crying so?"

so sadly

"Oh," answered the girl, "I have to spin straw into gold, and I do not know how to do it."

"What will you give me," said the little man, "if I do it for you?"

"My necklace," said the girl.

necklace

Stop & Think
Did the miller lie to the king?

CHECK UP | **True or false?**

1 The miller made himself appear important to the king. _____
2 The miller's daughter could spin straw into gold. _____
3 The miller's daughter offered the little man her ring. _____

GRAMMAR POINT

what to . . . / how to . . .
• She did not know **what to** do.
• I do not know **how to** do it.

31

The little man took the necklace, seated himself in front of the wheel, and "Whirr! Whirr! Whirr!" Three turns, and the reel was full. Then he put another on, and "Whirr! Whirr! Whirr!"

(a sound made when something spins fast and regularly)

Three times around, and the second was full too. And so it went on until the morning when all the straw had been spun and all the reels were full of gold.

the spinning wheel continued to spin

the straw had been changed into gold

By dawn the king was already there, and when he saw the gold he was amazed and delighted, but his heart only became greedier. He had the miller's daughter taken into another room full of straw, which was much larger, and commanded her to spin that also into gold in one night if she wanted to live.

the king wanted to have more gold

Stop & Think
What did the little man take from the miller's daughter the first time?

greedy

 WORDS

- **go on** to continue
- **amazed** very surprised

- **at the sight** at the moment of seeing something

The girl didn't know how to save herself. She was crying when the door opened again and the little man appeared and said, "What will you give me if I spin that straw into gold for you?"

"The ring on my finger," answered the girl.

The little man took the ring, again began to turn the wheel, and by morning had spun all the straw into shining gold.

The king rejoiced greatly at the sight, but still he was not
when he saw this
satisfied. He had the miller's daughter taken into a still larger room full of straw and said, "You must spin all of this into gold tonight, but if you succeed, you shall be my wife."

"Even if she is only a miller's daughter," he thought, "I could not find a richer wife in the whole world."
She would be the richest wife that I could have.

ring

Stop & Think
What will happen if the miller's daughter succeeds in spinning all of the straw into gold?

CHECK UP | Answer the questions.

1 What did the miller's daughter NOT give to the little man?
   a. A ring.   b. Gold.   c. A necklace.
2 What kind of a person was the king?
   a. He was kind.   b. He was greedy.   c. He was easily satisfied.

GRAMMAR POINT

---• **have someone / something p.p.**
   • He **had** the miller's daughter **taken** into another room full of straw.
     (= He ordered someone to take the miller's daughter into another room full of straw.)

When the girl was alone, the little man came for the third time and said, "What will you give me if I spin the straw for you this time, too?"

"I have nothing left that I can give," answered the girl.

"Then promise me, if you become a queen, to give me your first child."

"Who knows if that will ever happen?" thought the miller's daughter, and not knowing how else to help herself in this difficulty, she promised the little man what he wanted, and for that he once more spun the straw into gold.
one more time

And when the king came in the morning and found everything as he had wished, he took her hand in marriage, and
married the miller's daughter
the pretty miller's daughter became a queen.

A year later, she gave birth to a beautiful child, and she never thought about the little man. But suddenly he came into her
she forgot about her promise
room and said, "Now give me what you promised."

Stop & Think

What did the little man want from the miller's daughter the third time?

marriage

KEY WORDS

- **promise** to tell someone that you will do something; to give one's word
- **horrified** very frightened
- **pity** to feel sorry for someone
- **messenger** someone who takes a message from one person to another

The queen was horrified and offered the little man all the riches of the kingdom if
wealth
he would leave her the child. But the little
let her keep her child
man said, "No, a living thing is dearer to me than all the treasures in the world."
the most valuable thing in the world to me

Then the queen began to lament and cry,
behave sadly
so that the little man pitied her. "I will give you three days' time," he said, "and if in that time you can find out my name, then you shall keep your child."

So the queen thought all night long of all the names that she had ever heard, and she sent a messenger throughout the country to ask, far and wide, for any
over a large area
other names that there might be.

treasure

When the little man came the next day, she began with Caspar, Melchior, and Balthazar, and then said all the names she knew, one after another, but to every one the little man said, "That is not my name."

messenger

Stop & Think

How could the queen stop the little man from taking her baby away?

CHECK UP | **Choose the right words.**

1 The queen began to _____ and cry. (pity | lament)
2 The little man _____ the queen when she cried. (offered | pitied)
3 The queen sent a _____ throughout the country. (messenger | living thing)

GRAMMAR POINT

  • **offer someone something (= offer something to someone)**
    • The queen was horrified and **offered the little man all the riches** of the kingdom.
     (= The queen was horrified and **offered all the riches** of the kingdom **to the little man**.)

On the second day she had inquiries made in the
sent someone to ask for information
neighborhood about the names of the people there, and she

repeated to the little man the most unusual and curious.
strange
"Perhaps your name is Shortribs, or Sheepshanks, or Laceleg."

But he always answered, "That is not my name."

On the third day the messenger came back and said, "I have not been able to find a single new name, but as I came to a high mountain at the end of the forest, where the fox and the rabbit say good night to each other, I saw a little house, and in front of the house a fire was burning, and around the fire quite a
a fire had been lit
ridiculous little man was jumping. He hopped upon one leg and
silly
shouted, 'Today I bake, tomorrow I brew, and the next day I'll have the young queen's child. How glad I am that no one knew that Rumpelstiltskin is my name.'"

Stop & Think
Where did the little man live?

KEY WORDS

- **make an inquiry** to ask for information
- **neighborhood** the area around one's home
- **unusual** strange (≠ usual)
- **ridiculous** very silly or unreasonable
- **brew** to make beer or wine
- **mistress** a woman who has great power
- **the devil** the most powerful evil spirit; Satan
- **plunge** to push downwards suddenly; to fall
- **in (a) rage** in great anger

You can imagine how glad the queen was when she heard the name. And when soon afterwards the little man came in and asked, "Now, mistress queen, what is my name?" At first she said, "Is your name Conrad?"

"No."

"Is your name Harry?"

"No."

"Perhaps your name is Rumpelstiltskin."

"The devil has told you that! The devil has told you that!"

No one could possibly know my name unless the devil told you.

cried the little man, and in his anger he plunged his right foot

pushed

so deep into the earth that his whole leg went in, and then in

the ground

rage he pulled at his left leg so hard with both hands that he

tore himself in two.

killed himself

Stop & Think

How did Rumpelstiltskin feel when the queen told him his real name?

CHECK UP | Put the events in order by marking them 1, 2, 3, and 4.

_____ Rumpelstiltskin tore himself in two.
_____ The messenger told the queen he had seen a ridiculous little man jumping around.
_____ The queen said, "Perhaps your name is Rumpelstiltskin."
_____ The queen had inquiries made in the neighborhood about the names of the people there.

GRAMMAR POINT

be able to
• I have not **been able to** find a single new name.

6 The Frog King

well

In ancient times when wishing still helped
people, _people got help by making wishes_ there lived a king whose daughters
were all beautiful, but the youngest was
so beautiful that the sun itself, which
has seen so much, was astonished
very surprised
whenever it shone on her face. Near the
anytime
king's castle lay a great dark forest, and
under an old lime tree in the forest was a
well. When the day was very warm, the king's
child went out into the forest and sat down by the side of
the cool fountain. When she was bored, she took a golden
ball and threw it up high and caught it, and this ball was her
favorite toy.

Now on one occasion the princess's golden ball did
a particular time
not fall into the little hand which she was holding up for

it, but onto the ground beyond, and
rolled straight into the water. The
king's daughter watched it go, but it

Stop & Think
What did the youngest princess
do when she was bored?

KEY WORDS

- **whenever** anytime
- **fountain** a pool or well from which water flows out
- **bored** ≠ interested
- **pity** the feeling of sadness for someone else's difficult situation
- **splash** the sound made when someone or something falls into water

vanished, and the well was deep,
disappeared
so deep that the bottom could

not be seen. Then she began

to cry, and cried louder and

louder, and could not be

comforted. And as she thus

lamented, someone said to
showed how sad she was
her, "What is wrong, king's

daughter? You weep so that

even a stone would feel pity."
everyone would feel sorry for the princess

She looked around to the side

from which the voice had come, and

saw a frog stretching its big, ugly head from

the water. "Ah, old water-splasher, is it you?" she said. "I am
(A frog splashes, so the princess called it a splasher.)
weeping for my golden ball, which has fallen into the well."

Stop & Think
Why did the princess begin to cry?

CHECK UP | **True or false?**

1 The king's three daughters were ugly. _____
2 The golden ball rolled straight into the well. _____
3 The well was under an old lemon tree in the forest. _____

GRAMMAR POINT

whose (relative pronoun)
• There lived a king **whose** daughters were all beautiful king.

"Be quiet and do not weep," answered the frog. "I can help you, but what will you give me if I bring your toy up again?"

"Whatever you will have, dear frog," she said. "My clothes, my pearls and jewels, and even this golden crown which I am wearing."

The frog answered, "I do not care for your clothes, your
want
pearls and jewels, nor for your golden crown; but if you will love me and let me be your friend and companion, sit by you at your little table, eat off your little golden plate, drink out of
eat from
your little cup, and sleep in your little bed, I will go down below and bring your golden ball up again."

"Oh, yes," she said, "I promise you all you wish, if you will but bring me my ball again." But she thought, "How the silly

Stop & Think
What could the frog do to help the princess?

crown

golden plate

KEY WORDS

- **crown** the decoration that a member of a royal family wears on his or her head
- **care for** to like; to want
- **companion** a person or animal one spends a lot of time with

- **promise** the act of promising to do something

72 *Step 2*

frog talks! All he does is sit in the water with the other frogs and
He can only
croak. He can be no companion to any human being."
(the sound a frog makes)   *He cannot be any person's friend.*

But the frog, when he had received this promise, put his
head under the water and sank down, and in a little while he
a short time later
came swimming up again with the ball in his mouth and threw
it onto the grass. The king's daughter was delighted to see her
pretty toy once more, picked it up, and ran away with it.
again

"Wait, wait," said the frog. "Take me with you. I can't run as
you can." But what good did it do him to scream his "Croak!
how could his croaking help him
Croak!" after her, as loudly as he could? She did not listen to it,
but ran home and soon forgot the poor frog, who was forced to
≠ willing
go back into his well again.

croak

companion

Stop & Think

Did the princess take her promise seriously?

CHECK UP | **Answer the questions.**

1 What did the frog want?
   a. Jewels.   b. The princess's crown.   c. To be the princess's friend.

2 What did the princess do after the frog helped her?
   a. She ran away.   b. She gave him her toy.   c. She took him with her.

GRAMMAR POINT

   • **not . . . , nor . . . (conjunction)**
      • I do **not** care for your clothes, your pearls and jewels, **nor** for your golden crown.

   • **All one does is V (the only thing . . .)**
      • **All he does is sit** in the water with the other frogs and **croak**.

splash

marble

The next day when she had seated herself at the table with the king and all his royal court and was eating from her little golden plate, something came creeping with a "splish-splash, splish-splash" up the marble staircase, and when it had reached the top, it knocked at the door and cried, "Princess, youngest princess, open the door for me."

the king's family and advisors

a splashing sound

She ran to see who was outside, but when she opened the door, there sat the frog in front of her. Then she slammed the door, quickly sat down to dinner again, and was quite frightened. The king saw clearly that her heart was beating violently and said, "My child, what are you so afraid of? Is there perhaps a giant outside who wants to carry you away?"

loudly shut

hard and fast

"Ah, no," she replied. "It is no giant, but a disgusting frog."

there is no giant

"What does a frog want with you?"

Stop & Think

How did the princess feel when she saw the frog outside the door?

staircase

KEY WORDS

- **marble** a type of hard stone
- **staircase** a set of stairs inside a building
- **slam** to shut something hard and loudly
- **violently** with a lot of force

- **disgusting** very unpleasant
- **insist** to keep saying or doing something whether it is right or wrong
- **in the meantime** meanwhile

"Ah, dear father, yesterday when I was in the forest playing by the well, my golden ball fell into the water. And because I cried so much, the frog brought it out again for me, and because he insisted, I promised him he could be my companion, but I

he could be my friend and spend time with me

never thought he would be able to come out of the water. And now he is out there and wants to come in to be with me."

In the meantime the frog knocked again and cried, "Princess,

Meanwhile

youngest princess, open the door for me. Do you not remember what you said to me yesterday by the cool waters of the well?

an area of water

Princess, youngest princess, open the door for me."

Then the king said, "That which you have promised you

Whatever

must do. Go and let him in." So she went and opened the door, and the frog hopped in and followed her, step by step, to her chair. There he sat and cried, "Lift me up beside you."

knock on the door

Stop & Think

What did the king command the princess to do?

CHECK UP | Finish the sentences.

1 The princess
2 The frog
3 The princess was eating from
4 The frog came creeping up

a. the marble staircase.
b. her little golden plate.
c. hopped in and followed her.
d. slammed the door.

GRAMMAR POINT

to + V (purpose)
• She ran **to see** who was outside.

She hesitated, until at last the king commanded her to do it.
delayed

Once the frog was on the chair, he wanted to be on the table, and when he was on the table, he said, "Now push your little golden plate nearer to me so that we may eat together." She did this, but it was easy to see that she did not do it willingly. The frog enjoyed what he ate, but almost every mouthful she took made her

(she choked because she was eating with the frog)

choke. Finally he said, "I have eaten and am satisfied, and now I am tired. Carry me into your little room and make your little silken bed ready, and we will both lie down and go to sleep."

The king's daughter began to cry, for she was afraid of the cold frog which she did not want to touch, and which was now to sleep in her pretty, clean little bed. But the

was going to

Stop & Think
Where did the frog want to sleep after the meal?

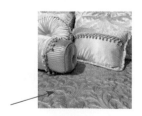

silken bed

 WORDS

- **hesitate** to pause or delay because one is nervous or not sure what to do
- **willingly** happily; readily; because one wants to do something
- **choke** to be unable to breathe
- **in trouble** ≠ out of trouble

king became angry and said, "He who helped you when you were in trouble should not afterwards be despised by you." *You should not look down on the frog that helped you.*

So she picked the frog up with two fingers, carried him upstairs, and put him in a corner, but when she was in bed, he crept over to her and said, "I am tired, and I want to sleep as well as you. *as comfortably as you* Lift me up or I will tell your father." When she heard this she became terribly angry. She picked the frog up and threw him as hard as she could against the wall. "Now will you be quiet, horrible frog?" she said.

But when he fell down, he was no longer a frog, but a king's son with kind and beautiful eyes.

Stop & Think
What did the frog turn into after he fell down?

CHECK UP | **Fill in the blanks with the correct words.**

> willingly   choke   satisfied   hesitated

1 Almost every mouthful she took made her _____.
2 The frog said, "I have eaten and am _____, and now I am tired."
3 She _____, until at last the king commanded her to do it.
4 She did this, but it was easy to see that she did not do it _____.

GRAMMAR POINT

as . . . as one can / could
- She picked the frog up and threw him **as hard as she could** against the wall.

And he, by her father's wish, was now her dear companion and husband. Then he told her how he had been cursed by a wicked witch, and how no one could have saved him from the well but herself, and that tomorrow they would go together into his kingdom.

a witch said magic words to bring him bad luck

except

Then they went to sleep, and the next morning when the sun awoke them, a carriage came driving up pulled by white horses, which had white ostrich feathers on their heads and were harnessed with golden chains, and behind them stood the young king's servant Faithful Henry.

attached to the carriage

Faithful Henry had been so unhappy when his master was turned into a frog that he had ordered three iron bands to be tied around his heart to prevent it from bursting with grief and sadness. The carriage was to carry the young king into his kingdom. Faithful Henry helped them both in, placed himself behind the horses again, and was full of joy because of this salvation.

changed

breaking open because of great sorrow

freedom from harm

Stop & Think
Why did the prince become a frog?

carriage

ostrich

KEY WORDS

- **curse** to bring others bad luck with magic words
- **carriage** a vehicle with wheels that is pulled by horses
- **faithful** always supporting someone
- **turn into** to change into
- **grief** great sorrow
- **salvation** freedom from harm; safety
- **crack** to split open and break
- **imprison** to put one in prison (≠ set free)

And when they had driven a part of the way, the young king heard a cracking sound behind him as if something

some distance

the sound of something breaking

had broken. So he turned around and cried, "Henry, the carriage is breaking."

"No, master, it is not the carriage. It is an iron band from my heart, which was put there in my great pain when you were a frog and imprisoned in the well."

trapped

Again and once again while they were on their way, something cracked, and each time the young king thought the carriage was breaking, but it was only the bands springing from the heart of Faithful Henry because his master had been set free and was happy.

popping

iron band

Stop & Think

When did Faithful Henry put iron bands on his heart?

CHECK UP | Choose the right words.

1. The prince had been _____ by a wicked witch. (cracked | cursed)
2. Faithful Henry was full of joy because of this _____ . (grief | salvation)
3. The prince had been _____ in the well. (imprisoned | set free)

GRAMMAR POINT

- **because of + N (noun)**
  - Faithful Henry helped them both in, placed himself behind the horses again, and was full of joy **because of this salvation**.
- **because S (subject) + V (verb)**
  - It was only the bands springing from the heart of Faithful Henry **because his master had been set** free and **was** happy.

7 Little Briar-Rose

A long time ago, there were a king and queen who said every day, "Ah, if only we had a child," but they never had one. But one day while the queen was bathing, a frog crept out of the water onto the land and said to her, "Your wish shall be fulfilled, and within a year you shall have a daughter."

(a phrase used to express a strong wish that hasn't come true)

realized

What the frog had said came true, and the queen had a little girl who was so pretty that the king could not contain his joy and ordered a great feast. He invited not only his relatives, friends and acquaintances, but also the wise women, so that they would be kind and helpful to the child.

control his feeling of happiness

witches who can do magic

There were thirteen of these wise women in his kingdom, but as he had only twelve golden plates for them to eat from, one of them had to stay at home.

Stop & Think
How many wise women did the king invite to the feast?

KEY WORDS

- **bathe** to wash one's body; to take a bath
- **fulfill** to complete or accomplish something
- **contain** to control one's feelings
- **acquaintance** a person you don't know very well
- **splendor** wonderful, fancy things or activities
- **virtue** good behavior
- **beauty** good looks
- **revenge** the act of punishing one who has hurt you
- **prick** to get hurt by touching something sharp

The feast was held with all sorts of
arranged as beautifully as possible
splendor and when it came to an end,
the wise women offered their magic
gifts to the baby. One gave her virtue,
another beauty, a third riches, and so
the third wise woman
on, with the child receiving everything
other similar gifts
in the world that one can wish for.

When eleven of the wise women
had made their promises, suddenly
the thirteenth came in. She wanted
revenge for not having been invited,
because of
and without greeting or even looking at
anyone, she cried in a loud voice, "The king's daughter shall
at the age of fifteen prick herself with a spindle and fall down
dead." And without saying a word more, she turned around and
left the room.

Stop & Think
Why did the thirteenth wise woman
want revenge?

prick   spindle

CHECK UP | Fill in the blanks with the correct words.

    revenge   splendor   fulfilled   contain

1 The frog said to the queen, "Your wish shall be _____."
2 The feast was held with all sorts of _____.
3 The king could not _____ his joy and ordered a great feast.
4 The thirteenth wise woman wanted _____.

GRAMMAR POINT

——• **not only . . . but also . . .**
• He invited **not only** his relatives, friends and acquaintances, **but also** the wise women.

They were all shocked, but the twelfth wise woman, whose
good wish still remained unspoken, came forward, and as she
(she hadn't said what her wish for the princess was yet)
could not undo the evil curse, but only soften it, she said, "It
undo-undid-undone
shall not be death, but a deep sleep of a hundred years, into
which the princess shall fall."
the sleep

The king, who eagerly wished to protect his dear child from
such misfortune, gave orders that every spindle in the whole
kingdom should be burned. Meanwhile, the gifts of the wise
women were abundantly fulfilled in the young girl, for she was
the wishes made by the wise women came true in the princess
so beautiful, modest, good-natured, and wise that everyone who
saw her simply had to love her.
certainly

On the very day that the girl turned fifteen years old, the
king and queen were not at home, and the maiden was left
in the palace quite alone. So she went around into all sorts of
places, looked into rooms and bedrooms just as she liked, and

protect

Stop & Think

How did the twelfth wise woman
prevent the princess from dying?

KEY WORDS

- **undo** to cancel the effects or results *undo–undid–undone
- **curse** magic words to bring others bad luck
- **soften** to make something less hard or less serious
- **eagerly** wanting to do something strongly
- **protect . . . from** to keep someone safe
- **abundantly** in large amounts
- **modest** not talking much about one's success
- **good-natured** kind and friendly
- **maiden** a young or unmarried girl
- **rusty** covered with rust
- **whirl** to spin very quickly
- **merrily** delightful

at last came to an old tower. She climbed up the narrow winding staircase and reached a little door. A rusty key was in the lock, and when she turned it the door opened and there in a little room sat an old woman with a spindle, busily spinning her flax.

winding staircase

"Good day, old mother," said the king's daughter.
(a polite way to greet old women)
"What are you doing there?"

"I am spinning," said the old woman, and nodded her head.

flax

"What sort of thing is that,
What is that
that whirls around so merrily?"
which
said the girl, and she took the spindle and wanted to spin too. But as soon as she had touched the spindle, the magic curse was fulfilled, and she pricked her
got hurt by touching the sharp top of the spindle
finger on it.

Stop & Think
Where did the princess find the old woman?

CHECK UP | True or false?

1 The princess shall fall into a sleep of a hundred years. _____
2 As soon as the princess had touched the rusty key, the magic curse was fulfilled. _____
3 The king gave orders that every spindle in the whole kingdom should not be burned. _____

GRAMMAR POINT

> **which** (relative pronoun)
> • It shall not be death, but a deep sleep of a hundred years, <u>into **which** the princess shall fall</u>.

7 Little Briar-Rose **83**

And at the very moment when she felt the prick, she fell
　　　　　　　exact
down upon the bed that stood there, and into a deep sleep. And
this sleep extended over the whole palace. The king and queen,
　　　　　　　(Everyone in the castle was cursed and fell asleep.)
who had just come home and entered the great hall, began to
fall asleep, and all of the court with them. The horses, too, went
　　　　　　　　the king's family and advisors
to sleep in the stable. The dogs in the yard, the pigeons upon the
roof, the flies on the walls, and even the fire that was flaming
in the fireplace, became quiet and slept. The roast meat stopped
roasting, and the cook, who was just going to pull the hair of
the dish-washing boy because he had forgotten something, let
him go and went to sleep. And the wind ceased to blow, and on
the trees before the castle not a leaf moved.

roast

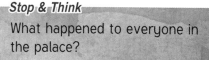

Stop & Think
What happened to everyone in
the palace?

KEY WORDS

- **prick** a pain one gets when touching
  something sharp
- **extend over** to cover an area
- **flame** to burn
- **roast** cooked over a fire; to cook over a fire
- **cease** to stop

- **hedge** small trees or bushes that form a wall
- **thorn** a sharp, pointed part of a stem or a
  plant's stem
- **from time to time** not often
- **thorny** having many thorns
- **get loose** to be free from; to escape

But all around the castle there began to grow a hedge of thorns, which every year became higher, and at last grew close up around the castle and all over it, so that there was nothing of the castle to be seen, not even the flag upon the roof. But the story of the beautiful sleeping Briar-Rose (for so the princess was named) went ~~about~~ *spread* the country, so that <u>from time to time</u> *sometimes* kings' sons came and tried to <u>get through</u> *pass* the thorny hedge into the castle.

But they found it impossible, for the thorns held fast together, as if they had hands, and the youths were caught in them, *stuck tightly* could not get loose again, and died a *young princes* miserable death.

Stop & Think
Why couldn't the princes get through the thorny hedge into the castle?

hedge   thorn   get through

CHECK UP | Put the events in order by marking them 1, 2, 3, and 4.

_____ All around the castle there began to grow a hedge of thorns.
_____ Kings' sons came and tried to get through the thorny hedge into the castle.
_____ The story of the beautiful sleeping Briar-Rose went about the country.
_____ The princess's sleep extended over the whole palace.

GRAMMAR POINT

• **stop -ing / try to**
  • The roast meat **stopped roasting**.
  • Kings' sons came and **tried to** get through the thorny hedge into the castle.

After many, many years, a king's son came once again to that country, and heard an old man talking about the thorny hedge, and how a castle was said to stand beneath it in which
under
a wonderfully beautiful princess named Briar-Rose had been asleep for a hundred years, and how the king and queen and the whole court were likewise asleep. The prince had heard too,
in the same way
from his grandfather, that many kings' sons had already come and tried to get through the thorny hedge, but had remained stuck fast in it and died a terrible death.
unable to move

Then the youth said, "I am not afraid. I will go and see the beautiful Briar-Rose." The good old man tried his best to dissuade him, but the prince did not listen to his words.
stop

Stop & Think
Why did the old man try his best to dissuade the prince from going to the castle?

youths

dissuade

 WORDS

- **dissuade** to stop one from doing something (≠ persuade)
- **awaken** to stop sleeping

- **part** to separate
- **pluck** to quickly remove something from its place

But by this time the hundred years had passed, and
the day had come when Briar-Rose was to awaken again.
the time of the curse had ended
When the king's son came near the thorny hedge, it was
nothing but large and beautiful flowers, which parted from
only
each other by themselves and let him pass unharmed,
not hurt
then closed again behind him like a hedge. In the castle
yard he saw the horses and the spotted hounds lying
dogs with spots
asleep; on the roof sat the pigeons with their heads under
their wings. And when he entered the house, the flies
were asleep upon the walls, the cook in the kitchen was
still holding out his hand to seize the boy, and the maid
stretching
was sitting by the black hen which she was going to pluck.
remove the feathers from

awaken

spotted hound

pluck

hen

Stop & Think

What did the thorny hedge turn into when the king's son came near it?

CHECK UP | **Answer the questions.**

1 What had the prince heard about from his grandfather?
   a. The spotted hounds.   b. The deaths of many princes.   c. The king's son.

2 What did the prince see when he was in the castle?
   a. Sleeping people and animals.   b. A spindle.   c. Thorns.

GRAMMAR POINT

try one's best to
• The good old man **tried his best to** dissuade him, but the prince did not listen to his words.

He went on farther, and in the great hall he saw the whole court lying asleep, while up by the throne lay the king and queen.

Then he went on still farther, and all was so quiet that a breath could be heard. At last he came to the tower, and opened the door to the little room where Briar-Rose was sleeping.

There she lay, so beautiful that he could not look away, and he stooped down and gave her a
<u>bent his body forward</u>
kiss. But as soon as he had kissed her, Briar-Rose opened her eyes, awoke and looked at him sweetly.
<u>with love</u>
Then they went downstairs together, and the king awoke, and the queen, and the whole court, and looked at each other in great astonishment. And the
<u>surprise</u>
horses in the yard stood up and shook themselves, the hounds
(the horses moved their bodies because they had slept for a long time)

Stop & Think
How did the princess awake?

throne   go downstairs

KEY WORDS

- **throne** a king's or queen's chair
- **breath** the air one breathes in and out
- **wag** to move something quickly from side to side or up and down

- **flicker** to burn or shine on and off quickly
- **smack** a hit with one's open hand
- **contentedly** feeling happy about one's life

jumped up and wagged their tails, the pigeons upon the roof pulled their heads out from under their wings, looked around and flew into the open country, the flies on the walls crept
wide countryside
again, the fire in the kitchen burned and flickered and cooked the meat, which began to turn and roast again, the cook gave the boy such a smack on the ear that he screamed, and
hit
the maid finished plucking the hen.

And then the marriage of the king's son to Briar-Rose was celebrated with all splendor, and they lived contentedly for the rest of their days. *(they felt happy for they had everything they wanted)*

open country

Stop & Think
How was the marriage of the prince and princess celebrated?

CHECK UP | **Choose the right words.**

1 The king and queen lay up by the _____. (smack | throne)
2 The hounds jumped up and _____ their tails. (wagged | flickered)
3 Briar-Rose and the prince lived _____ for the rest of their days. (sweetly | contentedly)

GRAMMAR POINT

finish -ing
• The maid **finished plucking** the hen.

8 Cinderella

The wife of a rich man became very sick, and as she felt that she would soon pass away she called her only daughter to her bedside and said, "Dear child, be good and pious, and then God will always protect you, and I will watch over you from heaven and be near you." Then she closed her eyes and died.

(a polite way to express dying)

believing in God

look after you

Every day the girl went out to her mother's grave and wept, and she remained pious and good. When winter came, the snow spread like a white sheet over the grave, and by the time the spring sun had melted it again, the man had a new wife.

there was a lot of snow

This woman had brought with her into the house her two daughters, who were beautiful and fair but also evil and cruel. Now began a bad time for the poor stepchild. "Is this stupid girl to sit in the living room with us?" they said. "Whoever wants to eat bread must earn it. Out with the kitchen maid." Then they took her pretty clothes away from her, put an old gray gown on

light-skinned

Everyone must work to get food.

Stop & Think

What kind of people were Cinderella's two sisters?

grave

gown

EY WORDS

- **pass away** to die
- **pious** showing belief in a religion
- **watch over someone** to look after someone
- **grave** a place underground where a dead body is put
- **melt** to become liquid

- **stepchild** the child of one's husband or wife
- **gown** a long dress
- **insult** to say or do something rude
- **pour** to make something go out
- **pea** a small green vegetable
- **dusty** covered in dust

her, and gave her wooden shoes. "Just look at the proud princess! How fancy she is!" they laughed, and led her into the kitchen.

(The two sisters were mocking Cinderella.)

peas

There she had to do hard work from morning till night: get up before dawn, carry water, light fires, cook, and wash. Besides this, the sisters did all they could to hurt her. They insulted her and poured her peas

said and did rude things to

and lentils into the ashes, so that she was forced to sit

lentils

and pick them out again. In the evening, when she had worked till she was exhausted, she had no bed to go to, but had to sleep by the fireplace in the cinders. And because she

small pieces of burnt wood

always looked dusty and dirty, they called her Cinderella.

Stop & Think
Why did the two sisters call the girl Cinderella?

cinders

CHECK UP | True or false?

1 The two sisters did all they could to help Cinderella. _____
2 Cinderella remained pious and good. _____
3 The two sisters poured Cinderella's peas and lentils into the fireplace. _____

GRAMMAR POINT

do all one can to
• The two sisters **did all they could to** hurt her.

One day the father was going to the fair, and he asked his two stepdaughters what he should bring back for them.

festival at which many things are sold

fair

"Beautiful dresses," said one.

"Pearls and jewels," said the other.

"And you, Cinderella?" he said. "What will you have?"

"Father, break off for me the first branch which knocks against your hat on your way home."

pull from the tree

touches

bushes

So he bought beautiful dresses, pearls and jewels for his two stepdaughters, and on his way home, as he was riding through some green bushes, a twig brushed against him and knocked off his hat. Then he broke off the branch and took it with him. When he got home, he gave his stepdaughters the things which they had asked for, and to Cinderella he gave the branch from the bush.

pushed off

Cinderella thanked him, went to her mother's grave, planted the branch on it, and wept so much that her

---

Stop & Think

What did Cinderella want from her father?

KEY WORDS

- **stepdaughter** one's daughter by marriage, but not by birth
- **bush** a plant with many small branches, like a small tree
- **perch** to sit on; to settle
- **express** to say
- **last** to continue (≠ stop)
- **fasten** to join together
- **buckle** the metal piece that fastens a belt

tears fell down on the branch and watered it. And so it grew and became a beautiful tree. Three times a day Cinderella went and sat beneath it and wept and prayed, and a little white bird always came and <u>perched</u> (*sat*) on the tree, and if Cinderella expressed a wish, the bird <u>threw down to her whatever she had wished for.</u> (*gave her her wish*)

buckle

One day, however, the king gave orders for a festival which was to <u>last</u> (*continue for*) three days, and to which all the beautiful young girls in the country were invited, so that his son might choose himself a bride. <mark>When Cinderella's two stepsisters heard that they too had been invited to appear at the festival, they were delighted.</mark> They called Cinderella and said, "Comb our hair for us, brush our shoes, and <u>fasten</u> (*join together*) our buckles, for we are going to the festival at the king's palace."

Stop & Think
How many days would the festival last?

CHECK UP | **Finish the sentences.**

1 The father was going to
2 Cinderella went to
3 The father was riding through
4 The stepsisters had been invited to

a. the festival.
b. some green bushes.
c. her mother's grave.
d. the fair.

GRAMMAR POINT

> • **hear that S (subject) + V (verb)** . . .
> • When Cinderella's two stepsisters **heard that they** too **had been invited** to appear at the festival, they were delighted.

pigeon

dove

Cinderella obeyed, but wept, because she too would have liked to go to the dance. She begged her stepmother to allow her to go. "Cinderella," she said, "you are covered in dust and dirt, yet you would go to the festival? You have no clothes or shoes, yet you would dance?"

but you still want to go to the festival

As Cinderella went on asking, however, her stepmother said at last, "I have poured a dish of lentils into the ashes for you. If you have picked them out again in two hours, you shall go with us."

Cinderella went through the back door into the garden and called, "You tame pigeons, you doves, and all you other birds beneath the sky, come and help me to pick the good lentils into the dish and the bad into the barrel."

≠ dangerous and wild

Stop & Think

Who did Cinderella ask to help her pick the lentils?

KEY WORDS

- **dust** small dry pieces of soil which can float in the air
- **dirt** small pieces of soil or mud
- **tame** ≠ dangerous and wild (animals)

- **dove** a white bird which is like a pigeon
- **flap** to move (wings) up and down
- **grain** seeds eaten as food, like rice or corn
- **joyful** happy; delighted

Then two pigeons came in through the kitchen window, and after them some doves, and finally all the birds beneath the sky came flapping and crowding in and landed

moving their wings up and down   *filling up the kitchen*   *settled on the ground*

among the ashes. And the pigeons nodded with their heads and began to pick, pick, pick, pick, and the rest began also to pick, pick, pick, pick, and they gathered all the good grains into the dish. In just one hour they had finished, and all flew out again. Joyful, the girl took the dish to her

Delighted

stepmother and thought that now she would be allowed to go to the festival.

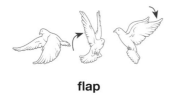

flap

bird landing

Stop & Think

Where did the birds gather all the good grains?

CHECK UP | Answer the questions.

1 What must Cinderella do if she wants to go to the festival?
  a. Remove dust and dirt.   b. Prepare clothes.   c. Pick out lentils.

2 How long did the birds take to finish gathering all the good grains?
  a. Two hours.   b. One hour.   c. A day.

GRAMMAR POINT

allow one to
  • She begged her stepmother to **allow her to** go.

But the stepmother said, "No, Cinderella, you have no clothes and you cannot dance. You would only be laughed at."

And as Cinderella wept at this, her stepmother said, "If you can pick two dishes of lentils out of the ashes for me in one hour, you shall go with us." And she thought to herself, "She most certainly cannot do that again." When the stepmother had

(The stepmother thought it would be impossible for Cinderella to do it.)

poured the two dishes of lentils among the ashes, the girl went through the back door into the garden and cried, "You tame pigeons, you doves, and all you other birds beneath the sky, come and help me to pick the good lentils into the dishes, and the bad into the barrel."

laugh at   **bad lentils**

Stop & Think

Do you think Cinderella will be able to go to the festival this time? Why or why not?

WORDS

- **certainly** of course; without doubt
- **ashamed of** embarrassed by (≠ proud of)

- **turn one's back on** to ignore; to refuse to help

Then two pigeons came in through the kitchen window, and after them some doves, and finally all the birds beneath the sky came flapping and crowding in and landed among the ashes. And the doves nodded with their heads and began to pick, pick, pick, pick, and the others began also to pick, pick, pick, pick, and they gathered all the good seeds into the dishes. In less
grains
than half an hour they had already finished, and all flew out again.

Then Cinderella was delighted and believed that she might now go to the festival. But her stepmother said, "All this will not help. You cannot go with us, for you have no clothes and
Everything you've done is of no use.
cannot dance. We would be ashamed of you." And she turned
embarrassed by
her back on Cinderella and hurried away with her two proud
ignored
daughters.

hurry away

Stop & Think
How long did the birds take to finish gathering all the good seeds this time?

CHECK UP | Fill in the blanks with the correct words.

> certainly   delighted   ashamed of

1 Cinderella was _____ and believed that she might now go to the festival.
2 The stepmother said, "We would be _____ you" to Cinderella.
3 The stepmother thought to herself, "She most _____ cannot do that again."

GRAMMAR POINT

- **believe that S (subject) + V (verb) . . .**
  - Then Cinderella was delighted and **believed that she might** now **go** to the festival.

As no one else was now at home, Cinderella went to her mother's grave beneath the tree and cried, "Shiver and quiver, little tree, throw silver and gold down over me."

(Cinderella said magic words to make her wish come true.)

Then the bird threw a gold and silver dress down to her, and slippers decorated with silk and silver. She quickly put on the dress and went to the festival. Her stepsisters and stepmother, however, did not know her and thought she must be a foreign princess, for she looked so beautiful in her golden dress. They never once thought of Cinderella and assumed that she was sitting at home in the dirt, picking lentils out of the ashes.

one time

Stop & Think

What did the white bird give Cinderella?

golden dress

slippers

(K)EY WORDS

- **shiver** to shake to a small degree, as if cold
- **quiver** to shake to a small degree; shiver
- **silk** a soft type of cloth of very high quality
- **assume** to think something is true
- **keep one company** to stay with someone
- **belong to** to be owned by
- **unknown** not known by others (≠ known)
- **leap** to jump *leap–leapt–leapt

The prince approached her, <u>took her by the hand</u>, *held her hand* and danced with her. He would dance with no other maiden and never let go of her hand, and if anyone else came to invite her, he said, "This is my partner." *stopped holding*

pigeon house

She danced till it was evening, and then she wanted to go home. But the king's son said, "I will go with you and keep you company," for <mark>he wished to see to whom this beautiful maiden belonged.</mark> She escaped from him, *stay with you so you won't be alone* however, and ran into the pigeon house.

pickaxe

The king's son waited until her father came, and then he told him that the <u>unknown</u> maiden had <u>leapt</u> *≠ known* *leap-leapt-leapt* into the pigeon house. The old man thought, "Can it be Cinderella?" They had to bring him an axe and a pickaxe so that he could <u>chop</u> the *cut* pigeon house into pieces, but no one was inside it.

Stop & Think
How did the prince feel about Cinderella?

CHECK UP | **Choose the right words.**

1 The stepmother and stepsisters _____ that Cinderella was at home. (leapt | assumed)
2 Cinderella had _____ into the pigeon house. (belonged | leapt)
3 The bird threw slippers decorated with _____ and silver. (gold | silk)

GRAMMAR POINT

whom (pronoun as the object of a preposition)
• He wished to see to **whom** this beautiful maiden belonged.

And when they got home, Cinderella lay in her dirty clothes among the ashes, and a dim little oil lamp was burning on the

≠ bright

giving off light

shelf, for she had jumped quickly down from the back of the pigeon house and run to the little tree, where she had taken off her beautiful clothes and laid them on the grave. The bird had taken them away again, and then Cinderella had seated herself

sat

in the kitchen among the ashes in her gray gown.

The next day when the festival began again and her parents and stepsisters had gone once more, Cinderella went to the tree and said, "Shiver and quiver, my little tree, throw silver and gold down over me."

Then the bird threw down a much more beautiful dress than the one from the day before. And when Cinderella appeared at the festival in this dress, everyone was astonished at her beauty. The king's son had waited for her to come, and he instantly took her by the hand and danced with no one but her. When others

only

Stop & Think
Why did Cinderella take off her beautiful clothes?

oil lamp

shelf

 WORDS

- **dim** giving off little light (≠ bright)
- **wish to** to want to do something
- **gracefully** beautifully and elegantly
- **squirrel** a small animal that eats nuts

came and invited her, he said, "This is my partner."

When evening came, she wished to leave. The king's
son followed her and wanted to see into which house
she went. But she sprang away from him and into the

moved quickly

garden behind the house. There stood a beautiful tall tree
on which hung the most magnificent pears. She moved so
gracefully between the branches, like a squirrel, that the

beautifully and elegantly

king's son did not know where she had gone. He waited
until her father came and said to him, "The unknown
maiden has escaped from me, and I believe she has climbed

run away

up the pear tree."

squirrel

Stop & Think
What was special about the tall tree?

CHECK UP | True or false?

1 The white bird had taken Cinderella's gray gown away again. ____
2 Cinderella had seated herself in the kitchen among the ashes in her gray gown. ____
3 Cinderella sprang away from the prince and into the pigeon house. ____

GRAMMAR POINT

be astonished at
• Everyone **was astonished at** her beauty.

The father thought, "Can it be Cinderella?"

And the father had an axe brought and cut the tree down,
asked someone to bring an axe
but no one was on it. And when they went into the kitchen
Cinderella lay there among the ashes, as usual, for she had
like always
jumped down off the other side of the tree, taken the beautiful
dress back to the bird on the little tree, and put on her gray
gown.

On the third day, when her parents and stepsisters had gone
away, Cinderella went once more to her mother's grave and said
to the little tree, "Shiver and quiver, my little tree, throw silver
and gold down over me."

And now the bird threw down to her a dress which was
more splendid and magnificent than any she had yet had, and
she had had before
golden slippers. And when she went to the festival in this dress,

axe   golden slipper

Stop & Think
What color were Cinderella's
slippers this time?

KEY WORDS

- **as usual** like what happens most or all of the
  time
- **splendid** excellent; wonderful; outstanding

- **anxious** worried and nervous
- **smear** to spread over, like butter on bread
- **pitch** a sticky black material

everyone was so astonished that no one could speak. The king's

everyone was too surprised to say anything

son danced with her only, and if anyone else invited her to

dance, he said, "This is my partner."

When evening came, Cinderella wished to leave, and the

king's son was anxious to go with her, but she escaped from

him so quickly that he could not follow her. The king's

son, however, had thought of

a clever trick, and ordered

smart plan

the whole staircase to be

smeared with pitch. And

covered

there, after Cinderella had

run down, her left slipper

remained stuck.

unable to move

anxious   **pitch**

Stop & Think
Why did Cinderella's left slipper
remain stuck?

CHECK UP | Put the events in order by marking them 1, 2, 3, and 4.

_____ Cinderella's left slipper remained stuck on the staircase.
_____ Cinderella took the beautiful dress back to the bird on the little tree.
_____ Cinderella's father had an axe brought and cut the pear tree down.
_____ The prince ordered the whole staircase to be smeared with pitch.

GRAMMAR POINT

• comparative adjective + than . . .
  • And now the bird threw down to her a dress which was **more splendid** and
  magnificent than any she had yet had.

51

The king's son picked it up, and it was small and delicate and
easily damaged
all golden. The next morning he went with it to Cinderella's
father and said to him, "No one shall be my wife but she whose
foot this golden slipper fits."
↳ only the one whose foot can fit in this shoe

Then the two sisters were glad, for they had pretty feet. The
eldest went into her room with the shoe to try it on, and her
mother watched. But she could not get her big toe into it as the
shoe was too small for her. Then her mother gave her a knife
and said, "Cut the toe off. When you are queen, you will never
need to walk again." So the girl cut her toe off, forced her foot
pushed her foot hard
into the shoe, hid her pain, and went out to the king's son.
didn't show any pain
Then he took her on his horse as his bride and rode away with
her.

big toe   cut off   pain

Stop & Think

What did the mother tell her
eldest daughter to do?

 EY WORDS

- **delicate** easily damaged
- **try on** to put something on and see if it fits
- **peep** to secretly look at something
- **drip** to fall slowly in drops (of liquid)
- **chamber** a room
- **heel** the rounded back part of the foot

They had to pass the grave, however, and there on the tree sat two white doves, who cried, "Turn and peep, turn and peep; there's blood within the shoe. The shoe is too small for her, and your true bride waits for you."

turn around and look secretly

peep

Then the king's son looked at her foot and saw how the blood was dripping from it. He turned his horse around, took the false bride home again and said that she was not the right one and the other sister was to put the shoe on. Then this one went into her chamber and got her toes safely into the shoe, but her heel was too large.

falling in drops

had to

room

drip

heel

Stop & Think
What will the mother probably tell her other daughter to do to fit her foot into the shoe?

CHECK UP | Fill in the blanks with the correct words.

> delicate   peep   dripping   heel

1 The two pigeons cried, "Turn and _____; there's blood within the shoe."
2 The king's son looked at the girl's foot and saw how the blood was _____ from it.
3 The other daughter got her toes safely into the shoe, but her _____ was too large.
4 The king's son picked the shoe up, and it was small and _____.

GRAMMAR POINT

> **S (subject) + V (present tense verb) . . . , S + will . . .**
> • When you **are** queen, you **will** never need to walk again.

52

So her mother gave her a knife and said, "Cut a bit off your heel. When you are queen, you will never need to walk again." So the girl cut a bit off her heel, forced her foot into the shoe, hid her pain, and went out to the king's son.

He took her on his horse as his bride and rode away with her, but when they passed by the tree, the two doves sat on it and cried, "Turn and peep, turn and peep; there's blood within the shoe. The shoe is too small for her, and your true bride waits for you."

He looked down at her foot and saw the blood running out
flowing out
of the shoe and how it had stained her white stocking quite red.
made her white stocking red
Then he turned his horse around and took the false bride home again. "This is not the right, one, either," he said. "Have you no other daughter?"
Don't you have another daughter?

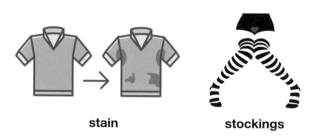

stain   stockings

 KEY WORDS

- **stain** to leave a mark; to change the color of something
- **stocking** thin clothing that covers one's leg and foot

- **stunted** not completely developed (≠ fully grown)
- **absolutely** in every way
- **fit like a glove** to fit perfectly
- **recognize** to know who someone is

"No," said the man. "There is still a little stunted kitchen

maid whom my late wife left behind, but she cannot possibly

be your bride."

≠ fully grown

dead

The king's son said he was to send the girl up to him, but

ordered the father to send Cinderella to him

the stepmother answered, "Oh, no! She is much too dirty; she

cannot show herself." But he absolutely insisted on it, and so

in every way

Cinderella had to be called.

She first washed her hands and face and then went and

bowed down before the king's son, who gave her the golden

shoe. Then she seated herself on a stool, pulled her foot out of

the heavy wooden shoe, and put it into the slipper, which fit

like a glove. And when she rose and the king's son looked at her

fit her foot perfectly

face, he recognized the beautiful maiden who had danced with

knew who the young girl was

him and cried, "This is my true bride."

kitchen maid　　　**stool**

Stop & Think
What did the prince insist on?

CHECK UP | Answer the questions.

1　What did the second daughter do to fit into the shoe?
　　a. She cut off her toe.　　b. She cut a bit off her heel.　　c. She took off her stocking.
2　What did Cinderella do before she met the king's son?
　　a. She put on a glove.　　b. She washed her hands and face　c. She seated herself.

GRAMMAR POINT

● **negative statement, either**
　● This is **not** the right one, **either**.

53

The stepmother and the two sisters were horrified and became pale with rage. **got so angry that their faces turned white** The king's son, however, took Cinderella on his horse and rode away with her.

As they passed by the tree, the two white doves cried, "Turn and peep, turn and peep; no blood is in the shoe. The shoe is not too small for her, and your true bride rides with you." When they had cried that, they came flying down and placed themselves on Cinderella's shoulders — one on the right, the **sat** other on the left — and remained sitting there.

When the wedding of Cinderella and the king's son was to be celebrated, the two false sisters came and tried to get into favor **≠ sincere** with Cinderella and share her good fortune. When the engaged **(they started being nice to Cinderella because they hoped she would give them things)**

pale

good fortune

Stop & Think
Why did the two false sisters come to Cinderella's wedding?

shoulder

peck

 KEY WORDS

- **get into favor with** to make someone like you
- **good fortune** good luck
- **engaged** having formally agreed to marry

- **peck out** to bite out with a beak
- **wickedness** being wicked (≠ kindness)
- **falsehood** a lie (≠ truth)

couple went to the church, the elder sister was on the right

side and the younger on the left, and the two pigeons pecked

out one eye from each of them. Afterwards, as they came back,

each of the two sisters lost one of her eyes

the elder was on the left and the younger on the right, and the

pigeons pecked out the other eye from each. And thus, for their

wickedness and falsehood, they were punished with blindness

And so the pigeons made them blind because they were evil and dishonest.

for the rest of their days.

Stop & Think

Will the two false sisters be able to see anymore?

CHECK UP | Finish the sentences.

1 The stepmother and the two sisters
2 The two white doves
3 The two pigeons
4 The two sisters

a. tried to share Cinderella's good fortune.
b. pecked out one eye from each of the sisters.
c. placed themselves on Cinderella's shoulders.
d. were horrified when the prince took Cinderella with him.

GRAMMAR POINT

with (by means of)
• They were punished **with** blindness for the rest of their days.

英文閱讀聽力素養訓練課

格|林|童|話

作者

原著 Brothers Grimm
(Jacob Ludwig Carl Grimm / Wilhelm Carl Grimm)
英譯 Margaret Hunt
改寫 Richard Luhrs
英英解釋與測驗題 Olanda Lin

譯者 丁宥榆

編輯 林晨禾

插畫 楊雅媛 Story 1, 2／楊盟玉 Story 3
許永和 Story 4, 6／夏萱 Story 5
宋雅圓 Story 7, 8

校對 黃詩韻

內文排版 林書玉（課本）／謝青秀（訓練書）

封面設計 林書玉

製程管理 洪巧玲

發行人 黃朝萍

出版者 語言工場出版有限公司

電話 +886-(0)2-2365-9739

傳真 +886-(0)2-2365-9835

網址 www.icosmos.com.tw

讀者服務 onlineservice@icosmos.com.tw

出版日期 2022 年11月　初版一刷　（寂天雲隨身聽APP版)

作者簡介

Margaret Hunt
為十九、二十世紀的英國小說家與翻譯，於1884年完成多篇格林童話之翻譯。

Richard Luhrs
紐約州立大學（State University of New York）英語寫作系與哲學系（BA in English Composition and Philosophy）雙學士，於日本、台灣、韓國等地從事英語教學二十餘年，曾替LTTC財團法人語言訓練測驗中心及各出版社編寫英語教材。

國家圖書館出版品預行編目(CIP)資料

英文閱讀聽力素養訓練課：格林童話(寂天雲隨身聽APP版) / ABrothers Grimm原著；Richard Luhrs改寫；Margaret Hunt英譯；丁宥榆譯. -- 初版. -- 臺北市：語言工場出版有限公司, 2022.11
ISBN 978-986-6963-84-1 (16K平裝)

1.CST: 英語 2.CST: 讀本
805.18　　　　　　　　111017364

* 本書由寂天文化授權出版，原書名《FUN 學格林童話：英語閱讀聽力訓練》。

劃撥帳號 1998620-0 寂天文化事業股份有限公司
訂書金額未滿 1000 元，請外加運費 100 元。
【若有破損，請寄回更換，謝謝】

英文閱讀聽力
素養訓練課
格│林│童│話

TRAINING BOOK + MP3

Table of Contents

Vocabulary & Listening Practice

Vocabulary & Listening Practice

1 Thumbling

pp. 2–3

1 Vocabulary Practice: Match.

_____	1. **peasant**	A	to turn around quickly
_____	2. **poke**	B	a loud, deep breath
_____	3. **spin**	C	having grace; elegant
_____	4. **thread**	D	an arm or leg
_____	5. **lively**	E	however
_____	6. **limb**	F	to push with a finger or an object
_____	7. **sigh**	G	a living thing
_____	8. **remain**	H	full of energy; energetic
_____	9. **nevertheless**	I	a poor farmer
_____	10. **sensibly**	J	to stay the same
_____	11. **graceful**	K	intelligently
_____	12. **creature**	L	a long, thin string to make clothes

② Listen and fill in the blanks with the correct words. Remember to change the form of verbs or nouns if necessary.

There was once a poor 1._____ who sat one evening by the fireplace and poked the fire as his wife sat spinning 2._____. Then he said, "How sad it is that we have no children. With us all is so quiet, and in other houses it is noisy and 3._____."

"Yes," replied his wife with a sigh. "Even if we had only one, and it were quite small, and only as big as a thumb, I should be quite satisfied, and we would still love it with all our hearts."

Now it happened that the woman fell ill, and after seven months she gave birth to a child that was perfect in all his 4._____, but no longer than a thumb.

Then the couple said, "It is as we wished it to be, and he shall be our dear child." And because of his size, they called him Thumbling.

Though the couple did not let him go without food, the child did not grow taller, but 5._____ as he had been at first. Nevertheless, he looked 6._____ at the world through his eyes and soon showed himself to be a wise and 7._____ creature, for everything he did turned out well.

One day the peasant was getting ready to go into the forest to cut wood when he said, as if to himself, "How I wish that there was someone who would bring my 8._____ to me."

"Oh, Father," cried Thumbling, "I will soon bring the cart. Trust me. It shall be in the forest when you need it."

The man smiled and said, "How can you do that? You are far too small to lead the horse by the reins."

❶ Vocabulary Practice: Match.

_____	1. **harness**	**A**	to connect one thing to another
_____	2. **attach**	**B**	to grab
_____	3. **place**	**C**	to show; to display
_____	4. **properly**	**D**	a great surprise
_____	5. **turn a corner**	**E**	to one side
_____	6. **exactly**	**F**	to tie an animal to a vehicle
_____	7. **get hold of**	**G**	to put
_____	8. **amazement**	**H**	correctly
_____	9. **aside**	**I**	right
_____	10. **exhibit**	**J**	to change direction at a corner

02 ❷ Listen and fill in the blanks with the correct words. Remember to change the form of verbs or nouns if necessary.

"That's not important, Father. If my mother will just harness the horse, I shall sit in the horse's ear and tell him where he must go."

"Well," answered the man, "let's give it a try."

When the time came, the mother **1.**_____ the horse to the cart and placed Thumbling in his ear, and then the little child cried, "Giddy-up! Giddy-up!"

Then the horse went quite **2.**_____ as if with his master, and the cart went the right way into the forest. It happened that just as the horse was **3.**_____ and the little one was crying, "Giddy-up," two strange men came towards him.

"My word," said one of them. "What is this?"

"There is a cart coming, and a driver is calling to the horse, but still he cannot be seen. That can't be right," said the other. "We will follow the cart and see where it stops."

The cart, however, drove right into the forest and **4.**_____ to the place where the wood had been cut. When Thumbling saw his father, he cried to him, "Do you see, Father? Here I am with the cart. Now take me down."

The father **5.**_____ the horse with his left hand and with the right took his little son out of the ear. Thumbling sat down quite happily on a straw, but when the two strange men saw him, they did not know what to say in their **6.**_____. Then one of them took the other aside and said, "Listen. The little fellow would make us rich if we **7.**_____ him in a large town for money. We will buy him."

Answers ❷

1. attached **2.** properly **3.** turning a corner **4.** exactly **5.** got hold of **6.** amazement **7.** exhibited

1 Vocabulary Practice: Match.

_____	1. creep	**A** good behavior; politeness
_____	2. whisper	**B** ≠ put . . . on
_____	3. sum	**C** to move slowly and carefully
_____	4. back and forth	**D** to speak quietly with one's breath, not the voice
_____	5. necessary	**E** to go quickly into a space
_____	6. good manners	**F** a disappointed feeling
_____	7. take . . . off	**G** amount
_____	8. slip into	**H** repeatedly from one side to the other
_____	9. stick	**I** to move slowly on the ground with your hands and knees
_____	10. no use	**J** to push something in
_____	11. crawl	**K** needing to be done
_____	12. frustration	**L** useless; in vain

🎧 03 ❷ **Listen and fill in the blanks with the correct words. Remember to change the form of verbs or nouns if necessary.**

They went to the peasant and said, "Sell us the little man. He shall be well treated with us."

"No," replied the father. "He is the apple of my eye, and all the money in the world cannot buy him from me." Thumbling, however, when he heard the men's idea, **1.**_____ up the folds of his father's coat, placed himself on his shoulder, and whispered in his ear, "Father, do give me away. I will soon come back again." Then the father sold him to the two men for a large **2.**_____ of money.

"Where will you sit?" the men asked Thumbling.

"Oh, just set me on the edge of your hat, and then I can walk **3.**_____ and look at the country and still not fall down." They did as he wished, and when Thumbling had said goodbye to his father, they went away with him.

They walked until it was dark, and then the little fellow said, "Do take me down. It is **4.**_____."

"Just stay up there," said the man on whose hat Thumbling sat. "I don't care. The birds sometimes drop things on me."

"No," said Thumbling. "I know **5.**_____. Take me down quickly."

The man took his hat off and put the little fellow on the ground by the side of the road. Thumbling jumped and crept around a little on the ground, and then he suddenly **6.**_____ a mousehole which he had been looking for. "Good evening, gentlemen. Just go home without me," he shouted to the men and laughed.

They ran to the mousehole and stuck their walking sticks into it, but it was **7.**_____. Thumbling crawled still farther in, and as it soon became quite dark, they had to go home with their **8.**_____ and their empty pockets.

Answers ❷

1. crept   2. sum   3. back and forth   4. necessary   5. good manners   6. slipped into   7. no use   8. frustration

Vocabulary & Listening Practice ❶ Thumbling **7**

pp. 8–9

1 Vocabulary Practice: Match.

_____	1. **underground**	**A**	≠ danger
_____	2. **fortunately**	**B**	fear
_____	3. **stumble**	**C**	to give
_____	4. **shell**	**D**	luckily
_____	5. **safety**	**E**	worried
_____	6. **interrupt**	**F**	the hard, outer part that protects an animal, egg, or seed
_____	7. **fright**	**G**	below the surface of the earth
_____	8. **hand out**	**H**	power; strength
_____	9. **might**	**I**	to speak when someone else is already speaking
_____	10. **alarmed**	**J**	to walk awkwardly

Answers

1

1. G   2. D   3. I   4. F   5. A
6. I   7. B   8. C   9. H   10. E

2 Listen and fill in the blanks with the correct words. Remember to change the form of verbs or nouns if necessary.

When Thumbling saw that they were gone, he crawled back out of the underground tunnel. "It is so dangerous to walk on the ground in the dark," he said, "and how easily a neck or a leg can be broken." **1.**_____ he soon stumbled against an empty snail shell. "Thank God," he said, "that I can spend the night in **2.**_____." And he got inside it.

Not long afterwards, as he was just falling asleep, he heard two men go by, and one of them was saying, "How shall we get hold of the rich pastor's silver and gold?"

"I could tell you that," cried Thumbling, **3.**_____ them.

"What was that?" said one of the thieves in fright. "I heard someone speaking."

They stood still listening, and Thumbling spoke again. "Take me with you, and I'll help you."

"But where are you?"

"Just look on the ground and see where my voice is coming from," he replied.

There the thieves finally found him and lifted him up. "You little imp, how will you help us?" they asked.

"Listen," he said. "I will creep into the pastor's room through the iron bars and will **4.**_____ to you whatever you want to have."

"Come on, then," they said, "and we will see what you can do."

When they got to the pastor's house, Thumbling crept into the room, but instantly cried out with all his **5.**_____, "Do you want to have everything that is here?"

The thieves were **6.**_____ and said, "Please speak softly, so as not to wake anyone up."

Thumbling, however, behaved as if he had not understood this and cried again, "What do you want? Do you want to have everything that is here?"

① Vocabulary Practice: Match.

_____	1. maid	**A**	to start a fire
_____	2. rascal	**B**	a naughty child or young man
_____	3. take off	**C**	to plan to do something
_____	4. light	**D**	to know; to realize
_____	5. examine	**E**	(sleep) deeply
_____	6. intend to	**F**	to leave
_____	7. arise	**G**	to wake up (≠ fall asleep)
_____	8. grab	**H**	to get up
_____	9. precisely	**I**	to check
_____	10. soundly	**J**	to get hold of
_____	11. be aware of	**K**	a female servant
_____	12. awake	**L**	exactly

🎧 **05** **②** Listen and fill in the blanks with the correct words. Remember to change the form of verbs or nouns if necessary.

The maid, who slept in the next room, heard this, sat up in bed, and listened. The thieves had run some distance away in their fright, but at last they felt braver and thought, "The little rascal wants to **1.**_____ us." They came back and whispered to him, "Be serious, and hand something out to us."

Then Thumbling again cried as loudly as he could, "I really will give you everything; just put your hands in." The maid, who was listening, heard this quite clearly, jumped out of bed, and rushed to the door. The thieves **2.**_____ and ran as if a wild animal were behind them, but as the maid could not see anything, she went to **3.**_____ a candle.

When she came back with it, Thumbling, unseen, went to the granary. The maid, after she had examined every corner and found nothing, lay down in her bed again and believed that, after all, she had only been dreaming with open eyes and ears.

Thumbling had climbed up into the hay and found a beautiful place to sleep. There he **4.**_____ rest until daylight and then go home again to his parents.

But that was not what happened.

Truly, there is much worry and pain in this world. When the day began, the maid **5.**_____ from her bed to feed the cows. Her first walk was into the barn, where she grabbed an armful of hay, and **6.**_____ that very one in which poor Thumbling was lying asleep. He, however, was sleeping so soundly that he was aware of nothing and did not **7.**_____ until he was in the mouth of a cow, who had picked him up with the hay.

1 Vocabulary Practice: Match.

_____	1. **mill**	**A**	the place around you
_____	2. **discover**	**B**	a factory that makes cloth or flour
_____	3. **tear apart**	**C**	to understand
_____	4. **be forced to**	**D**	extremely afraid; frightened
_____	5. **surroundings**	**E**	to realize; to find out
_____	6. **unpleasing**	**F**	to drop or pour liquid suddenly
_____	7. **realize**	**G**	ghost
_____	8. **terrified**	**H**	to do against one's will
_____	9. **stool**	**I**	to break something violently into small pieces
_____	10. **spill**	**J**	a seat without a back
_____	11. **evil**	**K**	≠ satisfying
_____	12. **spirit**	**L**	extremely bad; cruel

Answers

1

1. B   2. E   3. I   4. H   5. A   6. K
7. C   8. D   9. J   10. F   11. L   12. G

2 Listen and fill in the blanks with the correct words. Remember to change the form of verbs or nouns if necessary.

"Oh, no!" he cried. "How have I got into the wool-cleaning mill?"

But he soon **1.**_____ where he was. Then he had to take care not to let himself get between the cow's teeth and be **2.**_____, but he was therefore forced to slip down into the stomach with the hay.

"In this little room there are no windows," he said, "and no sun shines in, nor will a candle be lit." His **3.**_____ were especially unpleasing to him, and the worst was that more and more hay was always coming in through the door, and the space growing smaller and smaller. At last, in his anguish, he cried **4.**_____ he could, "Bring me no more fodder! Bring me no more fodder!"

The maid was just then milking the cow, and when she heard someone speaking and saw no one and **5.**_____ that it was the same voice that she had heard in the night. She was so terrified that she slipped off her stool and **6.**_____ the milk.

She ran quickly to her master and said, "Oh heavens, Pastor, the cow has been speaking."

"You are mad," replied the pastor, but he went himself to the cowshed to see what was there. He had just set his foot inside, however, when Thumbling again cried, "Bring me no more fodder! Bring me no more fodder!"

Then the pastor himself was alarmed, thinking that an **7.**_____ spirit had gone into the cow, and ordered her to be killed. She was killed, but her stomach, with Thumbling inside, was thrown on the dunghill.

1 Vocabulary Practice: Match.

_____	**1. difficulty**	**A**	excellent; wonderful
_____	**2. thrust**	**B**	loud and unpleasant (≠ soft)
_____	**3. misfortune**	**C**	in the same way
_____	**4. swallow**	**D**	a difficult thing or time; hardship
_____	**5. at one gulp**	**E**	the feeling of satisfaction
_____	**6. magnificent**	**F**	to try to get into a small place
_____	**7. squeeze in**	**G**	a terrible event
_____	**8. content**	**H**	≠ eat slowly
_____	**9. violent**	**I**	power and energy
_____	**10. rage**	**J**	to push forward
_____	**11. likewise**	**K**	to show great anger
_____	**12. strength**	**L**	to make food go down your throat

2 Listen and fill in the blanks with the correct words. Remember to change the form of verbs or nouns if necessary.

Thumbling had great difficulty in working his way out. He succeeded in getting some room, but just as he was going to thrust his head outsides a new 1._____ occurred. A hungry wolf ran up and swallowed the whole stomach at one gulp.

Thumbling did not 2._____. "Perhaps," he thought, "the wolf will listen to what I have got to say." And he called to the wolf from out of his belly, "Dear wolf, I know of a 3._____ feast for you."

"Where is it to be had?" said the wolf.

"In such and such a house. You must creep into it through the kitchen sink, and you will find cakes, bacon, and sausages, and as much of them as you can eat." And he described to the wolf exactly his father's house.

The wolf did not need to be told this twice. He 4._____ himself in at night through the sink, and ate to his heart's 5._____ in the pantry. When he had eaten his fill, he wanted to go out again, but he had become so big that he could not go out the same way. Thumbling had expected this, and now he began to make a 6._____ noise in the wolf's body and raged and screamed as loudly as he could.

"Will you be quiet?" said the wolf. "You will wake up the people."

"What do I care?" replied the little fellow. "You have eaten your fill, and I will celebrate likewise." And he began once more to scream with all his 7._____.

1 Vocabulary Practice: Match.

_____	1. **fetch**	**A**	money; wealth
_____	2. **chop**	**B**	to cut into pieces
_____	3. **sorrow**	**C**	to hug
_____	4. **go through**	**D**	a long trip
_____	5. **for one's sake**	**E**	to get something and bring it back
_____	6. **breathe**	**F**	to experience
_____	7. **riches**	**G**	to take air into your body
_____	8. **embrace**	**H**	to damage
_____	9. **spoil**	**I**	for one's good or benefit
_____	10. **journey**	**J**	sadness

1

6. G   7. A   8. C   9. H   10. D
1. E   2. B   3. I   4. F   5. I

⌂08 ❷ Listen and fill in the blanks with the correct words. Remember to change the form of verbs or nouns if necessary.

At last his father and mother were aroused by the noise, ran to the kitchen, and looked in through the opening in the door. When they saw that a wolf was inside, they ran away. The husband **1.**_____ his axe, and the wife fetched the scythe. "Stay behind," said the man when they entered the room. "When I have hit him with the axe, if he is not killed by it, you must cut him down and **2.**_____ his body to pieces."

Then Thumbling heard his parents' voices and cried, "Dear Father, I am here. I am in the wolf's body."

The father, full of joy, said, "Thank God, our dear child has found us again." And he told the woman to take away her scythe, so that Thumbling would not be hurt by it. After that he raised his arm and **3.**_____ the wolf so powerfully on his head that he fell down dead, and then the peasant and his wife got knives and scissors to cut the wolf's body open and bring the little fellow out.

"Ah," said the father, "what sorrow we have **4.**_____ for your sake."

"Yes, Father, I have traveled the world a great deal. Thank heaven, I **5.**_____ fresh air again."

"Where have you been, then?"

"Ah, Father, I have been in a mouse's hole, in a cow's stomach, and then in a wolf's belly. Now I will stay with you."

"And we will not sell you again, not for all the riches in the world," his parents said, and they **6.**_____ and kissed their dear Thumbling. Then they gave him something to eat and drink and had some new clothes made for him, for his old ones had been **7.**_____ on his journey.

Answers ❷
1. fetched 2. chop 3. struck 4. gone through 5. breathe 6. embraced 7. spoiled

2 Little Red Riding Hood

pp. 18–19

① Vocabulary Practice: Match.

_____	**1. suit one well**	**A**	to leave (≠ stay)
_____	**2. do one good**	**B**	should; must
_____	**3. set out**	**C**	to check; to investigate
_____	**4. run off**	**D**	to be good for one's health; to benefit one
_____	**5. look into**	**E**	to one's house
_____	**6. give one's word**	**F**	to promise
_____	**7. to one's**	**G**	(clothes) to look good on one
_____	**8. be to**	**H**	to start a journey

② Listen and fill in the blanks with the correct words. Remember to change the form of verbs or nouns if necessary.

Once upon a time, there was a dear little girl who was loved by everyone who looked at her, but most of all by her grandmother, and there was nothing that the grandmother would not have given the child. Once she gave the girl a little hood of red velvet, which **1.**_____ her so well that she would never wear anything else. So she was always called Little Red Riding Hood.

One day her mother said to her, "Come, Little Red Riding Hood. Here is a piece of cake and a bottle of wine. Take them to your grandmother. She is ill and weak, and they will do her good. **2.**_____ before it gets hot, and while you are going, walk nicely and quietly and do not run off the path, or you may fall and break the bottle, and then your grandmother will get nothing. And when you go into her room, don't forget to say good morning, and don't **3.**_____ every corner before you do it."

"I will take great care," said Little Red Riding Hood to her mother, and **4.**_____ on it.

The grandmother lived out in the woods, about two miles from the village, and just as Little Red Riding Hood entered the woods, a wolf met her. She did not know what an evil **5.**_____ he was, and was not at all afraid of him.

"Good day, Little Red Riding Hood," said the wolf.

"Thank you kindly, wolf."

"Where are you going so early?"

"To my grandmother's."

"What have you got in your apron?"

"Cake and wine. Yesterday was baking day, so my poor sick grandmother **6.**_____ have something good to make her stronger."

1 Vocabulary Practice: Match.

_____	1. **tender**	**A**	what if
_____	2. **so as to**	**B**	easy to eat and cut (≠ tough)
_____	3. **merry**	**C**	to arrive
_____	4. **suppose**	**D**	every time something happens
_____	5. **a bunch of**	**E**	right away; immediately
_____	6. **please**	**F**	a group of things
_____	7. **get (to)**	**G**	causing joy and happiness; pleasant
_____	8. **whenever**	**H**	while something else is happening
_____	9. **meanwhile**	**I**	to make one happy
_____	10. **straight**	**J**	in order to

10 **②** Listen and fill in the blanks with the correct words. Remember to change the form of verbs or nouns if necessary.

"Where does your grandmother live?"

"A good mile farther on in the woods. Her house stands under the three large oak trees, and the nut trees are just below. You surely must know it," replied Little Red Riding Hood.

The wolf thought to himself, "What a **1.**_____ young creature, and what a nice fat mouthful! She will be better to eat than the old woman. I must act cleverly, **2.**_____ catch both." So he walked for a short time by the side of Little Red Riding Hood, and then he said, "See, Little Red Riding Hood, how pretty the flowers are about here! Why do you not look around? I believe, too, that you do not hear how sweetly the little birds are singing. You walk seriously along as if you were going to school, while everything else out here in the woods is **3.**_____."

Little Red Riding Hood raised her eyes, and when she saw the sunlight dancing here and there through the trees and pretty flowers growing everywhere, she thought, "**4.**_____ I take Grandmother a fresh bunch of flowers? That would please her, too. It is so early in the day that I shall still get there in time." And so she ran from the path into the woods to look for flowers. And **5.**_____ she had picked one, she imagined that she saw a still prettier one farther on, and ran after it, and so went deeper and deeper into the woods.

Meanwhile, the wolf ran **6.**_____ to the grandmother's house and knocked at the door.

"Who is there?"

"Little Red Riding Hood," replied the wolf. "I am bringing cake and wine. Open the door."

"Lift the latch," called out the grandmother. "I am too **7.**_____ to get up."

pp. 22–23

1 Vocabulary Practice: Match.

_____	1. **run about**	**A**	≠ comfortable
_____	2. **gather**	**B**	an answer
_____	3. **cottage**	**C**	to run around
_____	4. **uncomfortable**	**D**	to get
_____	5. **receive**	**E**	a small house in the country
_____	6. **reply**	**F**	to collect

11

2 Listen and fill in the blanks with the correct words. Remember to change the form of verbs or nouns if necessary.

The wolf lifted the latch, the door flew open, and without saying a word he went straight to the grandmother's bed and ate her. Then he put on her clothes, dressed himself in her cap, laid himself on the bed, and closed the 1._____.

Little Red Riding Hood, however, had been running about picking flowers, and when she had 2._____ so many that she could carry no more, she remembered her grandmother and continued on the way to her house.

She was surprised to find the 3._____ door standing open, and when she went into the room she had such a strange feeling that she said to herself, "Oh dear, how uncomfortable I feel today, and at other times I like being with Grandmother."

She called out "Good morning," but 4._____ no answer. So she went to the bed and opened the curtains. There lay her grandmother with her cap pulled far over her face, looking very strange.

"Oh, Grandmother," she said, "what big ears you have."

"The better to hear you with, my child," was the 5._____.

"But Grandmother, what big eyes you have," she said.

"The better to see you with, my dear."

"But Grandmother, what large hands you have."

"The better to 6._____ you with."

"Oh, but Grandmother, what a terribly big mouth you have."

"The better to eat you with."

1 Vocabulary Practice: Match.

_____	1. **bound**	**A**	to look for
_____	2. **snore**	**B**	a quick, long jump
_____	3. **criminal**	**C**	to shoot
_____	4. **search for**	**D**	scared
_____	5. **fire at**	**E**	to fall down suddenly
_____	6. **pop out**	**F**	right away; immediately
_____	7. **frightened**	**G**	one who seriously breaks the law
_____	8. **barely**	**H**	very happy; very pleased
_____	9. **collapse**	**I**	almost not at all; hardly
_____	10. **at once**	**J**	to breathe loudly during sleep
_____	11. **delighted**	**K**	to come out suddenly

12

② Listen and fill in the blanks with the correct words. Remember to change the form of verbs or nouns if necessary.

And as soon as the wolf had said this, with one bound he was out of the bed and swallowed up Little Red Riding Hood.

When the wolf had satisfied his hunger, he lay down again in the bed, fell asleep and began to **1.**_____ very loudly. A hunter was just then passing the house, and thought to himself, "How the old woman is snoring! I must see if she wants anything."

So he went into the room, and when he came to the bed, he saw that the wolf was lying in it. "Do I find you here, you old **2.**_____?" he said. "I have searched for you for a long time." Then, just as he was going to **3.**_____ the wolf, he realized that the wolf might have eaten the grandmother and that she might still be saved, so he did not fire, but took a pair of scissors and began to cut open the stomach of the sleeping wolf. When he had made two snips, he saw the little red hood shining.

Then he made two more snips, and the little girl popped out, crying, "Ah, how **4.**_____ I have been. How dark it was inside the wolf." And after that the old grandmother also came out alive, but **5.**_____ able to breathe. Little Red Riding Hood, however, quickly fetched some great stones with which they filled the wolf's belly, and when he awoke he wanted to run away, but the stones were so heavy that he **6.**_____ at once and fell dead.

Then all three were **7.**_____. The hunter cut off the wolf's skin and went home with it. The grandmother ate the cake, drank the wine which Little Red Riding Hood had brought, and felt better. But Little Red Riding Hood thought to herself, "As long as I live, I will never again leave the path by myself to run into the woods when my mother has told me not to do so."

pp. 26–27

1 Vocabulary Practice: Match.

_____	1. **lure**	**A**	to go in secretly
_____	2. **onto**	**B**	a bucket
_____	3. **sneak (in)**	**C**	to pull one's body to full length
_____	4. **pail**	**D**	to die under water
_____	5. **sniff**	**E**	to hurt someone
_____	6. **stretch**	**F**	to persuade one to do something wrong
_____	7. **keep one's balance**	**G**	≠ fall down
_____	8. **drown**	**H**	to smell quickly
_____	9. **harm**	**I**	= on to

🎧 13 **②** Listen and fill in the blanks with the correct words. Remember to change the form of verbs or nouns if necessary.

It is also said that once when Little Red Riding Hood was again taking cakes to her old grandmother, another wolf spoke to her, and tried to **1.**_____ her away from the path. Little Red Riding Hood, however, was careful, went straight forward on her way, and told her grandmother that she had met the wolf and that he had said good morning to her, but with such an evil look in his eyes that she was certain he would have eaten her up if they had not been on a **2.**_____ road.

"Well," said the grandmother, "we will shut the door, and he may not come in."

Soon afterwards the wolf knocked and cried, "Open the door, Grandmother! I am Little Red Riding Hood, and I am bringing you some cakes." But they did not speak or open the door. The wolf crept two or three times around the house and at last jumped onto the roof, planning to wait until Little Red Riding Hood went home in the evening and then to **3.**_____ after her and eat her in the darkness. But the grandmother knew what he was thinking. In front of the house was a great stone trough, so she said to the child, "Take the **4.**_____, my dear. I made some sausages yesterday, so carry the water in which I boiled them to the trough." Little Red Riding Hood carried water until the great trough was quite full. Then the smell of the sausages reached the wolf, and he **5.**_____, looked down, and at last stretched out his neck so far that he could no longer keep his balance and began to slip, and slid down from the roof straight into the great trough, and he **6.**_____.

But Little Red Riding Hood went happily home, and no one ever did anything to **7.**_____ her again.

3 The Golden Goose

pp. 28–29

1 Vocabulary Practice: Match.

_____	1. despise	A	a time when something happens
_____	2. mock	B	a hit or strike at something
_____	3. sneer at	C	to cover a wound with a bandage
_____	4. occasion	D	to make fun of
_____	5. suffer from	E	the act of punishing
_____	6. thirst	F	be one's fault or responsibility
_____	7. stroke	G	to feel pain in one's body or mind
_____	8. bandage	H	to look down on (≠ respect)
_____	9. be one's doing	I	too
_____	10. as well	J	the feeling of needing to drink water
_____	11. punishment	K	to smile or speak in an unkind way

2 Listen and fill in the blanks with the correct words. Remember to change the form of verbs or nouns if necessary.

There was a man who had three sons, the youngest of whom, called Dummling, was despised, mocked, and sneered at on every **1.**_____.

One day the man's eldest son wanted to go into the forest to cut wood, and before he went, his mother gave him a beautiful sweet cake and a bottle of wine so that he would not **2.**_____ hunger or thirst.

When he entered the forest, he met a little grey-haired old man who wished him good day and said, "Do give me a piece of cake out of your pocket, and let me have a mouthful of your wine. I am so hungry and **3.**_____." But the clever son answered, "If I give you my cake and wine, I shall have none for myself. Go away." And he left the little man standing there and went on.

But when he began to chop down a tree, it was not long before he made a bad **4.**_____, and the axe cut him on the arm, so that he had to go home and have it **5.**_____ up. And this was the little grey man's doing.

After this the second son went into the forest, and his mother gave him, like the eldest, a cake and a bottle of wine. The little old grey man met him as well, and asked him for a piece of cake and a drink of wine. But the second son too said, **6.**_____ enough, "What I give you will be taken away from myself. Go away." And he left the little man standing there and went on. His **7.**_____, however, was not delayed. When he had made a few cuts at the tree, he struck himself in the leg, so that he had to be carried home.

1 Vocabulary Practice: Match.

_____	**1. beg**	**A**	to be a good person
_____	**2. ash**	**B**	to ask strongly for something
_____	**3. have a good heart**	**C**	the thing that cover a bird's body
_____	**4. feather**	**D**	not mixed with something else
_____	**5. pure**	**E**	a place to stay overnight; a small hotel
_____	**6. inn**	**F**	soft grey powder from burned things

2 Listen and fill in the blanks with the correct words. Remember to change the form of verbs or nouns if necessary.

Then Dummling said, "Father, do let me go and cut wood." The father answered, "Your brothers have hurt themselves doing it. Don't try it, because you do not understand anything about it." But Dummling **1.**_____ so long that at last his father said, "Just go, then; you will get wiser by hurting yourself." His mother gave him a cake made with water and baked in the **2.**_____, and with it a bottle of sour beer.

When Dummling came into the forest, the little old grey man met him, greeted him, and said, "Give me a piece of your cake and a drink out of your bottle. I am so hungry and thirsty."

Dummling answered, "I have only ash cake and sour beer. If that **3.**_____ you, we will sit down and eat." So they sat down, and when Dummling pulled out his ash cake, it was a fine sweet cake, and the sour beer had become good wine. So they ate and drank, and after that the little man said, "Since you **4.**_____ and are willing to share what you have, I will give you good luck. There stands an old tree; cut it down, and you will find something in its roots." Then the little man left him.

Dummling went and cut down the tree, and when it fell there was a goose sitting in the roots with feathers of **5.**_____ gold. He lifted her up, took her with him, and went to an inn where he thought he would stay for the night. The owner had three daughters, who saw the goose and were curious to know what such a wonderful bird could be, and each wanted to have one of its golden **6.**_____.

pp. 32–33

1 Vocabulary Practice: Match.

_____ **1. stuck**   **A** to or in any place

_____ **2. scream**   **B** the feeling of embarrassment or guilt

_____ **3. hang on to** **C** to shout very loudly with emotion

_____ **4. wherever**   **D** lazy and useless

_____ **5. shame**   **E** unable to separate; fixed

_____ **6. good-for-   F** to hold tightly
              nothing

16 **②** Listen and fill in the blanks with the correct words. Remember to change the form of verbs or nouns if necessary.

The eldest daughter thought, "I shall soon find an opportunity to pull out a feather." And as soon as Dummling had gone out, she grabbed the goose by the wing, but her fingers and hand remained stuck to it.

The second came soon afterwards, thinking only of how she might get a feather for herself, but as soon as she had touched her sister, she was stuck too.

At last the third daughter came with the same idea, and the others **1.**_____ out, "Keep away, for goodness' sake, keep away!" But she did not understand why she should keep away. "The others are there," she thought, "so I may as well be there too," and she ran to them, but as soon as she had touched her sister, she remained **2.**_____ to her. So they all had to spend the night with the goose.

The next morning Dummling took the goose under his arm and left, without worrying about the three girls who were **3.**_____ it. They had to run after him again and again, now left, now right, **4.**_____ his legs took him.

In the middle of the fields the parson met them, and when he saw them he said, "**5.**_____ on you, you good-for-nothing girls. Why are you running across the fields after this young man? Is that polite?" At the same time he **6.**_____ the youngest by the hand to pull her away, but as soon as he touched her, he too became stuck, and was himself forced to run behind them.

Answers

②

5. Shame
6. grabbed

1. screamed
2. stuck
3. hanging on to
4. wherever

❶ Vocabulary Practice: Match.

_____ 1. **sleeve** ⬛A to help one let go; to allow one to be free

_____ 2. **workman** ⬛B part of a shirt that covers one's arm

_____ 3. **set one free** ⬛C a person who follows

_____ 4. **whoever** ⬛D to offer reasons

_____ 5. **follower** ⬛E the husband of one's daughter

_____ 6. **son-in-law** ⬛F a worker who does physical work; a laborer

_____ 7. **make excuses** ⬛G anyone

Answers

❶

6. E   7. D

1. B   2. F   3. A   4. C   5. C

② Listen and fill in the blanks with the correct words. Remember to change the form of verbs or nouns if necessary.

Before long the bell-ringer came by and saw his master, the parson, running behind the three girls. He was **1.**_____ at this and called out, "Hi, Parson! Where are you going so quickly? Do not forget that we have a christening today." Running after the parson, he took him by the **2.**_____, and was stuck to it. While the five were running in this way one behind the other, two **3.**_____ came with their hoes from the fields, and the parson called out to them and begged that they would set him and the bell-ringer free. But they had just touched the bell-ringer when they were stuck fast, and now there were seven people running behind Dummling and the goose.

Soon afterwards Dummling came to a city, where the king had a daughter who was so serious that no one could make her laugh. So he had ordered that **4.**_____ could make her laugh should marry her. When Dummling heard this, he went with his goose and all her **5.**_____ before the king's daughter, and as soon as she saw the seven people running on and on, one behind the other, she began to laugh quite loudly, and as if she would never stop.

Dummling immediately asked to have her for his wife, but the king did not like this son-in-law, and made all sorts of **6.**_____ and said Dummling must first show him a man who could drink a cellarful of wine.

1 Vocabulary Practice: Match.

_____	1. **quench**	**A**	a large container
_____	2. **cellar**	**B**	very angry; very mad
_____	3. **barrel**	**C**	to satisfy one's thirst
_____	4. **groin**	**D**	something which must be done
_____	5. **bride**	**E**	a belt
_____	6. **furious**	**F**	a woman who is getting married
_____	7. **condition**	**G**	the area where your legs meet
_____	8. **strap**	**H**	a room under a house used to store things

Answers

1

1. C 2. H 3. A 4. G 5. F 6. B 7. D 8. E

2 Listen and fill in the blanks with the correct words. Remember to change the form of verbs or nouns if necessary.

Dummling thought of the little grey man, who could **1.**_____ help him, so he went into the forest, and in the same place where he had cut down the tree, he saw a man sitting who had a very sad face. Dummling asked the man what he was so unhappy about, and he answered, "I have such a great thirst and cannot **2.**_____ it. Cold water I cannot stand; a barrel of wine I have just emptied, but that to me is like a drop on a hot stone."

"There I can help you," said Dummling. "Just come with me, and you shall be satisfied."

He led him into the king's **3.**_____, and the man bent over the huge barrels and drank and drank till his groin hurt. Before the day was over, he had emptied all the barrels. Then Dummling asked once more for his bride, but the king was **4.**_____ that such an ugly fellow, whom everyone called Dummling, should take away his daughter, and so he set a new **5.**_____: Dummling must first find a man who could eat a whole mountain of bread.

Dummling did not think long, but went straight into the forest, where in the same place there sat a man who was tying up his body with a **6.**_____, making an awful face, and saying, "I have eaten a whole ovenful of rolls, but what good is that when one has such a hunger as I? My stomach remains empty, and I must tie myself up if I am not to **7.**_____ hunger."

At this Dummling was glad and said, "Get up and come with me, and you shall eat yourself full."

pp. 38–39

❶ Vocabulary Practice: Match.

______	**1. palace**	A	to receive money or property from someone after he or she has died
______	**2. vanish**	B	to stop . . . from . . .
______	**3. prevent . . . from . . .**	C	the official home of a king and queen; a castle
______	**4. inherit**	D	to disappear
______	**5. look for**	E	not . . . anymore
______	**6. no longer**	F	to search for

Answers ❶

1. C **2.** D **3.** B **4.** A
5. F **6.** E

2 Listen and fill in the blanks with the correct words. Remember to change the form of verbs or nouns if necessary.

He led him to the king's **1.**_____, where all the flour in the whole kingdom was collected, and from it he ordered a huge mountain of bread to be baked. The man from the forest stood before it, began to eat, and by the end of one day the whole mountain had **2.**_____.

Then Dummling for the third time asked for his bride, but the king again looked for a way out and ordered a ship which could **3.**_____ on land and on water. "As soon as you come sailing back in it," he said, "you shall have my daughter for your wife."

Dummling went **4.**_____ into the forest, and there sat the little grey man to whom he had given his cake. When he heard what Dummling wanted, he said, "Since you have given me food to eat and wine to drink, I will give you the ship, and I do all this because you once were kind to me."

Then he gave him a ship which could sail on land and water, and when the king saw that, he could no longer **5.**_____ Dummling from having his daughter. The wedding was celebrated, and after the king's death, Dummling **6.**_____ his kingdom and lived for a long time happily with his wife.

4 Hansel and Gretel

pp. 40–41

❶ Vocabulary Practice: Match.

_____	**1. toss**	**A**	to make a deep sound showing pain or worry
_____	**2. anxiety**	**B**	to turn one's body from side to side
_____	**3. groan**	**C**	≠ able
_____	**4. be (get) rid of**	**D**	one's father's wife, who is not one's real mother
_____	**5. trim**	**E**	nevertheless
_____	**6. coffin**	**F**	to cut something carefully
_____	**7. all the same**	**G**	a feeling of worry; concern
_____	**8. unable**	**H**	to make one feel worried
_____	**9. stepmother**	**I**	a long box in which a dead body is buried
_____	**10. upset**	**J**	to throw away; to desert

② Listen and fill in the blanks with the correct words. Remember to change the form of verbs or nouns if necessary.

Beside a great forest lived a poor wood-cutter with his wife and his two children. The boy was called Hansel and the girl Gretel.

He had little to eat, and once when there was great **1.**_____ throughout the land, he could no longer earn even his daily bread. Now when he thought about this at night in his bed and tossed about in his **2.**_____, he groaned and said to his wife, "What will happen to us? How are we going to feed our poor children when we no longer have anything even for ourselves?"

"I'll tell you what, husband," answered the woman. "Early tomorrow morning we will take the children out into the forest to where it is the thickest. There we will light a fire for them and give each of them one more piece of bread, and then we will go to our work and leave them alone. They will not find their way home again, and we shall **3.**_____ them."

"No, wife," said the man, "I will not do that. How could I stand to leave my children alone in the forest? The wild animals would soon come and tear them to pieces."

"Oh, you fool!" she said. "Then we must all four die of hunger, and you may as well **4.**_____ the boards for our coffins." And she gave him no peace until he agreed.

"But I feel very sorry for the poor children, all the same," said the man.

The two children had also been **5.**_____ to sleep because of hunger and had heard what their stepmother had said to their father. Gretel wept bitter tears and said to Hansel, "Now all is over for us."

"Be quiet, Gretel," said Hansel. "Do not **6.**_____ yourself, and I will soon find a way to help us."

pp. 42–43

1 Vocabulary Practice: Match.

_____ 1. **folks**   A a small one-cent coin

_____ 2. **glitter**   B to make one feel less worried or upset

_____ 3. **penny**   C to desert

_____ 4. **stoop**   D people

_____ 5. **stuff**   E to shine brightly

_____ 6. **comfort**   F all the time

_____ 7. **abandon**   G to put something into a small space

_____ 8. **chimney**   H a pipe that allows smoke to pass out
                                  of a building up into the air

_____ 9. **constantly**   I to bend one's body downward

② Listen and fill in the blanks with the correct words. Remember to change the form of verbs or nouns if necessary.

And when the old folks had fallen asleep, he got up, put on his little coat, opened the door downstairs, and crept outside. The moon shone brightly, and the white pebbles which lay in front of the house **1.**_____ like real silver pennies. Hansel **2.**_____ down and stuffed the little pocket of his coat with as many as he could fit in. Then he went back and said to Gretel, "Be comforted, dear little sister, and sleep in peace. God will not **3.**_____ us." And he lay down again in his bed.

When day dawned, but before the sun had risen, the woman came and awoke the two children, saying, "Get up, you lazy little ones. We are going into the forest to gather wood." She gave each a little piece of bread and said, "There is something for your dinner, but do not eat it up before then, for you will get nothing else."

Gretel put the bread under her apron, as Hansel had the pebbles in his pocket. Then they all **4.**_____ together on the way to the forest. When they had walked for a short time, Hansel stood still, looked back at the house, and then did so again and again. His father said, "Hansel, what are you looking at there and staying behind for? Pay attention, and do not **5.**_____ how to use your legs."

"Ah, Father," said Hansel, "I am looking at my little white cat, which is sitting up on the roof and wants to say goodbye to me."

The wife said, "Fool, that is not your little cat. That is the morning sun which is shining on the chimney."

Hansel, however, had not been looking back at his cat, but had been **6.**_____ throwing the white pebbles from his pocket onto the road.

1 Vocabulary Practice: Match.

_____	1. **pile up**	**A**	fire
_____	2. **flame**	**B**	tiredness
_____	3. **fatigue**	**C**	completely new
_____	4. **brand-new**	**D**	to put things in a pile
_____	5. **reach**	**E**	a hit or strike at something
_____	6. **stroke**	**F**	to get to

② Listen and fill in the blanks with the correct words. Remember to change the form of verbs or nouns if necessary.

When they had reached the middle of the forest, the father said, "Now, children, **1.**_____ some wood, and I will light a fire so that you will not be cold." Hansel and Gretel gathered twigs and branches together, as high as a little hill. The wood was lit, and then the **2.**_____ were burning very high.

The woman said, "Now, children, lie down by the fire and rest. We will go into the forest and cut some wood. When we have finished, we will come back and take you home."

Hansel and Gretel sat by the fire, and when noon came, each ate a little piece of bread, and as they heard the strokes of the axe, they believed that their father was near. It was not the axe, however, but a branch which he had **3.**_____ a dying tree, and which the wind was blowing backwards and forwards.

And as they had been sitting such a long time, their eyes closed with **4.**_____ and they fell fast asleep. When at last they awoke, it was already dark night. Gretel began to cry and said, "How are we to get out of the forest now?"

But Hansel **5.**_____ her and said, "Just wait a little until the moon has risen, and then we will soon find the way." And when the full moon had risen, Hansel took his little sister by the hand and followed the pebbles which shone like **6.**_____ silver pieces and showed them the way.

They walked the whole night long and by dawn had come once more to their father's house. They knocked at the door, and when the woman opened it and saw that it was Hansel and Gretel, she said, "You **7.**_____ children, why did you sleep so long in the forest? We thought you were never coming back at all."

1 Vocabulary Practice: Match.

_____	1. **rejoice**	**A**	feeling shame
_____	2. **break one's heart**	**B**	to talk angrily about someone's behavior
_____	3. **guilty**	**C**	to show or feel joy
_____	4. **scold**	**D**	to give up
_____	5. **reproach**	**E**	to break into small pieces
_____	6. **surrender**	**F**	to blame someone for something
_____	7. **crumble**	**G**	to make one feel very sad

② Listen and fill in the blanks with the correct words. Remember to change the form of verbs or nouns if necessary.

The father, however, rejoiced, for it had **1.**_____ to leave them behind alone.

Not long afterwards, there was once more great hunger throughout the land, and the children heard their mother saying at night to their father, "Everything is eaten again; we have one half loaf of bread left, and that is all. The children must go. We will take them farther into the woods, so that they will not find their way out again. There is no other way of saving ourselves."

The man felt **2.**_____, and he thought, "It would be better for you to share your last mouthful with your children."

The woman, however, would listen to nothing that he had to say, but scolded and **3.**_____ him. He who says this must likewise say that, and as he had **4.**_____ the first time, he had to do so a second time too.

The children, however, were still awake and had heard the conversation. When the old folks were asleep, Hansel again got up and wanted to go out to pick up pebbles as he had done before, but the woman had locked the door, and he could not get out. **5.**_____, he comforted his little sister and said, "Do not cry, Gretel. Go to sleep quietly, and the good God will help us."

Early in the morning the woman came and took the children out of their beds. Their piece of bread was given to them, but it was even smaller than it had been the time before. On the way into the forest Hansel **6.**_____ his in his pocket, often stood still, and threw the crumbs on the ground.

1 Vocabulary Practice: Match.

_____	1. **pigeon**	A	finished (≠ unfinished)
_____	2. **little by little**	B	to throw things in different directions
_____	3. **done**	C	slowly over a period of time; bit by bit
_____	4. **scatter**	D	to make one feel less worried or upset
_____	5. **awake**	E	to start a journey
_____	6. **comfort**	F	to wake up (≠ fall asleep)
_____	7. **set out**	G	a grey bird with short legs

2 Listen and fill in the blanks with the correct words. Remember to change the form of verbs or nouns if necessary.

"Hansel, why do you stop and look around?" said the father. "Go on."

"I am looking back at my little pigeon which is sitting on the roof and wants to say goodbye to me," answered Hansel.

"Fool," said the woman, "that is not your little pigeon; that is the morning sun that is shining on the **1.**_____." Hansel, however, little by little, threw all his crumbs on the path.

The woman led the children still **2.**_____ into the forest, where they had never in their lives been before. Then a great fire was again made, and the mother said, "Just sit there, you children, and when you are tired, you may sleep a little. We are going into the forest to cut wood, and in the evening when we are **3.**_____, we will come and take you home."

When it was noon, Gretel shared her piece of bread with Hansel, who had **4.**_____ his along the way. Then they fell asleep and evening passed, but no one came for the poor children. They did not awake until it was dark night, and Hansel **5.**_____ his little sister and said, "Just wait, Gretel, until the moon rises, and then we shall see the crumbs of bread which I have thrown about. They will show us our way home again."

When the moon came, they set out, but they found no **6.**_____, for the many thousands of birds which fly about in the woods and fields had picked them all up. Hansel said to Gretel, "We shall soon find the way." But they did not find it.

1 Vocabulary Practice: Match.

_____	1. **exhausted**	**A**	noon
_____	2. **beneath**	**B**	to sit or rest in a comfortable position
_____	3. **exhaustion**	**C**	to move toward
_____	4. **midday**	**D**	to start doing something
_____	5. **delightfully**	**E**	to take a small bite of food
_____	6. **settle**	**F**	under
_____	7. **approach**	**G**	to bite something hard repeatedly
_____	8. **be built of**	**H**	to move one's upper body backwards or forwards
_____	9. **work on**	**I**	very tired
_____	10. **lean**	**J**	joyfully; pleasingly
_____	11. **nibble**	**K**	to be made of certain materials
_____	12. **gnaw**	**L**	the feeling of being exhausted

2 Listen and fill in the blanks with the correct words. Remember to change the form of verbs or nouns if necessary.

They walked the whole night and all the next day too from morning till evening, but they did not get out of the forest. They were very hungry, for they had nothing to eat but two or three berries which grew on the ground. And as they were so **1.**_____ that their legs could carry them no longer, they lay down beneath a tree and fell asleep.

It was now three mornings since they had left their father's house. They began to walk again, but they always went deeper into the forest. If help did not come soon, they would surely die of hunger and exhaustion.

When it was **2.**_____, they saw a beautiful snow-white bird sitting on a branch, which sang so delightfully that they stood still and listened to it. And when its song was over, it spread its wings and flew away before them, and they followed it until they reached a little house, on the roof of which it **3.**_____.

And when they approached the little house they saw that it **4.**_____ bread and covered with cakes, and that the windows were made of clear sugar.

"We will go to **5.**_____ that," said Hansel, "and have a good meal. I will eat a bit of the roof, and you, Gretel, can eat some of the window. It will taste sweet."

Hansel reached up and broke off a little of the roof to see how it tasted, and Gretel **6.**_____ against the window and nibbled at the panes. Then a soft voice cried from the living room, "Nibble, nibble, gnaw; who is **7.**_____ at my little house?"

1 Vocabulary Practice: Match.

_____	1. heaven	A	a person
_____	2. crutch	B	to behave as if something were real when it's not
_____	3. harm	C	a stick that helps people walk
_____	4. pretend	D	the feeling of hate (≠ love)
_____	5. in reality	E	where God lives; paradise
_____	6. witch	F	to run away from
_____	7. keen	G	with unkind laughter
_____	8. human being	H	very strong (ability to see, smell, or hear)
_____	9. hatred	I	an evil woman who can do magic
_____	10. mockingly	J	in fact
_____	11. escape	K	injury; damage

2 Listen and fill in the blanks with the correct words. Remember to change the form of verbs or nouns if necessary.

The children answered, "The wind, the wind, the **1.**_____-born wind," and went on eating without worrying. Hansel, who liked the taste of the roof, tore down a great piece of it, and Gretel pushed out the whole of one round windowpane, sat down, and enjoyed herself with it. Suddenly the door opened and an ancient woman, who supported herself on **2.**_____, came creeping out. Hansel and Gretel were so terribly frightened that they dropped what they had in their hands. The old woman, however, nodded her head and said, "Oh, you dear children, who has brought you here? Do come in, and stay with me. No harm shall come to you."

She took them both by the hand and led them into her little house. Then good food was set before them: milk and pancakes with sugar, apples, and nuts. Afterwards, two pretty little beds were **3.**_____ with clean white sheets, and Hansel and Gretel lay down in them and thought they were in heaven.

The old woman had only **4.**_____ to be so kind. She was in reality an evil witch, who waited for children to pass and had only built the little house of bread in order to lure them there. When she caught a child, she killed, cooked, and ate it, and that was a feast day for her. Witches have red eyes and cannot see far, but they have a **5.**_____ sense of smell like animals and are aware when human beings come near. When Hansel and Gretel came into her neighborhood, she laughed with **6.**_____ and said mockingly, "I have them; they shall not escape me."

Answers

2

1. heaven   2. crutches   3. covered   4. pretended   5. keen   6. hatred

❶ Vocabulary Practice: Match.

_____	1. **cheek**	**A**	having lines and folds
_____	2. **tasty**	**B**	a place where horses are kept
_____	3. **seize**	**C**	evil (≠ kind)
_____	4. **wrinkled**	**D**	very surprised
_____	5. **stable**	**E**	≠ patient
_____	6. **weep**	**F**	delicious
_____	7. **in vain**	**G**	a large and dangerous animal
_____	8. **wicked**	**H**	to express how sad one is
_____	9. **astonished**	**I**	the soft part of face below the eye
_____	10. **impatient**	**J**	to cry
_____	11. **lament**	**K**	no use (≠ successful)
_____	12. **beast**	**L**	to grab suddenly

2 Listen and fill in the blanks with the correct words. Remember to change the form of verbs or nouns if necessary.

Early in the morning before the children were awake, she was already up, and when she saw both of them sleeping and looking so pretty, with their round and rosy cheeks, she whispered to herself, "That will be a tasty mouthful."

Then she **1.**_____ Hansel with her wrinkled hand, carried him into a little stable, and locked him in behind an iron door. All his screaming could not help him. Then she went to Gretel, shook her till she awoke, and cried, "Get up, lazy thing, fetch some water, and cook something good for your brother. He is in the **2.**_____ outside and is to be made fat. When he is fat, I will eat him."

Gretel began to weep bitterly, but it was all **3.**_____, for she was forced to do what the wicked witch commanded. And now the best food was cooked for poor Hansel, but Gretel got nothing but crab shells. Every morning the woman crept to the little stable and cried, "Hansel, **4.**_____ your finger so that I may feel if you will soon be fat." Hansel, however, always stretched out a little bone to her, and the old woman, who had weak eyes, could not see it, thought it was Hansel's finger, and was **5.**_____ that there was no way of making him fat.

When four weeks had gone by and Hansel still remained thin, she became **6.**_____ and would not wait any longer. "Now, then, Gretel," she cried to the girl, "move yourself, and bring some water. Let Hansel be fat or thin, tomorrow I will kill him and cook him."

Ah, how the poor little sister did lament when she had to fetch the water, and how her tears did flow down her cheeks. "Dear God, do help us," she cried. "If the wild **7.**_____ in the forest had eaten us, we would at least have died together."

Answers

2

		7. beasts	6. impatient	5. astonished
	4. stick out	3. in vain	2. stable	1. seized

Vocabulary & Listening Practice   **4** Hansel and Gretel   **55**

pp. 56–57

① Vocabulary Practice: Match.

_____ **1. dough**

_____ **2. dart**

_____ **3. bolt**

_____ **4. miserably**

_____ **5. spring**

_____ **6. chest**

_____ **7. pearl**

_____ **8. jewel**

A to lock by sliding a bolt

B thick flour ready to be baked into bread

C to jump suddenly

D a large box to put things in

E a precious stone

F a kind of jewel

G unhappily and painfully

H to move suddenly and quickly

2 Listen and fill in the blanks with the correct words. Remember to change the form of verbs or nouns if necessary.

"Just keep quiet," said the old woman. "Your noise won't help you at all."

Early in the morning Gretel had to go out, hang up the pot of water and light the fire. "We will bake first," said the old woman. "I have already heated the oven and rolled the **1.**_____."

She pushed poor Gretel out to the oven, from which flames were already darting. "Creep in," said the witch, "and see if it is properly heated, so that we can put the bread in." Once Gretel was inside, the old woman **2.**_____ shut the oven and let her bake in it, and then she would eat her, too.

But Gretel saw what she had in mind and said, "I do not know how to do it. How do I get in?"

"Silly goose," said the old woman. "The door is big enough. Just look; I can get in myself." And she crept up and **3.**_____ her head into the oven.

Then Gretel gave her a push that drove her far into it, shut the iron door, and **4.**_____ it.

"Oh!" Then she began to scream quite horribly, but Gretel ran away, and the evil witch was **5.**_____ burned to death.

Gretel, however, ran like lightning to Hansel, opened his little stable and cried, "Hansel, we are saved. The old witch is dead."

Then Hansel sprang like a bird from its cage when the door was opened. How they did rejoice and hug each other and dance about and kiss each other. As they no longer had any need to fear the witch, they went into her house, and in every corner there stood chests full of pearls and **6.**_____.

Answers

2

1. dough   2. planned to   3. stuck   4. bolted   5. miserably   6. jewels

1 Vocabulary Practice: Match.

_____ **1. ferry**   **A** knowing something or someone because you've seen it, him or her before

_____ **2. seat oneself**   **B** a story

_____ **3. familiar**   **C** the soft thick hair that covers the bodies of animals such as bears

_____ **4. handful**   **D** to put something into a small space

_____ **5. tale**   **E** a boat or ship which carries people from one place to another

_____ **6. fur**   **F** the amount of something that fills one's hand

_____ **7. stuff**   **G** to sit down

2 **Listen and fill in the blanks with the correct words. Remember to change the form of verbs or nouns if necessary.**

"These are far better than pebbles," said Hansel, and he stuffed into his pockets whatever could be put in. Gretel said, "I, too, will take something home with me," and **1.**_____ her apron full.

"But now we must go," said Hansel, "so that we may get out of the witch's forest."

When they had walked for two hours, they came to a great stream. "We cannot cross," said Hansel. "I see no boards and no bridge."

"And there is also no **2.**_____," answered Gretel, "but a white duck is swimming there. If I ask her, she will help us over." Then she cried, "Little duck, little duck, do you see? Hansel and Gretel are waiting for you. There's neither a board nor a bridge **3.**_____. Take us across on your back so white."

The duck came to them, and Hansel seated himself on its back and told his sister to sit by him. "No," replied Gretel, "that will be too heavy for the little duck. She shall take us across, one after the other."

The good little duck did so, and once they were safely across and had walked for a short time, the forest seemed to become more and more **4.**_____ to them, and after a while they saw their father's house far in the distance.

Then they began to run, rushed into the living room, and threw their arms around their father's neck. The man had not had one happy hour since he had left the children in the forest. The woman, however, was dead. Gretel emptied her apron until pearls and precious stones ran about the room, and Hansel threw one **5.**_____ after another out of his pocket to add to them. Then all sorrow was at an end, and they lived together in perfect happiness.

My tale is done. There runs a mouse, and whoever catches it may make himself a big **6.**_____ cap out of it.

5 Rumpelstiltskin

pp. 62–63

1 Vocabulary Practice: Match.

_____	1. **miller**	A	to make one happy
_____	2. **spin . . . into . . .**	B	immediately
_____	3. **reel**	C	to produce something by spinning
_____	4. **have no idea**	D	a person who owns or works in a factory that makes flour
_____	5. **please**	E	a round object onto which thread can be rolled
_____	6. **at once**	F	not to know

2 Listen and fill in the blanks with the correct words. Remember to change the form of verbs or nouns if necessary.

Once there was a miller who was poor, but who had a beautiful daughter. One day he had to go and speak to the king, and in order to make himself appear important, he said to the king, "I have a daughter who can 1._____ straw into gold."

The king said to the miller, "That is a skill which pleases me well. If your daughter is as 2._____ as you say, bring her tomorrow to my palace, and I will see what she can do."

And when the girl was brought to the king, he took her into a room which was quite full of straw, gave her a spinning wheel and a 3._____, and said, "Now get to work, and if by early tomorrow morning you have not spun this straw into gold, you must die."

Then he himself locked up the room and left her in it alone. So there sat the poor miller's daughter. She did not know what to do, and she 4._____ how straw could be spun into gold. She grew more and more frightened until at last she began to 5._____.

But all at once the door opened, and in came a little man who said, "Good evening, Miss 6._____. Why are you crying so?"

"Oh," answered the girl, "I have to spin straw into gold, and I do not know how to do it."

"What will you give me," said the little man, "if I do it for you?"

"My necklace," said the girl.

pp. 64–65

1 Vocabulary Practice: Match.

_____	**1. go on**	**A**	very surprised
_____	**2. amazed**	**B**	at the moment of seeing something
_____	**3. at the sight**	**C**	always wanting more things than one needs
_____	**4. greedy**	**D**	to show or feel joy
_____	**5. rejoice**	**E**	to sit down
_____	**6. seat oneself**	**F**	to continue

31

❷ Listen and fill in the blanks with the correct words. Remember to change the form of verbs or nouns if necessary.

The little man took the necklace, seated himself in front of the wheel, and "Whirr! Whirr! Whirr!" Three turns, and the reel was full. Then he put another on, and "Whirr! Whirr! Whirr!" Three times around, and the second was full too. And so it **1.**_____ until the morning when all the straw had been spun and all the reels were full of gold.

By dawn the king was already there, and when he saw the gold he was **2.**_____ and delighted, but his heart only became greedier. He had the miller's daughter taken into another room full of straw, which was much larger, and **3.**_____ her to spin that also into gold in one night if she wanted to live.

The girl didn't know how to save herself. She was crying when the door opened again and the little man appeared and said, "What will you give me if I spin that straw into gold for you?"

"The ring on my finger," answered the girl.

The little man took the ring, again **4.**_____ turn the wheel, and by morning had spun all the straw into shining gold.

The king rejoiced greatly **5.**_____, but still he was not satisfied. He had the miller's daughter taken into a still larger room full of straw and said, "You must spin all of this into gold tonight, but if you **6.**_____, you shall be my wife."

"Even if she is only a miller's daughter," he thought, "I could not find a richer wife in the whole world."

❷

5. at the sight

6. succeed

1. went on

4. began to   3. commanded   2. amazed

1 Vocabulary Practice: Match.

_____ **1. promise**   **A** to feel sorry for someone

_____ **2. horrified**   **B** someone who takes a message from one person to another

_____ **3. pity**   **C** very frightened

_____ **4. messenger**   **D** wealth

_____ **5. difficulty**   **E** a legal relationship between two people who get married

_____ **6. marriage**   **F** a difficult thing or time; hardship

_____ **7. riches**   **G** to tell someone that you will do something; to give one's word

32

❷ Listen and fill in the blanks with the correct words. Remember to change the form of verbs or nouns if necessary.

When the girl was alone, the little man came for the third time and said, "What will you give me if I spin the straw for you this time, too?"

"I have nothing left that I can give," answered the girl.

"Then **1.**_____ me, if you become a queen, to give me your first child."

"Who knows if that will ever happen?" thought the miller's daughter, and not knowing how else to help herself in this **2.**_____, she promised the little man what he wanted, and for that he once more spun the straw into gold.

And when the king came in the morning and found everything as he had wished, he took her hand in marriage, and the pretty miller's daughter became a queen.

A year later, she **3.**_____ a beautiful child, and she never thought about the little man. But suddenly he came into her room and said, "Now give me what you promised."

The queen was **4.**_____ and offered the little man all the riches of the kingdom if he would leave her the child. But the little man said, "No, a living thing is dearer to me than all the treasures in the world."

Then the queen began to **5.**_____ and cry, so that the little man pitied her. "I will give you three days' time," he said, "and if in that time you can find out my name, then you shall keep your child."

So the queen thought all night long of all the names that she had ever heard, and she sent a **6.**_____ throughout the country to ask, far and wide, for any other names that there might be.

When the little man came the next day, she began with Caspar, Melchior, and Balthazar, and then said all the names she knew, one after another, but to every one the little man said, "That is not my name."

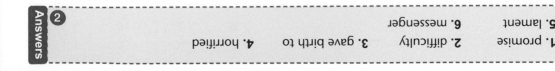

Answers

❷

1. promise 2. difficulty 3. gave birth to 4. horrified 5. lament 6. messenger

pp. 68–69

1 Vocabulary Practice: Match.

_____	**1.** **make an inquiry**	**A**	strange (≠ usual)
_____	**2.** **neighborhood**	**B**	a woman who has great power
_____	**3.** **unusual**	**C**	very silly or unreasonable
_____	**4.** **ridiculous**	**D**	the most powerful evil spirit; Satan
_____	**5.** **brew**	**E**	to push downwards suddenly; to fall
_____	**6.** **mistress**	**F**	to ask for information
_____	**7.** **the devil**	**G**	in great anger
_____	**8.** **plunge**	**H**	to make beer or wine
_____	**9.** **in (a) rage**	**I**	the area around one's home

❷ Listen and fill in the blanks with the correct words. Remember to change the form of verbs or nouns if necessary.

On the second day she had **1.**_____ made in the neighborhood about the names of the people there, and she repeated to the little man the most unusual and **2.**_____. "Perhaps your name is Shortribs, or Sheepshanks, or Laceleg."

But he always answered, "That is not my name."

On the third day the messenger came back and said, "I have not been able to find a single new name, but as I came to a high mountain at the end of the forest, where the fox and the rabbit say good night to each other, I saw a little house, and in front of the house a fire was burning, and around the fire quite a **3.**_____ little man was jumping. He hopped upon one leg and shouted, 'Today I bake, tomorrow I brew, and the next day I'll have the young queen's child. How glad I am that no one knew that Rumpelstiltskin is my name.'"

You can **4.**_____ how glad the queen was when she heard the name. And when soon afterwards the little man came in and asked, "Now, mistress queen, what is my name?" At first she said, "Is your name Conrad?"

"No."

"Is your name Harry?"

"No."

"Perhaps your name is Rumpelstiltskin."

"The devil has told you that! The devil has told you that!" cried the little man, and in his anger he **5.**_____ his right foot so deep into the earth that his whole leg went in, and then in rage he pulled at his left leg so hard with both hands that he **6.**_____ himself in two.

6 The Frog King

❶ Vocabulary Practice: Match.

_____ **1. whenever**   **A** ≠ interested

_____ **2. fountain**   **B** the feeling of sadness for someone
                              else's difficult situation

_____ **3. bored**   **C** the sound made when someone or
                              something falls into water

_____ **4. pity**   **D** anytime

_____ **5. splash**   **E** a pool or well from which water flows
                              out

_____ **6. vanish**   **F** to disappear

2 **Listen and fill in the blanks with the correct words. Remember to change the form of verbs or nouns if necessary.**

In ancient times when wishing still helped people, there lived a king whose daughters were all beautiful, but the youngest was so beautiful that the sun itself, which has seen so much, was **1.**_____ whenever it shone on her face. Near the king's castle lay a great dark forest, and under an old lime tree in the forest was a **2.**_____. When the day was very warm, the king's child went out into the forest and sat down by the side of the cool **3.**_____. When she was bored, she took a golden ball and threw it up high and caught it, and this ball was her favorite toy.

Now on one occasion the princess's golden ball did not fall into the little hand which she was holding up for it, but onto the ground beyond, and rolled straight into the water. The king's daughter watched it go, but it **4.**_____, and the well was deep, so deep that the bottom could not be seen. Then she began to cry, and cried louder and louder, and could not be **5.**_____. And as she thus lamented, someone said to her, "What is wrong, king's daughter? You weep so that even a stone would feel **6.**_____."

She looked around to the side from which the voice had come, and saw a frog **7.**_____ its big, ugly head from the water. "Ah, old water-splasher, is it you?" she said. "I am weeping for my golden ball, which has fallen into the well."

pp. 72–73

1 Vocabulary Practice: Match.

_____	1. **crown**	A	a person or animal one spends a lot of time with
_____	2. **care for**	B	to like; to want
_____	3. **companion**	C	the act of promising to do something
_____	4. **promise**	D	the decoration that a member of a royal family wears on his or her head
_____	5. **jewel**	E	a person
_____	6. **human being**	F	a precious stone

2 Listen and fill in the blanks with the correct words. Remember to change the form of verbs or nouns if necessary.

"Be quiet and do not weep," answered the frog. "I can help you, but what will you give me if I bring your toy up again?"

"Whatever you will have, dear frog," she said. "My clothes, my pearls and jewels, and even this golden crown which I am wearing."

The frog answered, "I do not **1.**_____ your clothes, your pearls and jewels, nor for your golden crown; but if you will love me and let me be your friend and companion, sit by you at your little table, eat off your little golden plate, drink out of your little cup, and sleep in your little bed, I will go down below and bring your golden ball up again."

"Oh, yes," she said, "I **2.**_____ you all you wish, if you will but bring me my ball again." But she thought, "How the silly frog talks! All he does is sit in the water with the other frogs and croak. He can be no **3.**_____ to any human being."

But the frog, when he had received this promise, put his head under the water and sank down, and in a little while he came swimming up again with the ball in his mouth and threw it onto the grass. The king's daughter was **4.**_____ to see her pretty toy once more, picked it up, and ran away with it.

"Wait, wait," said the frog. "Take me with you. I can't run as you can." But what good did it do him to **5.**_____ his "Croak! Croak!" after her, as loudly as he could? She did not listen to it, but ran home and soon forgot the poor frog, who **6.**_____ go back into his well again.

1 Vocabulary Practice: Match.

_____	**1. marble**	**A**	with a lot of force
_____	**2. staircase**	**B**	very unpleasant
_____	**3. slam**	**C**	a type of hard stone
_____	**4. violently**	**D**	to keep saying or doing something whether it is right or wrong
_____	**5. disgusting**	**E**	to shut something hard and loudly
_____	**6. insist**	**F**	meanwhile
_____	**7. in the meantime**	**G**	a set of stairs inside a building

❷ Listen and fill in the blanks with the correct words. Remember to change the form of verbs or nouns if necessary.

The next day when she had seated herself at the table with the king and all his royal court and was eating from her little golden plate, something came creeping with a "splish-splash, splish-splash" up the marble **1.**_____, and when it had reached the top, it knocked at the door and cried, "Princess, youngest princess, open the door for me."

She ran to see who was outside, but when she opened the door, there sat the frog in front of her. Then she **2.**_____ the door, quickly sat down to dinner again, and was quite frightened. The king saw clearly that her heart was beating violently and said, "My child, what are you so afraid of? Is there perhaps a giant outside who wants to carry you away?"

"Ah, no," she replied. "It is no giant, but a **3.**_____ frog."

"What does a frog want with you?"

"Ah, dear father, yesterday when I was in the forest playing by the well, my golden ball fell into the water. And because I cried so much, the frog brought it out again for me, and because he **4.**_____, I promised him he could be my companion, but I never thought he would be able to come out of the water. And now he is out there and wants to come in to be with me."

5._____ the frog knocked again and cried, "Princess, youngest princess, open the door for me. Do you not remember what you said to me yesterday by the cool waters of the well? Princess, youngest princess, open the door for me."

Then the king said, "That which you have promised you must do. Go and let him in." So she went and opened the door, and the frog **6.**_____ in and followed her, step by step, to her chair. There he sat and cried, "Lift me up beside you."

Answers

❷

			6. hopped
			5. In the meantime
4. insisted	**3.** disgusting	**2.** slammed	**1.** staircase

pp. 76–77

❶ Vocabulary Practice: Match.

_____   **1. hesitate**   **A** happily; readily; because one wants to do something

_____   **2. willingly**   **B** to pause or delay because one is nervous or not sure what to do

_____   **3. choke**   **C** ≠ out of trouble

_____   **4. in trouble**   **D** to be unable to breathe

_____   **5. despise**   **E** to move slowly and carefully

_____   **6. creep**   **F** to look down on (≠ to respect)

🎧 **37** ❷ Listen and fill in the blanks with the correct words. Remember to change the form of verbs or nouns if necessary.

She hesitated, until at last the king commanded her to do it. Once the frog was on the chair, he wanted to be on the table, and when he was on the table, he said, "Now push your little golden plate nearer to me so that we may eat together." She did this, but it was easy to see that she did not do it **1.**_____. The frog enjoyed what he ate, but almost every mouthful she took made her **2.**_____. Finally he said, "I have eaten and am satisfied, and now I am tired. Carry me into your little room and make your little silken bed ready, and we will both lie down and go to sleep."

The king's daughter began to cry, for she **3.**_____ the cold frog which she did not want to touch, and which was now to sleep in her pretty, clean little bed. But the king became angry and said, "He who helped you when you were **4.**_____ should not afterwards be despised by you."

So she picked the frog up with two fingers, carried him upstairs, and put him in a corner, but when she was in bed, he **5.**_____ to her and said, "I am tired, and I want to sleep as well as you. Lift me up or I will tell your father." When she heard this she became terribly angry. She picked the frog up and threw him as hard as she could against the wall. "Now will you be quiet, horrible frog?" she said.

But when he fell down, he was **6.**_____ a frog, but a king's son with kind and beautiful eyes.

pp. 78–79

1 Vocabulary Practice: Match.

_____	1. **curse**	**A**	to change into
_____	2. **carriage**	**B**	freedom from harm; safety
_____	3. **faithful**	**C**	to bring others bad luck with magic words
_____	4. **turn into**	**D**	always supporting someone
_____	5. **grief**	**E**	to split open and break
_____	6. **salvation**	**F**	a vehicle with wheels that is pulled by horses
_____	7. **crack**	**G**	to put one in prison (≠ set free)
_____	8. **imprison**	**H**	great sorrow

38 ❷ Listen and fill in the blanks with the correct words. Remember to change the form of verbs or nouns if necessary.

And he, by her father's wish, was now her dear companion and husband. Then he told her how he had been cursed by a **1.**_____ witch, and how no one could have saved him from the well but herself, and that tomorrow they would go together into his kingdom.

Then they went to sleep, and the next morning when the sun awoke them, a **2.**_____ came driving up pulled by white horses, which had white ostrich feathers on their heads and were harnessed with golden chains, and behind them stood the young king's servant Faithful Henry.

Faithful Henry had been so unhappy when his master was **3.**_____ a frog that he had ordered three iron bands to be tied around his heart to prevent it from bursting with **4.**_____ and sadness. The carriage was to carry the young king into his kingdom. Faithful Henry helped them both in, placed himself behind the horses again, and was full of joy because of this **5.**_____.

And when they had driven a part of the way, the young king heard a **6.**_____ sound behind him as if something had broken. So he turned around and cried, "Henry, the carriage is breaking."

"No, master, it is not the carriage. It is an iron band from my heart, which was put there in my great pain when you were a frog and **7.**_____ in the well."

Again and once again while they were on their way, something cracked, and each time the young king thought the carriage was breaking, but it was only the bands springing from the heart of Faithful Henry because his master had been **8.**_____ and was happy.

Answers ❷

8. set free	7. imprisoned	6. cracking	5. salvation
4. grief	3. turned into	2. carriage	1. wicked

7 Little Briar Rose

pp. 80–81

1 Vocabulary Practice: Match.

_____	1.	**bathe**	**A** to complete or accomplish something
_____	2.	**fulfill**	**B** a person you don't know very well
_____	3.	**contain**	**C** to wash one's body; to take a bath
_____	4.	**acquaintance**	**D** good behavior
_____	5.	**splendor**	**E** good looks
_____	6.	**virtue**	**F** the act of punishing one who has hurt you
_____	7.	**beauty**	**G** to get hurt by touching something sharp
_____	8.	**revenge**	**H** wonderful, fancy things or activities
_____	9.	**prick**	**I** to control one's feelings

Answers

1

1. C   2. A   3. I   4. B   5. H
6. D   7. E   8. F   9. G

2 Listen and fill in the blanks with the correct words. Remember to change the form of verbs or nouns if necessary.

A long time ago, there were a king and queen who said every day, "Ah, if only we had a child," but they never had one. But one day while the queen was bathing, a frog crept out of the water onto the land and said to her, "Your wish shall be **1.**_____, and within a year you shall have a daughter."

What the frog had said came true, and the queen had a little girl who was so pretty that the king could not **2.**_____ his joy and ordered a great feast. He invited not only his relatives, friends and acquaintances, but also the wise women, so that they would be kind and **3.**_____ to the child.

There were thirteen of these wise women in his kingdom, but as he had only twelve golden plates for them to eat from, one of them had to stay at home.

The feast was held with all sorts of **4.**_____ and when it came to an end, the wise women offered their magic gifts to the baby. One gave her virtue, another beauty, a third **5.**_____, and so on, with the child receiving everything in the world that one can wish for.

When eleven of the wise women had made their promises, suddenly the thirteenth came in. She wanted **6.**_____ for not having been invited, and without greeting or even looking at anyone, she cried in a loud voice, "The king's daughter shall at the age of fifteen **7.**_____ herself with a spindle and fall down dead." And without saying a word more, she turned around and left the room.

1 Vocabulary Practice: Match.

_____	1. **undo**	**A**	magic words to bring others bad luck
_____	2. **curse**	**B**	a young or unmarried girl
_____	3. **soften**	**C**	not talking much about one's success
_____	4. **eagerly**	**D**	covered with rust
_____	5. **protect . . . from . . .**	**E**	wanting to do something strongly
_____	6. **abundantly**	**F**	to keep someone safe
_____	7. **modest**	**G**	to spin very quickly
_____	8. **good-natured**	**H**	delightful
_____	9. **maiden**	**I**	to cancel the effects or results
_____	10. **rusty**	**J**	kind and friendly
_____	11. **whirl**	**K**	to make something less hard or less serious
_____	12. **merrily**	**L**	in large amounts

2 Listen and fill in the blanks with the correct words. Remember to change the form of verbs or nouns if necessary.

They were all shocked, but the twelfth wise woman, whose good wish still remained unspoken, came forward, and as she could not undo the evil curse, but only **1.**_____ it, she said, "It shall not be death, but a deep sleep of a hundred years, into which the princess shall fall."

The king, who **2.**_____ wished to protect his dear child from such misfortune, gave orders that every spindle in the whole kingdom should be burned. Meanwhile, the gifts of the wise women were abundantly fulfilled in the young girl, for she was so beautiful, **3.**_____, good-natured, and wise that everyone who saw her simply had to love her.

On the very day that the girl turned fifteen years old, the king and queen were not at home, and the maiden was left in the palace quite alone. So she went around into all sorts of places, **4.**_____ rooms and bedrooms just as she liked, and at last came to an old tower. She climbed up the narrow winding **5.**_____ and reached a little door. A rusty key was in the lock, and when she turned it the door opened and there in a little room sat an old woman with a spindle, busily spinning her flax.

"Good day, old mother," said the king's daughter. "What are you doing there?"

"I am spinning," said the old woman, and nodded her head.

"What sort of thing is that, that whirls around so **6.**_____?" said the girl, and she took the spindle and wanted to spin too. But as soon as she had touched the spindle, the magic **7.**_____ was fulfilled, and she pricked her finger on it.

pp. 84–85

1 Vocabulary Practice: Match.

_____	1. **prick**	**A**	to burn
_____	2. **extend over**	**B**	to stop
_____	3. **flame**	**C**	not often
_____	4. **roast**	**D**	a pain one gets when touching something sharp
_____	5. **cease**	**E**	to be free from; to escape
_____	6. **hedge**	**F**	having many thorns
_____	7. **thorn**	**G**	a sharp, pointed part of a stem or a plant's stem
_____	8. **from time to time**	**H**	cooked over a fire; to cook over a fire
_____	9. **thorny**	**I**	small trees or bushes that form a wall
_____	10. **get loose**	**J**	to cover an area

2 Listen and fill in the blanks with the correct words. Remember to change the form of verbs or nouns if necessary.

And at the very moment when she felt the prick, she fell down upon the bed that stood there, and into a deep sleep. And this sleep 1._____ the whole palace. The king and queen, who had just come home and entered the great hall, began to fall asleep, and all of the court with them. The horses, too, went to sleep in the stable. The dogs in the yard, the pigeons upon the roof, the flies on the walls, and even the fire that was 2._____ in the fireplace, became quiet and slept. The roast meat stopped 3._____, and the cook, who was just going to pull the hair of the dish-washing boy because he had forgotten something, let him go and went to sleep. And the wind 4._____ to blow, and on the trees before the castle not a leaf moved.

But all around the castle there began to grow a hedge of 5._____, which every year became higher, and at last grew close up around the castle and all over it, so that there was nothing of the castle to be seen, not even the flag upon the roof. But the story of the beautiful sleeping Briar-Rose (for so the princess was named) 6._____ the country, so that from time to time kings' sons came and tried to get through the thorny hedge into the castle.

But they found it impossible, for the thorns held fast together, as if they had hands, and the youths were caught in them, could not 7._____ again, and died a miserable death.

Answers

2

1. extended over   2. flaming   3. roasting   4. ceased   5. thorns   6. went about   7. get loose

pp. 86–87

❶ Vocabulary Practice: Match.

_____	**1. dissuade**	**A**	to separate
_____	**2. awaken**	**B**	in the same way
_____	**3. part**	**C**	unable to move
_____	**4. pluck**	**D**	to stop sleeping
_____	**5. likewise**	**E**	to quickly remove something from its place
_____	**6. stuck**	**F**	to stop one from doing something; ≠ persuade

🎧 **42** ❷ Listen and fill in the blanks with the correct words. Remember to change the form of verbs or nouns if necessary.

After many, many years, a king's son came once again to that country, and heard an old man talking about the thorny hedge, and how a castle was said to stand beneath it in which a **1.**_____ beautiful princess named Briar-Rose had been asleep for a hundred years, and how the king and queen and the whole court were likewise asleep. The prince had heard too, from his grandfather, that many kings' sons had already come and tried to **2.** _____ the thorny hedge, but had remained stuck fast in it and died a terrible death.

Then the youth said, "I am not afraid. I will go and see the beautiful Briar-Rose." The good old man tried his best to **3.**_____ him, but the prince did not listen to his words.

But by this time the hundred years had passed, and the day had come when Briar-Rose was to **4.**_____ again. When the king's son came near the thorny hedge, it was nothing but large and beautiful flowers, which parted from each other by themselves and let him pass **5.**_____, then closed again behind him like a hedge. In the castle yard he saw the horses and the spotted hounds lying asleep; on the roof sat the pigeons with their heads under their wings. And when he entered the house, the flies were asleep upon the walls, the cook in the kitchen was still holding out his hand to seize the boy, and the maid was sitting by the black hen which she was going to **6.**_____.

❶ Vocabulary Practice: Match.

_____	1.	**throne**	**A** to move something quickly from side to side or up and down
_____	2.	**breath**	**B** to burn or shine on and off quickly
_____	3.	**wag**	**C** feeling happy about one's life
_____	4.	**flicker**	**D** a hit with one's open hand
_____	5.	**smack**	**E** a king's or queen's chair
_____	6.	**contentedly**	**F** the air one breathes in and out

2 Listen and fill in the blanks with the correct words. Remember to change the form of verbs or nouns if necessary.

He went on farther, and in the great hall he saw the whole court
1._____ asleep, while up by the throne lay the king and queen.

Then he went on still farther, and all was so quiet that a 2._____
could be heard. At last he came to the tower, and opened the door to the little
room where Briar-Rose was sleeping.

There she lay, so beautiful that he could not look away, and he
3._____ and gave her a kiss. But as soon as he had kissed her,
Briar-Rose opened her eyes, awoke and looked at him sweetly.

Then they went downstairs together, and the king awoke, and the queen,
and the whole court, and looked at each other in great astonishment. And the
horses in the yard stood up and shook themselves, the hounds jumped up and
4._____ their tails, the pigeons upon the roof pulled their heads out
from under their wings, looked around and flew into the open country, the flies
on the walls crept again, the fire in the kitchen burned and 5._____
and cooked the meat, which began to turn and roast again, the cook gave the
boy such a smack on the ear that he screamed, and the maid finished plucking
the hen.

And then the marriage of the king's son to Briar-Rose was celebrated with
all splendor, and they lived 6._____ for the rest of their days.

8 Cinderella

pp. 90–91

1 Vocabulary Practice: Match.

_____ 1. **pass away** **A** a place underground where a dead body is put

_____ 2. **pious** **B** a long dress

_____ 3. **watch over someone** **C** the child of one's husband or wife

_____ 4. **grave** **D** to die

_____ 5. **melt** **E** to make something go out

_____ 6. **stepchild** **F** a small green vegetable

_____ 7. **gown** **G** to become liquid

_____ 8. **insult** **H** to look after someone

_____ 9. **pour** **I** covered in dust

_____ 10. **pea** **J** to say or do something rude

_____ 11. **dusty** **K** showing belief in a religion

2 Listen and fill in the blanks with the correct words. Remember to change the form of verbs or nouns if necessary.

The wife of a rich man became very sick, and as she felt that she would soon pass away she called her only daughter to her bedside and said, "Dear child, be good and pious, and then God will always protect you, and I will 1._____ from heaven and be near you." Then she closed her eyes and died.

Every day the girl went out to her mother's grave and wept, and she remained pious and good. When winter came, the snow spread like a white sheet over the grave, and by the time the spring sun had 2._____ it again, the man had a new wife.

This woman had brought with her into the house her two daughters, who were beautiful and fair but also evil and 3._____. Now began a bad time for the poor stepchild. "Is this stupid girl to sit in the living room with us?" they said. "Whoever wants to eat bread must earn it. Out with the kitchen maid." Then they took her pretty clothes away from her, put an old gray 4._____ on her, and gave her wooden shoes. "Just look at the proud princess! How fancy she is!" they laughed, and led her into the kitchen.

There she had to do hard work from morning till night: get up before dawn, carry water, light fires, cook, and wash. Besides this, the sisters did all they could to hurt her. They 5._____ her and poured her peas and lentils into the ashes, so that she was forced to sit and pick them out again. In the evening, when she had worked till she was 6._____, she had no bed to go to, but had to sleep by the fireplace in the cinders. And because she always looked 7._____ and dirty, they called her Cinderella.

pp. 92–93

❶ Vocabulary Practice: Match.

_____	**1. stepdaughter**	**A**	to sit on; to settle
_____	**2. bush**	**B**	to say
_____	**3. perch**	**C**	to continue (≠ stop)
_____	**4. express**	**D**	to join together
_____	**5. last**	**E**	the metal piece that fastens a belt
_____	**6. fasten**	**F**	one's daughter by marriage, but not by birth
_____	**7. buckle**	**G**	a plant with many small branches, like a small tree

🎧 **45** ❷ **Listen and fill in the blanks with the correct words. Remember to change the form of verbs or nouns if necessary.**

One day the father was going to the **1.**_____, and he asked his two stepdaughters what he should bring back for them.

"Beautiful dresses," said one.

"Pearls and jewels," said the other.

"And you, Cinderella?" he said. "What will you have?"

"Father, break off for me the first branch which **2.**_____ your hat on your way home."

So he bought beautiful dresses, pearls and jewels for his two stepdaughters, and on his way home, as he was riding through some green **3.**_____, a twig brushed against him and knocked off his hat. Then he broke off the branch and took it with him. When he got home, he gave his stepdaughters the things which they had asked for, and to Cinderella he gave the branch from the bush.

Cinderella thanked him, went to her mother's **4.**_____, planted the branch on it, and wept so much that her tears fell down on the branch and watered it. And so it grew and became a beautiful tree. Three times a day Cinderella went and sat beneath it and wept and prayed, and a little white bird always came and perched on the tree, and if Cinderella **5.**_____ a wish, the bird threw down to her whatever she had wished for.

One day, however, the king gave orders for a festival which was to **6.**_____ three days, and to which all the beautiful young girls in the country were invited, so that his son might choose himself a bride. When Cinderella's two stepsisters heard that they too had been invited to appear at the festival, they were delighted. They called Cinderella and said, "Comb our hair for us, brush our shoes, and **7.**_____ our buckles, for we are going to the festival at the king's palace."

Answers ❷

1. fair 2. knocks against 3. bushes 4. grave 5. expressed 6. last 7. fasten

Vocabulary & Listening Practice ❽ Cinderella **91**

pp. 94–95

1 Vocabulary Practice: Match.

_____ 1. **dust**

_____ 2. **dirt**

_____ 3. **tame**

_____ 4. **dove**

_____ 5. **flap**

_____ 6. **grain**

_____ 7. **joyful**

A ≠ dangerous and wild (animals)

B to move (wings) up and down

C small pieces of soil or mud

D seeds eaten as food, like rice or corn

E happy; delighted

F a white bird which is like a pigeon

G small dry pieces of soil which can float in the air

2 **Listen and fill in the blanks with the correct words. Remember to change the form of verbs or nouns if necessary.**

Cinderella obeyed, but wept, because she too would have liked to go to the dance. She begged her stepmother to allow her to go. "Cinderella," she said, "you are covered in **1.**_____ and dirt, yet you would go to the festival? You have no clothes or shoes, yet you would dance?"

As Cinderella went on asking, however, her stepmother said at last, "I have **2.**_____ a dish of lentils into the ashes for you. If you have picked them out again in two hours, you shall go with us."

Cinderella went through the back door into the garden and called, "You **3.**_____ pigeons, you doves, and all you other birds beneath the sky, come and help me to pick the good lentils into the dish and the bad into the barrel."

Then two pigeons came in through the kitchen window, and after them some doves, and finally all the birds beneath the sky came **4.**_____ and crowding in and landed among the ashes. And the pigeons nodded with their heads and began to pick, pick, pick, pick, and the rest began also to pick, pick, pick, pick, and they gathered all the good **5.**_____ into the dish. In just one hour they had finished, and all flew out again. Joyful, the girl took the dish to her stepmother and thought that now she would be **6.**_____ to go to the festival.

pp. 96–97

1 Vocabulary Practice: Match.

_____	1. **certainly**	**A**	embarrassed by (≠ proud of)
_____	2. **ashamed of**	**B**	to cry
_____	3. **turn one's back on**	**C**	to collect
_____	4. **weep**	**D**	very happy; very pleased
_____	5. **gather**	**E**	of course; without doubt
_____	6. **delighted**	**F**	to ignore; to refuse to help

2 Listen and fill in the blanks with the correct words. Remember to change the form of verbs or nouns if necessary.

But the stepmother said, "No, Cinderella, you have no clothes and you cannot dance. You would only be **1.**_____."

And as Cinderella wept at this, her stepmother said, "If you can pick two dishes of lentils out of the ashes for me in one hour, you shall go with us." And she thought to herself, "She most **2.**_____ cannot do that again." When the stepmother had poured the two dishes of lentils among the ashes, the girl went through the back door into the garden and cried, "You tame **3.**_____, you doves, and all you other birds beneath the sky, come and help me to pick the good lentils into the dishes, and the bad into the barrel."

Then two pigeons came in through the kitchen window, and after them some doves, and finally all the birds beneath the sky came flapping and crowding in and landed among the ashes. And the doves nodded with their heads and began to pick, pick, pick, pick, and the others began also to pick, pick, pick, pick, and they **4.**_____ all the good seeds into the dishes. In less than half an hour they had already finished, and all flew out again.

Then Cinderella was **5.**_____ and believed that she might now go to the festival. But her stepmother said, "All this will not help. You cannot go with us, for you have no clothes and cannot dance. We would be ashamed of you." And she **6.**_____ on Cinderella and hurried away with her two proud daughters.

1 Vocabulary Practice: Match.

_____	**1. shiver**	**A**	a soft type of cloth of very high quality
_____	**2. quiver**	**B**	to stay with someone
_____	**3. silk**	**C**	not known by others
_____	**4. assume**	**D**	to jump
_____	**5. keep one company**	**E**	to shake to a small degree, as if cold
_____	**6. belong to**	**F**	to think something is true
_____	**7. unknown**	**G**	to be owned by
_____	**8. leap**	**H**	to shake to a small degree; shiver

48 **2** Listen and fill in the blanks with the correct words. Remember to change the form of verbs or nouns if necessary.

As no one else was now at home, Cinderella went to her mother's grave beneath the tree and cried, "Shiver and 1._____, little tree, throw silver and gold down over me."

Then the bird threw a gold and silver dress down to her, and slippers 2._____ with silk and silver. She quickly put on the dress and went to the festival. Her stepsisters and stepmother, however, did not know her and thought she must be a foreign princess, for she looked so beautiful in her golden dress. They never once thought of Cinderella and 3._____ that she was sitting at home in the dirt, picking lentils out of the ashes.

The prince approached her, took her by the hand, and danced with her. He would dance with no other maiden and never 4._____ her hand, and if anyone else came to invite her, he said, "This is my partner."

She danced till it was evening, and then she wanted to go home. But the king's son said, "I will go with you and 5._____," for he wished to see to whom this beautiful maiden belonged. She escaped from him, however, and ran into the pigeon house.

The king's son waited until her father came, and then he told him that the unknown maiden had 6._____ into the pigeon house. The old man thought, "Can it be Cinderella?" They had to bring him an axe and a pickaxe so that he could 7._____ the pigeon house into pieces, but no one was inside it.

1 Vocabulary Practice: Match.

_____	1. **dim**	**A**	excellent; wonderful
_____	2. **wish to**	**B**	very surprised
_____	3. **magnificent**	**C**	to want to do something
_____	4. **squirrel**	**D**	giving off little light (≠ bright)
_____	5. **astonished**	**E**	beautifully and elegantly
_____	6. **gracefully**	**F**	a small animal that eats nuts

② Listen and fill in the blanks with the correct words. Remember to change the form of verbs or nouns if necessary.

And when they got home, Cinderella lay in her dirty clothes among the ashes, and a **1.**_____ little oil lamp was burning on the shelf, for she had jumped quickly down from the back of the pigeon house and run to the little tree, where she had taken off her beautiful clothes and laid them on the grave. The bird had taken them away again, and then Cinderella had **2.**_____ herself in the kitchen among the ashes in her gray gown.

The next day when the festival began again and her parents and stepsisters had gone once more, Cinderella went to the tree and said, "**3.**_____ and quiver, my little tree, throw silver and gold down over me."

Then the bird threw down a much more beautiful dress than the one from the day before. And when Cinderella appeared at the festival in this dress, everyone was **4.**_____ at her beauty. The king's son had waited for her to come, and he instantly took her by the hand and danced with no one but her. When others came and invited her, he said, "This is my partner."

When evening came, she **5.**_____ leave. The king's son followed her and wanted to see into which house she went. But she sprang away from him and into the garden behind the house. There stood a beautiful tall tree on which hung the most magnificent pears. She moved so **6.**_____ between the branches, like a squirrel, that the king's son did not know where she had gone. He waited until her father came and said to him, "The **7.**_____ maiden has escaped from me, and I believe she has climbed up the pear tree."

1 Vocabulary Practice: Match.

_____	**1. as usual**	**A**	worried and nervous
_____	**2. splendid**	**B**	to spread over, like butter on bread
_____	**3. anxious**	**C**	to run away from
_____	**4. smear**	**D**	excellent; wonderful; outstanding
_____	**5. pitch**	**E**	like what happens most or all of the time
_____	**6. escape**	**F**	a sticky black material

2 Listen and fill in the blanks with the correct words. Remember to change the form of verbs or nouns if necessary.

The father thought, "Can it be Cinderella?"

And the father had an axe brought and cut the tree down, but no one was on it. And when they went into the kitchen Cinderella lay there among the ashes, 1._____, for she had jumped down off the other side of the tree, taken the beautiful dress back to the bird on the little tree, and 2._____ her gray gown.

On the third day, when her parents and stepsisters had gone away, Cinderella went once more to her mother's grave and said to the little tree, "Shiver and quiver, my little tree, throw silver and gold down over me."

And now the bird threw down to her a dress which was more 3._____ and magnificent than any she had yet had, and golden slippers. And when she went to the festival in this dress, everyone was so astonished that no one could speak. The king's son danced with her only, and if anyone else invited her to dance, he said, "This is my partner."

When evening came, Cinderella wished to leave, and the king's son was 4._____ to go with her, but she escaped from him so quickly that he could not follow her. The king's son, however, had thought of a clever 5._____, and ordered the whole staircase to be 6._____ with pitch. And there, after Cinderella had run down, her left slipper remained stuck.

pp. 104–105

1 Vocabulary Practice: Match.

_____	1. **delicate**	A	to fall slowly in drops (of liquid)
_____	2. **try on**	B	easily damaged
_____	3. **peep**	C	a room
_____	4. **drip**	D	to secretly look at something
_____	5. **chamber**	E	the rounded back part of the foot
_____	6. **heel**	F	to put something on and see if it fits

51 **2** **Listen and fill in the blanks with the correct words. Remember to change the form of verbs or nouns if necessary.**

The king's son picked it up, and it was small and **1.** ______________ and all golden. The next morning he went with it to Cinderella's father and said to him, "No one shall be my wife but she whose foot this golden slipper fits."

Then the two sisters were glad, for they had pretty feet. The eldest went into her room with the shoe to **2.** ______________, and her mother watched. But she could not get her big toe into it as the shoe was too small for her. Then her mother gave her a knife and said, "Cut the toe off. When you are queen, you will never need to walk again." So the girl cut her toe off, forced her foot into the shoe, **3.** ______________ her pain, and went out to the king's son. Then he took her on his horse as his bride and rode away with her.

They had to pass the grave, however, and there on the tree sat two white doves, who cried, "Turn and peep, turn and peep; there's blood within the shoe. The shoe is too small for her, and your true bride **4.** ______________ you."

Then the king's son looked at her foot and saw how the blood was dripping from it. He turned his horse around, took the **5.** ______________ bride home again and said that she was not the right one and the other sister was to put the shoe on. Then this one went into her chamber and got her toes safely into the shoe, but her **6.** ______________ was too large.

Answers **2**

1. delicate **2.** try it on **3.** hid **4.** waits for
5. false **6.** heel

1 Vocabulary Practice: Match.

_____	**1. stain**	**A**	not completely developed (≠ fully grown)
_____	**2. stocking**	**B**	to leave a mark; to change the color of something
_____	**3. stunted**	**C**	in every way
_____	**4. absolutely**	**D**	to fit perfectly
_____	**5. fit like a glove**	**E**	to know who someone is
_____	**6. recognize**	**F**	thin clothing that covers one's leg and foot

2 Listen and fill in the blanks with the correct words. Remember to change the form of verbs or nouns if necessary.

So her mother gave her a knife and said, "Cut a bit off your heel. When you are queen, you will never need to walk again." So the girl cut a bit off her heel, forced her foot into the shoe, hid her pain, and went out to the king's son.

He took her on his horse as his bride and **1.**_____ with her, but when they passed by the tree, the two doves sat on it and cried, "Turn and peep, turn and peep; there's blood within the shoe. The shoe is too small for her, and your true bride waits for you."

He looked down at her foot and saw the blood running out of the shoe and how it had **2.**_____ her white stocking quite red. Then he turned his horse around and took the false bride home again. "This is not the right one, either," he said. "Have you no other daughter?"

"No," said the man. "There is still a little stunted kitchen maid whom my late wife left behind, but she cannot **3.**_____ be your bride."

The king's son said he was to send the girl up to him, but the stepmother answered, "Oh, no! She is much too dirty; she cannot show herself." But he **4.**_____ insisted on it, and so Cinderella had to be called.

She first washed her hands and face and then went and bowed down before the king's son, who gave her the golden shoe. Then she seated herself on a stool, pulled her foot out of the heavy wooden shoe, and put it into the slipper, which **5.**_____. And when she rose and the king's son looked at her face, he **6.**_____ the beautiful maiden who had danced with him and cried, "This is my true bride."

1 Vocabulary Practice: Match.

_____ 1. **get into favor with**   A having formally agreed to marry

_____ 2. **good fortune**   B to make someone like you

_____ 3. **engaged**   C being wicked (≠ kindness)

_____ 4. **peck out**   D a lie (≠ truth)

_____ 5. **wickedness**   E good luck

_____ 6. **falsehood**   F to bite out with a beak

🎧 **53** ❷ Listen and fill in the blanks with the correct words. Remember to change the form of verbs or nouns if necessary.

The stepmother and the two sisters were **1.**_____ and became pale with rage. The king's son, however, took Cinderella on his horse and rode away with her.

As they passed by the tree, the two white doves cried, "Turn and peep, turn and peep; no blood is in the shoe. The shoe is not too small for her, and your true bride rides with you." When they had cried that, they came flying down and **2.**_____ themselves on Cinderella's shoulders — one on the right, the other on the left — and remained sitting there.

When the wedding of Cinderella and the king's son was to be celebrated, the two false sisters came and tried to **3.**_____ Cinderella and share her good fortune. When the engaged couple went to the church, the elder sister was on the right side and the younger on the left, and the two pigeons **4.**_____ one eye from each of them. Afterwards, as they came back, the elder was on the left and the younger on the right, and the pigeons pecked out the other eye from each. And thus, for their **5.**_____ and falsehood, they were punished with **6.**_____ for the rest of their days.

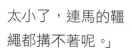

Translations

1 大拇哥

pp. 2–3 從前有個貧窮的農夫。一天晚上，他坐在壁爐旁撥著爐火，妻子則紡著紗。農夫說道：「我們膝下無子，家裡好冷清啊，看看別人家，吵吵鬧鬧多活潑啊！」

「可不是嗎？」妻子心有同感，嘆了一口氣說：「要是只有一個孩子也好！就算他像拇指一樣小，我也會心滿意足的，我們還是會全心愛他的呀。」

有一天，這位婦人生病了，七個月後，果真生下一個孩子。這孩子四肢健全，個頭卻就只有拇指大小。

不過他們還是說：「我們的願望還真的實現了，這是我們寶貝的孩子呀。」因為個子大小的關係，他們就叫他大拇哥。

雖然他們盡量讓他多吃，可他就是長不高，始終和他生下時一樣大。不過他能慧黠地觀察這個世界，也很快就表現出他的聰明敏捷，因為他做什麼事都能做得很好。

有一天，農夫準備到森林裡砍柴，他自言自語地說：「真希望有人能幫我驅馬車來這。」

「噢，老爸！」大拇哥叫道：「放心吧，我不久就會把馬車駕到森林裡去的。相信我，等你要用時就會出現。」

農夫笑道：「這怎麼可能呢？你個頭太小了，連馬的韁繩都搆不著呢。」

pp. 4–5 「爸爸，這不成問題的，」大拇哥說道：「只要媽媽把馬套上輓具，我就可以坐在馬的耳朵裡，告訴牠往哪條路走。」

「好吧，」農夫說：「那就試一次看看吧。」

到了要出發時，媽媽將馬接上馬車，將大拇哥放進馬的耳朵裡。這小傢伙就大聲地喊著：「走吧！駕！」

結果馬車好像真有人駕馭一般，就朝正確的方向進了林子。就在馬匹轉彎、小傢伙大叫：「駕！」時，兩個陌生人正朝牠過來。

其中一個說：「天啊！那是什麼啊！」另一個說道：「前面有一輛馬車駛過來，可以聽到車夫在對馬喊著，可是卻看不到車夫。這是不可能的啊！我們就跟著這輛馬車，看它要到哪兒去。」

馬車逕駛入森林，果然來到了農夫砍柴的地方。大拇哥看見爸爸，馬上喊道：「老爸，你看到沒？我把馬車駕來了，抱我下來吧。」

他爸爸便用左手抓住馬，右手將小小的兒子從馬耳朵裡接出來，大拇哥就高興地坐在麥稈上，而那兩個陌生人一見到他，驚訝得說不出話。後來，其中的一個把另一個拉到一邊，說道：「喂，要是我們把這小傢伙帶到大城市裡去展示，準會發財的。不如把他買下來吧。」

pp. 6–7 於是他們走到農夫面前，對他說：「能不能把這小傢伙賣給我們呀？我們會好好待他的。」

「不行！」父親答道：「他可是我的心肝寶貝，就算給我全世界的財富，我也不賣。」

大拇哥聽到這個交易，便沿著父親大衣上的摺痕爬上，站在他的肩上，悄悄地在他耳邊說：「老爸，先把我賣了吧，我會溜回來的。」

於是，農夫同意以一大筆錢成交，把大拇哥賣給這兩個人。

陌生人問大拇哥說：「你想坐在哪兒？」

「喔，就把我放在你的帽簷上吧，這樣我就可以走來走去，看看田園風光，也不至於摔倒啦。」

於是他們依了他。大拇哥和他父親告別後，兩個陌生人便帶著大拇哥上路了。

他們一直走到了傍晚，這時小傢伙說：「讓我下來好不好？這很重要，我想小便。」

「乖乖待在上面，」戴這頂帽子的人說：「我可沒差，反正鳥兒也常在我頭上拉屎。」

「不行啦，」大拇哥說：「我要有禮貌，快放我下來。」

這人脫下帽子，把這小傢伙放在路邊的地上。大拇哥跳到地上並悄悄地四處走走，最後找到一個老鼠洞鑽了進去。「晚安囉，各位，我先走一步。」他叫道，把他們嘲弄了一番。

他們跑了過來，用手杖往老鼠洞裡捅，但這是白費力氣，大拇哥已經爬到更裡面去了。不久，天整個暗下來，他們只得口袋空空回家，懊惱不已。

pp. 8–9 大拇哥看他們離去之後，從地道裡爬了出來。「要摸黑趕路，還真是危險。」他說：「很容易摔斷脖子、摔斷腿的。」幸好這時他被一個空的蝸牛殼給絆倒，他說道：「謝天謝地！這樣我就可以待在裡面安然地過夜了。」說完就爬了進去。

過了不久，在他正要入睡時，他聽到有兩個人打這兒經過，其中一個人說：「我們怎麼把那個有錢牧師的金銀財寶給弄到手呢？」

大拇哥聽了馬上插嘴叫道：「我知道！」

其中一個小偷聽見後嚇了一跳，問道：「這是什麼聲音？我明明聽見有人說話。」他倆停下腳步留神靜聽。而大拇哥又說了：「帶

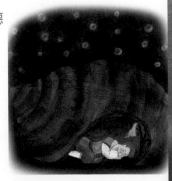

我一起去，我可以幫你們。」

「可是你在哪兒啊？」

「往地上找找，注意聽聲音是從哪兒發出的。」大拇哥答道。

他們終於找到了大拇哥，把他拎起來道：「你這個調皮鬼，幫得上什麼忙啊？」

「聽好了，」大拇哥說：「我能從牧師房間的鐵欄杆中間溜爬進去，把你們所要的東西扔出來。」

「那就來吧，」小偷說道：「我們倒要看看你有什麼能耐。」

當他們來到牧師的房子後，大拇哥悄悄地走爬進屋子，卻馬上使勁兒喊道：「是不是要搬個精光呀？」

聽到他的叫喊聲，兩個小偷一陣驚慌，說道：「小聲點，你會把屋裡的人叫醒的。」

但大拇哥卻裝傻，繼續大叫：「要什麼？要搬個精光嗎？」

pp. 10–11 這回，睡在隔壁的廚娘聽到了，便從床上坐起來聽著動靜。這時，嚇得跑得遠遠的兩個小偷，又鼓起了勇氣，想著說道：「這小無賴想耍我們。」於是他們又回來，輕聲地對大拇哥說：「現在不是開玩笑的時候，快扔點東西出來。」

大拇哥再度扯開嗓門叫道：「我會遞給你們，把手伸過來吧。」廚娘這回聽得可清楚了，她跳下床，衝到門邊，兩個

小偷就像有野獸在追捕似地逃之夭夭了。廚娘什麼都看不清楚，就走去點了一盞燈。

等她回來時，大拇哥已經溜進穀倉裡了。廚娘將屋子的每一個角落都仔細察看了一遍，也沒有發現異常，就又躺上了床，當自己是張著眼睛和耳朵在做夢呢。

大拇哥爬上一堆稻草，找到了一個舒適的地方睡覺，他打算等天亮後，再回到爸媽身邊。

怎知還有事情等著他呢？

老實說，這世上的麻煩事還真多。天才剛破曉，廚娘就起床餵牛。她第一件事是來穀倉抱乾草，好巧不巧，她抱的正是大拇哥睡覺的那堆乾草。而大拇哥睡得正甜，渾然不知，一直到自己和乾草一起進牛嘴裡時，才醒了過來。

pp. 12–13 「哇！」大拇哥叫了起來：「我怎麼滾進羊毛清洗廠裡來了呀？」

不過他一下就明白自己被困在哪兒了。他得小心翼翼不讓自己被牛牙齒咬到，卻還是和乾草一起進了牛肚。

「這裡沒有窗戶，」大拇哥說著：「陽光照不進來，蠟燭也點不起來。」這地方已經很不合他的意了，更慘的是，一堆一堆的乾草還不斷地往門裡送，使得空間越來越小。情急之下，他終於放聲大叫：「不要再給我送飼料來了！不要再給我送飼料來了！」

那廚娘這時正在擠牛奶，她聽到說話聲，卻沒看見什麼人影，又發覺這聲音分明就跟她昨晚聽到的一樣，就嚇得從凳子上跌下來，把牛奶都給打翻了

她慌慌張張地跑到主人那兒說：「噢，天啊，先生，那牛在說話哩！」

牧師回說：「我看你是昏頭了。」隨即親自來牛棚一看究竟。而當他前腳才剛踏進去，大拇哥又叫道：「不要再給我送飼料來了！不要再給我送飼料來了！」

這下牧師也嚇了一大跳，他認為這條母牛一定是邪靈附身了，急忙叫人把牛宰了。牛被宰了之後，裝著大拇哥的牛肚被扔到糞堆上。

pp. 14–15 大拇哥費了九牛二虎之力才爬了出來。不過禍不單行，他才剛要探出頭，一隻餓狼便跳了過來，把整個牛肚一口吞了下去。

然而大拇哥並沒有灰心喪氣，他想：「說不定這隻狼願意聽聽我說的話。」於是，他從狼的肚子裡大聲叫道：「親愛的狼啊，我能帶你去一個地方，那兒有好多美味的食物。」

「在哪裡？」狼說道。

大拇哥說道：「有這麼個房子，你可以從廚房的水槽爬進去，那裡有蛋糕、培根、香腸，你要吃多少就有多少。」然後把他爸爸住的地方一五一十地描述給狼聽。

狼不等他說第二遍，在夜裡就硬穿

進水槽，在貯藏室裡吃個過癮。待狼吃飽喝足想出去時，卻因為把肚子吃撐得太大，沒辦法沿著原路出去。大拇哥早料到如此，就在狼的肚子裡，拉開嗓門怒喊大叫了起來。

狼急忙說：「你安靜點行不行？你會把屋裡的人吵醒的。」

這小傢伙便說：「有什麼關係？你現在吃飽了，我也想快活快活呀。」說完，大拇哥再次用盡全力、扯著嗓子大吼大叫。

pp. 16–17 大拇哥的爸媽終於被吵醒了，他們往廚房跑來，從門縫往裡一瞧，看見裡面竟是一條狼，馬上跑了開來，農夫趕忙拿了一把斧頭，妻子則拿了一把長柄的鐮刀。他們走進貯藏室時，農夫對妻子說：「你跟在後面，我會先朝牠砍下去，要是牠還沒死，你就再補上一刀，把牠砍成碎片。」

大拇哥聽到爸媽的聲音，喊道：「親愛的爸爸，我在這兒，狼把我吞到肚子裡來了。」

他爸爸一聽，欣喜地說道：「謝天謝地，我們的寶貝兒子回來了。」他擔心鐮刀會傷到大拇哥，馬上要妻子把鐮刀扔了，自己拿著斧頭，對準狼頭給牠致命的一擊，然後和妻子用刀子和剪刀切開狼的肚子，拉出這個小傢伙。

「啊！」爸爸說道：「我們真為你擔驚受怕啊！」

「是啊，爸爸，我周遊了不少地方，真謝天謝地，我又能呼吸、重見天日了。」

「那麼你去了哪些地方呀？」

「喔，老爸，我鑽過老鼠洞，進過牛的胃，又到了狼的肚皮裡。不過我又回到你們身邊了。」

大拇哥的父母親於是說道：「我們再也不把你賣出去了，即使用世界上所有的財富來換，我們也不賣。」他們緊緊相擁，親吻著他們寶貝的大拇哥。他們為他準備吃的喝的，讓他換上新衣服，因為他一身的衣服在這次的歷險中已經破得差不多了。

2 小紅帽

pp. 18–19 從前從前，有位人見人愛的可愛女孩，其中就屬她的奶奶最疼她，什麼都願意給她。有一次，奶奶送她一頂紅絲絨風帽，她戴起來好看極了，因此，小女孩再也不願意戴別的帽子，於是大家就叫她「小紅帽」。

有一天，媽媽對小紅帽說：「來，小紅帽，這裡有一塊蛋糕和一瓶葡萄酒，把這拿去給奶奶，她病了，身子很虛弱，而這些食物對她身體很好。趁天氣還沒變熱之前出發吧。走的時候，要小心輕聲地走，不要走出了小徑，不然

很容易跌倒打破酒瓶的，那就沒東西給奶奶了。當你走進她的房間，別忘了說早安，還沒打招呼之前，不要東瞧西瞧的。」

「我會非常小心的。」小紅帽對媽媽承諾。

奶奶住在森林裡，離村子大約有兩里遠。正當小紅帽走進森林，一匹狼遇見了她。小紅帽不知道狼很壞，一點也不怕牠。

「你好啊，小紅帽。」牠說。

「謝謝你的關心，狼先生。」

「這麼早要去哪兒呀？」

「去奶奶家。」

「你圍裙裡放了什麼東西呀？」

「蛋糕和葡萄酒。昨天烘焙的，可憐的奶奶生病了，要吃點有營養的東西才能恢復體力。」

pp. 20–21「你奶奶住在哪裡呀？」

「再往森林走一里多就到了。她的房子就在三棵大橡樹下，樹下還有核桃樹，你一定找得到的。」小紅帽回答著。

狼在心中盤算著：「多麼細皮嫩肉的小傢伙，大口咬下去多麼美味可口呀，比老太婆好吃呢。我要小心行事，把兩個人都給逮著。」於是牠跟在小紅帽身旁走了一會兒，然後說：「看哪，小紅帽，這附近的花多美啊！你怎麼不瞧一瞧呢？我想你也沒聽到小鳥唱歌唱得多好聽吧。森林裡什麼都會令人感到愉悅，

可是你卻好像要去上學一樣，腳步那麼沈重。」

小紅帽抬眼往上瞧，當她看到從樹枝間灑下的陽光四處閃爍，遍地開滿美麗的花朵時，她想：「我想我要是帶束鮮花給奶奶呢？她也會很高興的。現在還很早，我還是可以及時趕到的。」於是她離開大路，跑進森林裡去摘花。她每摘了一朵花，就覺得前面看到的花更美，便跑過去，結果，她就往林子裡越走越進去了。

就在此時，狼直接跑到奶奶家敲門。

「是誰呀？」

「是小紅帽。」狼回答：「我帶了蛋糕和葡萄酒，開門哪。」

「你拉一下門閂就好了，」奶奶大聲說：「我沒力氣，下不了床。」

`pp. 22–23` 狼一拉起門閂，門就開了，狼二話不說就走到奶奶床前，把奶奶吞進了肚子。然後牠穿上奶奶的衣服，戴上她的帽子，躺在床上，拉下了簾子。

而小紅帽一直跑來跑去在採花，等到她花多到都拿不動時，才想起奶奶，重新上路去奶奶家。

看到小屋的門開著，她很驚訝，當她一走進房間，她就覺得怪怪的，她自言自語說著：「天哪！我今天怎麼會覺得不自在，以前我很喜歡跟奶奶在一起的啊。」

她大聲說：「早安！」，可是沒有人回答。於是她走到床邊拉開簾子，只見奶奶躺在床上，帽子拉得低低的，把臉都遮住了，看起來非常奇怪。

「啊！奶奶，」她說：「你的耳朵怎麼這麼大呀。」

「這樣才能更聽清楚你的聲音啊，我的孩子。」野狼回答說。

「可是奶奶，你的眼睛也好大呀。」小紅帽說。

「這樣才能更看清楚你的臉呀，親愛的。」

「可是奶奶，你的手怎麼這麼大呀。」

「這樣才能把你抱得更緊呀。」

「噢，但是奶奶，你的嘴巴怎麼大得這麼嚇人呀。」

「這樣才好把你吃掉呀！」

`pp. 24–25` 話一說完，狼就從床上跳起來，把小紅帽吞進了肚子。

當狼滿足了口腹之欲，便躺回床上睡覺，開始鼾聲震天。一位獵人此時正好經過房子，心想：「老婆婆怎麼打呼這麼大聲啊！我得進去看看她是不是有什麼需要。」

獵人進了房間，當他來到床前，他看到狼躺在床上。「我找到你了，你這老壞蛋，」他說：「我已經找你很久了！」就在他準備向牠開槍時，他突然想到，

狼可能已經吃了奶奶，或許她還有救，所以他就沒有開槍，而是拿了一把剪刀，開始剪開沈睡中的狼肚皮。當他剪了兩下，他看到發亮的紅色小帽子。

他又剪了兩下，小女孩便跳了出來，哭著說：「噢，我好害怕！狼的肚子裡烏漆抹黑的。」接著，老奶奶也活著出來了，只是有點呼吸困難。這時小紅帽很快拿來一些大石頭，三人將石頭塞進狼的肚子裡。狼醒來之後，想逃走，但是石頭實在太重了，牠一站起來就跌在地上，一命嗚呼。

他們三個人看了非常高興。獵人剝下狼皮，把它帶回家；奶奶吃了小紅帽帶來的蛋糕和葡萄酒，身體好多了；而小紅帽暗自想著：「這一輩子，沒有得到媽媽的允許，我再也不獨自走出大路，跑進森林裡了。」

pp. 26–27 之後聽說，小紅帽有一次又要送蛋糕給老奶奶，有另一隻狼又跟她講話，想把她誘離開大路。可是小紅帽這次提高警覺，逕自往前走。她告訴奶奶她碰到了狼，狼對她說：「早安」，眼神卻很邪惡，當時要不是在大馬路上，她相信狼一定會把她吃掉的。

「那麼，」奶奶說：「我們把門關緊，牠就進不來了。」

過了不久，狼敲著門叫道：「快開門呀，奶奶，我是小紅帽，給你送蛋糕來了。」但她們不應話，也不開門。狼圍著房子轉了兩三圈，最後跳上屋頂，打算等小紅帽在傍晚回家時，偷偷跟在她的後面，趁天黑把她吃掉。可是奶奶看穿了牠的心思。

屋子前有一個大石槽，於是她對孩子說：「把桶子拿來，小紅帽，我昨天做了一些香腸，去提一些煮香腸的水倒進石槽裡。」小紅帽提水把大石槽裝滿水，香腸的香味就飄進了狼的鼻孔，牠聞呀聞，往下張望，最後因為把脖子伸得太長而站不穩，開始往下滑。牠從屋頂上滑了下來，直接掉進大石槽裡淹死了。

而小紅帽呢，她高高興興地回家，再也沒有誰傷害她了。

3 金鵝

pp. 28–29 從前，有個人有三個兒子，最小的叫做傻子，大家總是瞧不起他，對他冷嘲熱諷。

有一天，大兒子要去森林裡砍柴，出發之前，母親給了他一塊美味的蛋糕和一瓶酒，免得他口渴或餓著了。

他進了森林裡遇到一位灰白髮小老翁向他道早安，還跟他說：「給我一塊你口袋裡的蛋糕吧，讓我喝一口酒吧，我好餓好渴啊。」但是這位精明的兒子回答:「如果我把蛋糕和酒給你,我自己就沒得吃了,你走開吧!」於是他不理會站在那的老人,繼續往前走。

然而當他才開始砍樹,沒多久竟失手砍在自己的手臂上,他只好回家包紮。這全是那小老翁的傑作。

後來,第二位兒子來到了森林,他母親也給他一塊蛋糕和一瓶酒。這位灰白髮老翁同樣出現在他面前,向他討塊蛋糕吃,要口酒來喝。可是第二位兒子也很精明地說:「給你,那我喝西北風嗎?走開!」他拋下站在那的老翁,繼續往前走。然而他馬上就遭到報應,他才往樹上砍了幾下,就砍傷自己的腿,結果他只好被抬回家。

pp. 30–31 於是傻子便說:「爸爸呀,讓我去砍柴吧。」父親回答道:「你的哥哥們都為此而受了傷,算了吧,你又不懂。」然而最終他禁不住傻子的苦苦哀求,只好說:「那就去吧,受個傷你就會學乖了。」他母親給了他一塊用碳灰烤出來的餅,還有一瓶酸啤酒。

當傻子來到了森林,老翁又出現了,向他問聲好,便說:「給我一塊蛋糕,讓我喝你的酒吧,我好餓又好渴。」

傻子回答說:「我只有碳灰玉米餅和酸啤酒,如果你不嫌棄的話,就坐下來吃吧。」

於是他們坐了

下來。當傻子拿出那塊用碳渣烤的蛋糕時,竟發現是個美味好吃的蛋糕,酸啤酒也變成了美酒。他們酒足飯飽之後,矮小的老人開口道:「你心腸真好,肯分享你的東西,我將賜給你好運。那兒有棵老樹,砍下它,你會在樹根找到一些東西。」老人說完便離開。

傻子走過去砍倒了那棵樹,發現有隻鵝坐著樹根裡,覆著金色的羽毛。他抱起金鵝,帶著牠到一間小旅館過夜。店老闆有三個女兒,看到這隻鵝,都很好奇這麼神奇的鳥到底是什麼鳥,每人都想拔一根牠的金羽毛。

pp. 32–33 大女兒心想:「我應該很快可以找到機會拔根羽毛。」趁傻子一離開,她便抓住鵝的翅膀,沒料到她的手和手指卻被緊緊地黏在上面。

過了一會兒,二女兒來了,一心只想弄一根羽毛到手,不過,她才一碰她姊姊,也被牢牢地黏住了。

最後,小女兒也來了,她的意圖和兩位姊姊一樣。姐姐們尖叫地說:「走開,天啊,走開啊。」但她不明白為什麼要走開,心想:「其他人都在那兒,我也要過去。」於是她向她們跑去,才碰了姊姊一下,就被黏得緊緊的。她們三人只好和這隻鵝一道過夜。

次日早晨,傻子把鵝夾在腋下就啟程,完全不管黏在上面的三姊妹。她們只得跟在傻子後面一直跑,一下往左,

一下往右，就看傻子怎麼走。

到了田野裡，有一位牧師見著他們，說道：「真不知害臊，你們這些沒用的女孩，跟著這個年輕小伙子在田野裡跑，成何體統？」說話的同時，他一把抓住小女兒的手，想拉開她，可是他一觸碰她，也同樣被緊緊黏住，只得跟在後面跑。

pp. 34–35 沒多久，教堂裡的敲鐘者從旁邊經過，看見他的牧師主人跟在三位小姐後面跑，他嚇了一跳，大喊著：「嗨，牧師大人，跑這麼快要去哪裡？別忘了今天還得參加洗禮啊。」說著他跑了過去，抓住牧師的袖子，結果也被緊緊黏住。這五個人一個黏著一個，小跑步前進的同時，兩個工人荷著鋤頭從田地那兒過來，牧師大叫著拜託他們解開他和敲鐘者，可是他們一碰這位敲鐘者，馬上就被緊緊黏住，現在，一共是七個人跟著鵝和傻子跑。

不久之後，傻子來到一個城市，那兒的國王有一個女兒，生性嚴肅，誰都沒辦法逗她笑。於是國王下達一道命令，只要誰能逗公主笑，誰就能成為駙馬。傻子聽到這個消息，就帶著他的鵝和鵝身後那一串人，來到公主面前。公主一看到這七個人，一個接著一個，不停地跑，她馬上大笑了起來，笑個沒完沒了。

於是傻子提出要求，要娶公主為妻，可是國王並不中意這位女婿，便編造出各種藉口，還說他得先帶來一個能喝掉酒窖裡所有的酒的人。

pp. 36–37 傻子想到那位小老翁，他一定幫得上忙，於是他回到森林裡，找到他砍樹的地方，他看到一個人坐在那兒，滿面愁容。傻子問他為什麼這麼傷心，他回答：「我渴得要命，卻止不了渴，我不能喝冷水，雖然才剛喝掉一桶酒，卻好像一滴水落在滾燙的石子上一樣，一點用也沒有。」

「好啦，我可以幫你，」傻子說：「跟我走，包你喝個夠。」

傻子引領他來到了國王的酒窖，他彎腰靠向大酒桶，不斷地喝，喝到腹股溝痛了為止，這天還沒結束，他就喝光了所有酒桶的酒。於是傻子再度要求迎娶他的新娘，可是國王還是很憤怒，這個人稱傻子的醜八怪，竟然要帶走他的女兒。於是他又開出新的條件，傻子必須先找到一個能吃掉一整座麵包山的人才行。

傻子也沒怎麼去想，就往森林裡走，在同樣的地方坐著一個人，全身用繩子綁了起來，表情十分痛苦，他說：「我已經吃掉一整爐的麵包捲了，可是我太餓了，那連塞牙縫都不夠。我的肚子還是空空的，我得把自己綁住才不會餓死。」

傻子一聽到這句話，十分地高興，

便說：「起來，跟我走，你絕對可以填飽肚皮。」

pp. 38–39 傻子帶他來到國王的宮殿，國王把全國的麵粉都集中到這兒，下令烘烤了一座麵包山。從森林來的這個人站在麵包山前面，開始大快朵頤。一天還沒過去，整座山已被吃得一乾二淨。

傻子再次提出迎娶新娘的要求，這已經是第三次了。可是國王依舊又想出一個點子，他要一艘海陸兩棲的船艦：「只要你乘著這種船回來，」他說：「我就把女兒嫁給你。」

傻子馬上回到森林，看到那位小老翁坐在那，當初他就是把自己的蛋糕給了那位老翁。老翁聽了傻子的心聲，跟他說：「既然你曾供我吃喝，我就賜你這艘船吧。因為你曾經善待過我，所以我才這麼做的。」

於是，老翁給了他一艘海陸兩棲的船隻。當國王看到這艘船，再也無法阻止傻子娶走自己的女兒。傻子和公主舉行了婚禮。國王死後，傻子繼承了他的王國，心滿意足地與妻子生活了好久好久。

4 糖果屋

pp. 40–41 靠近一座大森林的地方，住著一個貧窮的樵夫，他與妻子及兩個孩子相依為命，兒子叫漢瑟爾，女兒叫做葛萊特。

樵夫一貧如洗，碰到饑荒時，更是連一日都不得溫飽。夜裡，他躺在床上左思右想，焦慮得輾轉難眠，他對妻子抱怨說：「怎麼辦呢？我們連自己都吃不飽了，要拿什麼養我們可憐的孩子呢？」

婦人回答說：「老公，我告訴你該怎麼辦，明兒個一早，把兩個孩子帶到森林最深處，幫他們生一堆火，多給他們每人一塊麵包，然後我們上工去，把他們丟在那裡。他們找不到路回家的，這樣就可以擺脫兩個孩子了。」

「老婆，不行！」樵夫說：「我做不出這種事，我怎麼可以把孩子獨自丟在森林裡，野獸會把他們撕成碎片的！」

「噢，你這蠢蛋！」妻子回答說：「不這樣我們四個都會餓死的，你不妨把我們的棺材也裁好準備一下好了！」她不停地說到他同意為止。

「我還是覺得對不起可憐的孩子們。」樵夫說。

兩個孩子因為肚子餓，也無法入睡，所以聽見了繼母與父親的對話。葛萊特難過得哭了起來，對漢瑟爾說：「我們完了！」

「安靜點，葛萊特，」漢瑟爾説：「別難過了，我很快就會想到辦法的。」

pp. 42–43 當他們的父母睡著以後，漢瑟爾起床穿上小外套，打開下面的門爬出去。月光皎潔地映照著，屋前的白鵝卵石像銀幣一樣地閃閃發光。他彎下腰來，盡可能地把小口袋裝滿了石頭。回來之後，他告訴葛萊特説：「親愛的小妹，放心吧，好好睡，上帝不會遺棄我們的。」説完他也躺回床上。

黎明時分，太陽都還沒升起，婦人就把兩個孩子叫醒：「起床，你們這兩個懶蟲，我們要到森林去拾些木柴。」繼母給他們每人一點麵包，並説：「這是你們的晚餐，可別太早吃掉，否則就要餓肚子了。」

葛萊特把麵包放在她的圍裙下，因為漢瑟爾口袋裡裝有鵝卵石，然後他們出發一起往森林走去。走了一會兒，漢瑟爾停下來回頭往家的方向瞄了一眼，一路上走走停停的。他的父親説了：「漢瑟爾，你在後面是在看什麼呀？專心一點，別忘記該怎麼走路了。」

「哦，爸爸，」漢瑟爾回答説：「我在看屋頂上的小白貓，牠想跟我説再見呢。」

樵夫的妻子説：「笨蛋，那不是你的小貓，那是朝陽照在煙囪上的反光。」

然而，漢瑟爾並不是在看貓，而是沿路不斷地從口袋裡拿出小卵石來丟。

pp. 44–45 到了森林裡，樵夫説：「現在呀，孩子們，去堆一些木柴，我幫你們生個火，免得你們著涼了。」漢瑟爾和葛萊特把細枝與樹枝堆得跟小山一樣高，柴火一點燃，便熊熊地燃燒了起來。

繼母説：「孩子們，到火堆旁躺著休息吧，我們去森林裡砍點柴，砍完後再回來接你們。」

漢瑟爾和葛萊特坐在火堆旁，中午吃了一點麵包。聽到斧頭揮砍的聲音，他們以為父親就在附近，然而那才不是斧頭，那只是父親綁在枯樹上的樹枝被風吹得前後搖晃的聲音。

他們坐了很久，眼皮因為疲倦而闔了起來，很快就睡著了。醒來的時候，已經是深夜，葛萊特開始哭著説：「現在我們要怎麼逃出森林呢？」

漢瑟爾安慰她説：「再等一會兒，等月亮升起，我們很快就可以找到路了。」當滿月升起，漢瑟爾牽著妹妹的手，尋著像新銀幣般發亮的鵝卵石走回家。

他們走了一整夜，終於在天亮之前回到了家。他們敲了敲門，繼母開門一看到是漢瑟爾和葛萊特，就説：「你們這兩個頑皮鬼，怎麼在森林裡睡那麼久，我們還以為你們不會回來了。」

pp. 46–47 然而父親卻滿心歡喜，對他而言，因為把孩子獨自丟在森林裡，簡直是心如刀割。

　　不久之後，又遇到了全國大饑荒，孩子們又在夜裡聽到繼母對父親說：「什麼都沒得吃了，我們只剩半條麵包，死到臨頭了啦。非得將孩子弄走不可，我們把他們帶到林子的更裡面，他們不會再找到路回來的。不這樣做，我們會餓死的。」

　　樵夫內心感到十分愧疚，認為還是跟孩子們分享最後一口麵包吧。

　　然而婦人什麼也聽不進去，只是對他大聲叫罵。有一就有二，同樣地，既然樵夫都依了她一次，也得再聽她的。

　　還醒著的孩子們聽到了他們的談話。等老夫婦睡著，漢瑟爾又爬了起來，想要像上次一樣出去撿小卵石，不過繼母卻鎖住門了，根本出不去。不過，他還是安慰著小妹妹說：「葛萊特，別哭，安心地睡吧，上帝會幫我們的。」

　　一大早，婦人把兩個孩子叫起床，給他們比上次還小的麵包。在往森林的路上，漢瑟爾把口袋裡的麵包捏碎，然後三不五時停下腳步，丟一小塊麵包在地上。

pp. 48–49 「漢瑟爾，你怎麼停下來四處張望？」父親說道：「快跟上啊。」

　　「我是回頭看屋頂上的小鴿子，牠想跟我說再見。」漢瑟爾回答。

　　「笨蛋，」婦人說：「那不是你的小鴿子，那是朝陽照在煙囪上的反光。」然而

漢瑟爾還是一點一點地把所有的麵包屑都丟在路上。

　　婦人把孩子帶到森林的更深處，孩子們以前都還沒去過那裡呢。他們照樣生了一堆熊熊營火，然後繼母說道：「孩子們，就坐在這兒吧，要是累了，可以睡一會兒。我們去林裡砍柴，等我們晚上砍好柴，會回來接你們。」

　　正午時分，葛萊特把自己的麵包和哥哥分著吃，因為漢瑟爾把自己的麵包都撒在路上了。接著他們就睡覺，直到過了傍晚，也沒有人來接走這兩個可憐的孩子。他們睡到深夜才醒，漢瑟爾安慰著妹妹說：「等一等吧，葛萊特。等月亮升起，我們就看得到我沿途丟的麵包屑了，麵包屑會帶我們回家的。」

　　月亮初升，兩人便出發。可是，他們卻什麼麵包屑也沒看到，森林裡數以千計、飛來飛去的小鳥，早就把它們吃光了。漢瑟爾對葛萊特說：「我們很快就會找到路的。」可是他們根本找不到。

pp. 50–51 兩人走了一整夜，第二天又從早走到晚，就是走不出這片森林。他們肚子很餓，卻只有地上長出的兩、三粒莓果可以充飢。當他們累得走不動了，就倒在樹下睡覺。

　　現在，他們已經離家三天了，他們繼續趕路，卻只是往森林的更深處走進去，要是再沒有人伸出援手，他們恐怕就要餓死累死了。

中午時，他們看見一隻雪白的小鳥棲在一根樹枝上，叫聲十分優美，就停下腳步來聽。小鳥一唱完，便振翅從他們面前飛走，於是他們跟著牠來到了一間小屋，而牠就棲落在屋頂上。

他們走近小屋，發現房子竟是用麵包與蛋糕所做成的，窗戶還是透明的糖呢。

「開始吃吧，」漢瑟爾說道：「好好吃一頓，我吃屋頂，葛萊特，你吃窗戶，那一定很甜的。」

於是漢瑟爾爬到房子上面，敲下一小塊屋頂，嚐了嚐味道。葛萊特則靠在窗邊，小口小口地啃著窗玻璃。這時，屋子客廳裡卻傳來一陣低低的聲音——還吃，還吃，誰在啃我的小房子啊？

pp. 52–53 孩子們答道：「是風，是風，天堂吹來的風。」然後只管繼續吃。漢瑟爾很喜歡屋頂的味道，扯了一大片來吃。葛萊特也拆下了一整個圓窗片，坐下來大快朵頤。突然間，房門開了，一位老婦人拄著柺杖慢慢地走了出來。漢瑟爾和葛萊特嚇得手中的東西都掉了下去。不過這位老婦人卻點點頭說：「噢，親愛的孩子們，誰帶你們來的呀？進來吧，待在我這兒，沒有人會傷害你們的。」

她牽起他們的手，把他們帶進小房子裡，把美食擺在他們面前，有牛奶和煎餅，煎餅上灑了糖、蘋果和核桃。接著還有兩張漂亮的小床，覆著乾淨的白床單。漢瑟爾和葛萊特躺在小床上，彷彿置身天堂一般。

然而，老婦人只是假好心而已，她其實是個惡毒的女巫，造了這間小麵包屋，目的就是要引誘小孩子上門。一旦有小孩上當，便會送掉小命，被她煮來吃掉，而這樣的一天便是她飽餐的日子。女巫的眼睛是紅色的，視力不好看不遠，不過他們的嗅覺卻像野獸一般敏銳，一有人類接近，就能聞到。漢瑟爾和葛萊特來到附近時，她便露出邪惡的笑容，嘲諷地說：「他們中計了，休想逃出我的手掌心。」

pp. 54–55 一大清早，孩子們還在睡，老婦人就已經起床，她看著沈睡中的兩個孩子，他們是那麼地美麗，圓鼓鼓的兩頰還透著紅潤，她喃喃自語道：「這吃起來一定很美味呀。」

於是她用她皺巴巴的手把漢瑟爾抓到馬廄裡，漢瑟爾大喊大叫，還是被鎖進了鐵柵欄裡。接著，老婦人來到葛萊特面前，將她搖醒，並大叫道：「起床，懶蟲，去挑點水，幫妳哥哥煮點好吃的，他在外面的馬廄裡，得吃胖點。等他被養肥，就是我的盤中飧了。」

葛萊特傷心地哭了起來，可是哭也是白哭，她得服從惡毒女巫的命令。可憐的漢瑟爾現在吃的是上好的食物，而葛萊特只能吃螃蟹殼。每天早晨，那婦人都會爬到小馬廄前，喊著：「漢瑟爾，伸出你的手指頭來，讓我看看你是不是就快夠胖了。」然而漢瑟爾拿出的都是一根小骨頭，老婦人眼花看不清楚，以為那就是漢瑟爾的手指，很驚訝竟然沒辦法把他養肥。

四個星期過去了，漢瑟爾還是瘦巴巴的，老婦人耐不住性子，再也等不下去了，便對著葛萊特吼道：「喂，葛萊特，給我醒醒，去挑點水，不管漢瑟爾是胖是瘦，明天我都要把他宰掉煮來吃。」

噢，可憐的小妹妹還得去挑水，她傷心欲絕，哭得滿頰是淚。「親愛的上帝啊，救救我們吧，」她哭著說：「我們如果是被森林裡的野獸給吃掉，都還能死在一起呢。」

pp. 56–57「你省省吧，」老婦人說：「哭是沒有用的。」

一早，葛萊特就得出來把鍋子裝水掛好，並且生好火。老婦人說道：「我們就先來烤東西吧。我已經把烤箱熱好了，麵團也揉好了。」

她把可憐的葛萊特推到烤箱前，烤箱裡火已經很旺了。女巫說道：「爬進去看看夠不夠熱，我們才好放麵包進去。」女巫心裡算計著，等葛萊特一爬進去，就關上烤箱，把她關在裡面烘烤，然後也把她給吃了。

不過葛萊特看出了她的詭計，便說：「我不知道要怎麼弄，我怎麼才進得去呢？」

「笨蛋！」老婦人說道：「看，這門大得連我都進得去。」說著便爬起來，把頭探進烤箱裡。

接著，葛萊特推了她一把，把她推到更裡面去，然後關上鐵門，鎖上閂子。

「噢！」老婦人接著發出可怕的哀號聲，但葛萊特只管跑開，邪惡的女巫就慘死在火舌之中了。

葛萊特像閃電般很快地跑向漢瑟爾，打開小馬廄的門，大叫著：「漢瑟爾，我們得救了，老女巫死了。」

門一打開，漢瑟爾像隻掙脫牢籠的小鳥一般雀躍著，兩人高興得又抱又跳，相互親吻。他們不必再怕女巫了，他們走進她的房子，發現每個角落的櫃子裡都裝滿了珍珠和寶石。

pp. 58–59 漢瑟爾說道：「這些比小卵石珍貴得多喔。」說著便把口袋塞得滿滿的。葛萊特說：「我也要帶點東西回家。」說著也把她的圍裙塞得滿滿的。

「我們該走了，」漢瑟爾說道：「我們得走出女巫的森林。」

他們走了兩個小時，來到一條大河。漢瑟爾開口道：「我們過不去，既沒看到有木板，也沒看到橋樑。」

「而且連個渡輪也沒。」葛萊特回應道：「不過有隻白鴨在划水，我去問問，牠會幫助我們的。」於是她便大喊：「小鴨子，小鴨子，你看見沒呀？漢瑟爾和葛萊特在等著你呀！這裡沒有木板，也不見任何橋樑，讓我們坐在你那麼白皙的背上渡河吧。」

鴨子朝他們游了過來，漢瑟爾坐上鴨背，叫妹妹坐在他身邊。「不行，」葛萊特回道：「這樣對這隻小鴨子來說，可就太重了，牠一次只能載一個人過河。」

好心的小鴨照辦了，兄妹倆安全地渡過河，走了一小段路，森林的景致越來越熟悉，終於，他們遠遠地望見父親的房子了。

於是兩人便跑了起來，衝進客廳裡，抱著父親的脖子。這位樵夫，自從把孩子扔在森林裡之後，就沒再快樂過，而那婦人則去世了。葛萊特把口袋裡的珍珠和寶石倒出來，落得滿地都是，漢瑟爾也把自己口袋裡的珠寶一把一把掏出來。他們所有的憂慮都煙消雲散，幸福快樂地生活在一起。

故事說完了，有隻老鼠跑來，誰捉得到牠，就可以用牠的毛皮做一頂大帽子喔！

5 壞矮人

pp. 62–63 從前，有一位磨坊主，他雖然貧窮，卻有一位美麗的女兒。有一天，他得去晉見國王，為了顯示自己的重要性，他便與國王說：「我有一個女兒，她能將麥稈紡成黃金。」

國王跟這位磨坊主說：「這種技藝很合我意，如果你女兒真如你說的那麼聰明，明天把她帶到我的宮殿裡來吧，我要考考她。」

女孩被帶到國王面前，國王帶著她來到一間滿是麥稈的房間，給了她一台紡車和捲軸，便說：「現在就開始吧，要是明晨以前，你不能在夜晚期間將這些麥稈紡成黃金，你就得被處死。」

國王隨即把門一鎖，留下她獨自一人。可憐的磨匠女兒坐在那裡，她不知道該怎麼辦，她根本不知道如何將麥稈紡成黃金，越想越害怕，終於哭了起來。

但是突然之間，門開了，一個矮人走了進來，說道：「晚安啊，磨坊姑娘，妳怎麼在哭呢？」

「唉，」女孩回答道：「我必須把麥稈紡成黃金，可是我根本不會啊。」

「如果我幫妳做的話呢，」矮人說道：「妳要給我什麼？」

「我的項鍊吧。」女孩回答。

pp. 64–65 小矮人拿了項鍊，便在紡車前坐了下來，呼呼地轉啊，轉啊，轉啊，轉了三次，捲軸便纏得滿滿的。然後他又放了一個上去，呼呼地轉啊，轉啊，轉啊，轉了三次，第二捲又滿了。就這樣直到天亮，所有的麥稈都被紡完了，所有的捲軸上也都是金線。國王早在破曉之前就到了，他看到這些黃金，真是又驚又喜，然而他的心卻益發貪婪。他把磨坊主的女兒帶到另一間裝滿稻草的房間，這間可更大了，他命令她，如果還珍惜自己的生命，就得在一個晚上之內紡好。

女孩不知道該如何是好，又哭了起來。這時，門又再度開啟，小矮人出現了，說道：「我幫妳把那麥稈紡成黃金的話，妳要拿什麼報答我？」

「我手指上的戒指。」女孩回答。矮人拿了戒指，再度開始轉動紡車，早晨來臨之前，所有的麥稈都變成了閃閃發亮的黃金。

國王見到眼前的景象，不知道有多高興。可是他還不滿足，又將磨坊主的女兒帶到一間更大的房間，房裡充滿了麥稈，告訴她說：「妳也要在今晚紡好這些麥稈，如果你做到了，我就娶妳為妻。」

「雖然她只是個磨坊主的女兒，」他心裡想：「但我不可能在這世上找到更富有的妻子了。」

pp. 66-67 女孩獨自一人留了下來，矮人

再度出現，這是第三次了。他說：「如果這次也一樣，我幫妳紡這些麥稈，妳要給我什麼？」

「我已經沒有什麼可以給你了。」女孩回答。

「那麼妳得答應我，等你當上皇后，把妳的第一個孩子送我吧。」

「誰知道我能不能當上皇后呢？」磨坊主女兒心裡想著，況且她也走投無路了，於是便答應了矮人的要求。矮人為了得到想要的東西，又再一次將麥稈紡成黃金。

早晨國王來時，看到一切如他所願，便與她結婚，於是，美麗的磨坊主之女成了皇后。

一年過後，她生下一個美麗的寶寶，卻早已把矮人忘得一乾二淨。突然間，矮人出現在她房裡，說道：「現在，實現你對我的承諾吧。」

皇后嚇壞了，她願意把全國的財富都交給這位矮人，只求他把孩子留給她。但是這位矮人卻說：「不行，對我來說，活生生的東西，比世上所有的寶物都還要珍貴。」

皇后於是痛哭了起來，矮人心一軟，便說道：「我給你三天時間，要是三天內，妳能猜出我的名字，那麼，妳就可以把孩子留下。」

皇后想了一整夜，想遍所有她聽過的名字，並遣了一位信使到處打聽各種

可能的名字。

次日當矮人來到時，她說出了所有她知道的名字，從凱士柏、梅契爾、拜爾沙札，開始一個接著一個地唸，但是矮人聽了每一個名字，都說：「我不叫那個名字。」

pp. 68–69 第二天，皇后到附近打聽一些關於當地人的名字，然後把這些古怪又罕見的名字報給矮人聽：「你大概叫做短肋骨、羊小腿或蕾絲腿吧。」

但他總是回答：「我不叫那個名字。」

第三天，使者又回來了，告訴皇后說：「我找不到什麼新名字了，不過我走到森林盡頭的高山那兒，在狐狸和野兔互道晚安的地方，發現一間小屋子，屋子前面燃燒著一堆營火，一個相當滑稽的矮人正用單腳圍著營火跳躍著，還一邊喊道：『今天烘麵包，明天釀美酒，再來年輕皇后的孩子就歸我。哈哈多快活，沒人知道我，就叫魯貝爾史提斯欽。』」

你大概可以想見，皇后聽到這個名字時，是多麼地雀躍。過了不久，矮人來了，問道：「皇后娘娘，我叫什麼名字啊？」一開始皇后先說：「你叫康瑞德嗎？」

「錯。」

「你叫哈利嗎？」

「不是。」

「或許你叫魯貝爾史提斯欽吧。」

「是魔鬼告訴你的！是魔鬼告訴你的！」矮人叫喊著，一氣之下，他把右腳踏在地上，踏得太用力，整隻腿都陷進地面。他更是火大，就用兩手扯左腿，結果竟把自己撕成了兩半。

6 青蛙王子

pp. 70–71 在那遠古的時代，人們的願望總還能成真。那時，有一位國王，他的女兒個個都非常美麗，尤其是最小的女兒，連見多識廣的太陽照耀在她臉上時，都要對她的美震驚不已。緊鄰於國王的城堡旁，有一片幽暗的大森林，林中一棵菩提樹下有一口泉，天氣一熱起來，這位小公主總會來到林裡，坐在冷泉邊。要是覺得無聊，她就會拿出一顆金球，把它高高拋起，再接住，這顆球可是她最愛的玩物呢。

有一次，公主舉著小手，準備接住金球時，金球竟然沒落回她的手裡，卻落到遠遠的地上，直接滾進水裡。公主眼睜睜地看著球消失在眼前，井水又是那麼地深不見底，於是就哭了起來，越哭越大聲，沒人安慰得了她。就在她嚎啕大哭時，有人對她說：「公主，什麼事情讓你難過了？你這樣哭，連石頭都會心疼的。」

　　她環顧四周，尋找聲音的來源，卻看到一隻青蛙從水裡伸出牠醜陋的大腦袋。「哦，古老的噗通濺水者，是你嗎？」她説：「我是在哭我的金球，它掉進井水裡了。」

pp. 72–73 「好啦，別哭了。」青蛙回答道：「我可以幫得上忙，要是我幫你把那玩意兒撈上來，你要給我什麼呢？」

　　「親愛的青蛙，你要什麼都行啊。」她説著：「我的衣服、珍珠和首飾，就連我頭上戴的金冠都可以給你。」

　　青蛙回答：「我才不要你的衣服、珍珠和首飾，也不要你的金冠，只要你對我付出愛心，讓我做你的朋友和玩伴，與你比鄰坐在小桌前，讓我吃你那小金盤裡的食物，喝你小杯子裡的飲料，睡在你的小床上，如果你答應讓我這麼做，我就下去幫你把金球再取回來。」

　　「喔，沒問題，」她説：「我會如你所願，只要你幫我把金球拿回來。」不過她心想：「這隻笨青蛙話可真多，牠只能和其他青蛙一起蹲在水裡、呱呱叫罷了，哪能跟人類作朋友。」

　　青蛙一得到公主的承諾，便一頭鑽進水裡，潛了下去。不出一會兒功夫，青蛙就啣著金球浮了出來，並且把金球吐在草地上。公主看到她可愛的玩物又回來了，

開心不已，撿起金球就跑了。

　　「等等，等等啊。」青蛙説著：「帶我一起走啊，我可不能像你那樣跑。」可是牠也只能跟在公主後面，扯著嗓子大聲地呱呱、呱呱叫。小公主根本不理會牠，跑回了家，馬上就把那可憐的青蛙忘得一乾二淨。可憐的青蛙只好再回到牠的井水裡。

pp. 74–75 第二天，公主和國王及其他王室成員一同坐在桌前，用著小金盤在吃飯。這時有樣東西順著大理石階往上爬了過來，發出啪啦噗嗒的聲音，等牠爬到了梯頂，便敲門大喊：「公主啊，小公主，幫我開門啊。」

　　公主跑去看外頭是誰，一開門，竟發現蹲在門前的是那隻青蛙。她急忙把門砰地一聲關上，很快坐回去吃晚餐，心裡害怕極了。國王顯然看見她的心跳得很厲害，便問道：「孩子啊，什麼事把你嚇成這樣？該不會門外有個巨人想把你擄走吧？」

　　「沒有，沒有，」她回答，「沒什麼巨人，只有一隻噁心的青蛙。」

　　「青蛙找你要幹嘛？」

　　「噢，親愛的父王，昨兒個我在森林的井邊玩耍時，金球掉到水裡去了。因為我哭得很傷心，青蛙就幫我撈回來。可是牠又硬要跟我作朋友，我只好答應牠了。我壓根兒沒想到牠可以從水裡跳出來。結果現在牠找上門來了呀。」

這時，再度傳來了敲門和喊叫聲：「公主啊，小公主，幫我開開門啊，你忘了你昨天在井邊，是怎麼跟我說的嗎？公主啊，小公主，幫我開門嘛。」

於是國王開口道：「你得遵守你的諾言，讓牠進來吧。」公主開了門，青蛙便跳了進來，亦步亦趨地跟著她來到椅子旁，然後坐下來，嘴裡喊著：「抱我上去，我要坐在你旁邊。」

pp. 76–77 她拖延了好久，不肯動手，直到國王命令她，她才照做。青蛙才坐上椅子，又想坐到桌上去，上了桌之後，牠就說：「把你的小金盤推過來一點嘛，這樣我們就能一塊兒吃啦。」她雖然照做了，卻顯然是千百個不願意。青蛙吃得津津有味，公主卻是一口也難以下嚥。終於，青蛙開口說道：「我吃得很飽足了，現在我累了，帶我到你的小房間，鋪好你那絲緞小床，我們一同就寢吧。」

公主哭了，她很怕冷冰冰的青蛙，連碰都不想碰，牠現在竟然還要睡在她可愛乾淨的小床上。可是國王卻生氣了，跟她說：「當你遇上了麻煩，是牠幫你解危的，事後你怎麼能看不起牠？」

於是公主用兩隻手指拎著青蛙，帶牠上樓，把牠放在牆角。公主才躺上床，青蛙就爬過來說：「我累了，我也要在床上睡覺，抱我上去，不然我要跟你父王告狀。」一聽到這句話，公主勃然大怒，一把抓起青蛙，用力丟到牆上。「你

這可惡的青蛙，現在你給我閉嘴。」她說著。

然而，等青蛙跌在地上時，已經不再是一隻青蛙，而是一位王子，他的眼眸和善而美麗。

pp. 78–79 遵照國王的旨意，王子娶了公主為妻，成為她最親密的伴侶。他告訴公主，他被一位邪惡的女巫施了魔咒，除了公主之外，沒有人能將他從井中救出來。明天，他們將一同回到王子的國度裡。

然後他們就上床睡覺了。次日清晨，陽光喚醒了小倆口，一輛由白馬拉載的馬車已經在等著他們。白馬頭上插著白色的鴕鳥羽毛，身上套著金色項圈，王子的僕人「忠僕亨利」就站在後面。

打從他的主子變成了青蛙以後，忠僕亨利就一直悶悶不樂，他在胸口套了三條鐵箍，以免他的心因悲慟與傷感而破裂。這輛馬車將引領這位年輕的國王回到自己的家園。忠僕亨利護著兩人上車，自己位在馬後，為這次王子能回復原形而滿心歡喜。

他們上路後，走了不遠，年輕的國王聽到身後傳來一陣爆裂聲，好像有什麼東西斷掉了，於是他回頭大喊：「亨利，馬車裂了。」

「不是的，主子，並不是馬車，是我心上的枷鎖。從您變成青蛙被困在井裡之後，我十分痛楚，便在胸口套上了鐵箍。」

在他們回程的路上，爆裂聲一次又一次地傳來，每次年輕的國王都以為馬車壞了，其實，那只是忠僕亨利掙脫心上鎖鍊的聲音，因為，他的主子獲得自由，過著幸福快樂的日子了。

7 睡美人

pp. 80–81 很久很久以前，有位國王和皇后，他們每天都會說著：「哎呀，要是我們能有個孩子，那該有多好啊！」但他們從未有過小孩。有一次，當皇后正在沐浴，一隻青蛙從水面爬到陸地上，對她說：「你的願望將會實現，在一年之內，你會生下一個女兒。」

青蛙說的話應驗了，皇后生下了一個非常漂亮的小女孩，國王樂不可支，便下令舉行盛大筵席來慶祝。他不僅邀請了親朋好友，也邀請了女巫師們，希望她們能善待並祝福這個小孩。

這個王國有十三位女巫師，可是因為國王只有十二個金盤子，可供女巫在宴會上用餐時使用，所以有一位女巫就得留在家裡，沒能受到邀請。

筵席盛大舉行，在接近尾聲時，十二位女巫以魔法賜福給小嬰兒——一位賜給她美德，一位賜給她美貌，第三位賜給她財富，其他人也陸續送上世人最想得到的東西給小女孩。

在十一位女巫都賜福完之後，第十三位女巫突然走了進來。為了報復自己沒被邀請的事，她招呼也不打，甚至沒瞄任何人一眼，就扯開嗓門大喊：「國王的女兒將在十五歲時被紡錘扎到，然後倒下死去。」她話一說完，就轉身離去。

pp. 82–83 大家聽了都很震驚，不過還未賜福的第十二位女巫師站了出來。雖然她無法解除這個惡毒的詛咒，但她能夠減輕魔咒的威力，於是她說：「小公主不會死去，她只是會沈睡上一百年。」

國王非常希望能讓寶貝孩子免於不幸，便下令把全國的紡錘都燒毀。就此期間，女巫們的祝福在小女孩身上一一實現，她如此美麗、謙虛、善良又聰明，每個看到她的人都一定會喜歡她。

就在她十五歲生日的那天，國王和皇后恰巧不在家，皇宮裡只剩下這位少女，於是她到處走走，隨興看看房間與臥室，最後來到了一座老塔樓。她爬上狹窄的迴旋式樓梯，來到一扇小門前，鑰匙孔上插著生鏽的鑰匙，當她轉動鑰匙時，門就自動打開了。在小房間裡，坐著一位拿著紡錘的老婆婆，正忙著紡亞麻。

「你好，老婆婆！」國王的女兒說：

「你在那裡做什麼呀？」

「我在紡紗啊！」老婆婆點點頭回答。

「那是什麼東西呀？轉動得這麼好聽？」女孩說完，便拿起紡錘也想紡紗。然而她一碰到紡錘，魔咒便生效了，她的手指被紡錘給扎到了。

pp. 84–85 她感到一陣刺痛，接著就倒在旁邊的床上，沈沈睡去。這陣睡眠擴及至整個皇宮，才剛回到家的國王與皇后，一踏進大廳就睡著了。宮廷裡全部的人也跟著睡著。馬兒也是一樣，走進馬棚裡睡著了，庭院裡的狗，屋頂上的鴿子，牆上的蒼蠅，甚至連爐灶上燃燒的熊熊火焰，都靜靜地睡去。烤肉不再煎得吱吱作響，洗碗的男孩忘了廚師交待的事情，廚師正要拉他的頭髮時，也放手睡著了；風不再吹了，城堡前樹木上的葉子，也停止了晃動。

然而，城堡四周的荊棘叢卻開始生長，它們一年長得比一年高，最後把整個城堡都給包圍覆蓋住，什麼都看不到了，連屋頂上的旗子也看不見。但是沈睡中美麗的荊棘薔薇——人們給公主取的名字，她的故事傳遍全國，所以不時會有王子來這裡，想穿過荊棘叢進到城堡裡去。

但他們發現這是不可能的，因為這些荊棘緊密地交纏在一起，就好像它們有手一樣，把王子們困住，無法掙開而慘死。

pp. 86–87 很多年以後，又有一位王子來到這個國家，他聽見一位老人談到荊棘叢的事，據說在荊棘叢下的城堡裡面有著一位非常美麗的公主，名字叫做薔薇，已經沈睡了一百年，而國王、皇后及整個宮廷的人也同樣地睡著了。王子也曾聽祖父說過，曾有許多國王的王子都來到這裡，想穿越荊棘叢，但緊緊深困其中，可憐地死去。

這位年輕人說：「我不怕，我要去看美麗的薔薇公主。」那位好心的老人極力勸阻他，但王子沒聽他的話。

就在這時，一百年的時間剛好到了，這天正是薔薇公主要醒來的日子。當王子走近荊棘叢，只見綻放的美麗花朵，花叢自動分開讓他得以毫髮無傷地通過，然後又像樹籬般在他身後密合。在城堡庭院裡，他看見馬兒和身上有斑點的獵犬趴睡著，停在屋頂上的鴿子也把頭埋在翅膀下。走進房子後，他看見蒼蠅在牆上睡著了，廚房裡的廚師還伸手要抓男孩，而女僕坐在黑母雞旁正準備要拔雞毛。

pp. 88–89 他再往前走，在大廳裡看見人們都睡著，王座旁躺著國王與皇后。

128

他繼續往前走，一切寂靜無聲，連呼吸聲都聽得到，最後他來到塔樓，打開門進入薔薇公主所睡的小房間。

公主就躺在那裡，她如此美麗，王子看得目不轉睛。他彎下腰吻了她，就在此時，薔薇公主張開雙眼醒來，溫柔地看著王子。

接著，他們倆一起下樓，國王、皇后以及整個宮廷的人，都跟著醒了過來，大家驚訝地互視。庭院裡的馬兒站起來抖抖身體，獵犬也跳起來搖搖尾巴，屋頂上的鴿子把頭從翅膀下抬起來，張望一下之後便展翅向開闊的郊外飛去，牆上的蒼蠅又開始爬來爬去，廚房裡的火焰也開始燃燒了起來，搖曳閃爍，烹煮著肉，肉翻著面火烤。廚師給了男孩一記耳光，打得他哇哇大叫，而女僕也拔完了雞毛。

之後，王子與薔薇公主舉行了盛大的婚禮，心滿意足地過了一生。

8 灰姑娘

pp. 90–91 有位富人的妻子病了，臨終前，她把自己的獨生女叫到床邊說：「乖孩子，你要聽話，要虔誠，老天爺會永遠庇佑你的，我也會在天上看著你，守在你身邊。」說完她就闔眼離開人世了。

小姑娘每天都會到母親的墳前哭泣，而她也一直乖巧而虔誠。冬天來臨時，降雪為墳墓鋪上了白色的床單；春日來時，陽光又將它卸去，而這時，那位富人也另續了新弦。

新妻子帶來了她的兩個女兒。她們長得很美麗、皮膚白皙，心腸卻很醜惡狠毒，可憐的小姑娘就要大難臨頭了。她們說：「這個笨女孩該不會要跟我們一同坐在客廳裡吧？想吃麵包就得自己掙，滾到廚房跟女僕作伴吧！」她們拿走她漂亮的衣裳，給她換上灰色長外衣，讓她穿木鞋，還大聲嘲笑說：「瞧瞧那位高傲的公主，現在這身時髦打扮！」然後便趕她到廚房去。

她在廚房裡，從早到晚都得辛苦幹活，天還沒亮就要起床挑水、生火、做飯、洗衣，除此之外，那兩姊妹還對她極盡欺負之能事——嘲弄羞辱她啊，把豌豆與扁豆倒進灰燼裡啊，讓她只得坐在那裡再把豆子給挑出來。到了晚上，她累得筋疲力盡時，卻連睡覺的床鋪也沒有，只好靠在爐火旁，睡在碳渣裡。也因此她看起來總是髒兮兮的，所以大家就叫她灰姑娘。

pp. 92–93 有一天，父親要上市集，他問妻子的兩個女兒，要帶什麼回來給她們。

第一個說：「我要漂亮的衣裳。」

第二個叫道：「我要珍珠和寶石。」

「那你呢？灰姑娘，」他問灰姑娘說：「你想要什麼呢？」

「父親，就把你回家路上第一根碰到你帽子的樹枝折給我吧。」

於是父親為前兩個女兒買了漂亮衣服和珍珠寶石。在回家的路上，他穿過一片綠油油的矮樹林，有一根細枝碰到了他，把帽子給掃了下來，於是他便折下這根樹枝，帶在身上。回到家裡時，他把前兩個女兒要的東西給了她們，並把樹枝交給灰姑娘。

灰姑娘向父親道了謝，來到母親的墳前，將樹枝種在墳上。她哭了又哭，淚水落在樹枝上，澆灌著它，於是樹枝長成了一棵漂亮的大樹。灰姑娘每天都要上墳三次，坐在墳邊哭泣禱告。而這時都會有一隻白色的小鳥棲在樹上，每當灰姑娘許下心願，小鳥都會為她實現。

有一天，國王為了幫王子選王妃，下令舉辦一個為期三天的節慶宴會，邀請全國年輕漂亮的女子前來參加。灰姑娘的兩個姐姐看到自己列在邀請單上，很是興奮，她們把灰姑娘叫來，說道：

「幫我們梳好頭髮，擦亮鞋子，繫好扣環，我們要去參加皇宮舉辦的宴會。」

pp. 94–95 灰姑娘一邊照著做，一邊哭了起來，因為她也想和她們一起去參加舞會。她哀求繼母讓她去，可繼母說道：「灰姑娘，你也想去？穿這身髒兮兮的衣服去嗎？你沒有衣服，又沒有鞋子，竟然還想跳舞。」

然而灰姑娘不停地哀求，繼母終於說道：「我把一盤扁豆倒進灰爐裡了，如果你能在兩小時內把它們揀出來，你就可以跟我們一起去。」

灰姑娘走出後門來到花園，喊著：「你們這些溫順的鴿子，還有天上所有的小鳥呀，來吧！幫我把好的扁豆挑到盤子裡，不好的裝進桶子裡吧。」

兩隻鴿子從廚房窗戶飛了進來，接著白鴿也來了，最後天空中所有的小鳥都撲打翅膀湧進來，落在灰爐上。鴿子們點著頭開始揀，一直揀啊，不停地揀，其他的鳥兒也開始揀，一直揀啊，不停地揀！牠們把所有好的穀子都揀到盤子裡，才一個小時就揀完，然後飛走。灰姑娘懷著興奮的心情，端著盤子去找繼母，以為自己可以跟她們一起去參加舞會了。

pp. 96–97 但繼母卻說：「不行！灰姑娘，你沒有衣服，又不會跳舞，只會被當成笑話的。」

灰姑娘哭了起來，繼母只好說：「如

果你能在一個小時之內把兩盤扁豆從灰燼裡揀出來，你就可以跟我們去。」繼母心想，這下她不可能再辦到了。在繼母將兩盤扁豆倒進灰燼時，灰姑娘走出後門到花園裡喊道：「你們這些溫順的鴿子、還有天上所有的小鳥呀，來吧！幫我把好的扁豆挑到盤子裡來，不好的裝進桶子裡吧。」

於是兩隻鴿子從廚房窗戶飛了進來，接著白鴿也來了，最後天上所有的小鳥都撲打翅膀湧進來，飛到灰燼上。鴿子們點著頭開始在灰燼裡揀起來，一顆一顆地揀，不停地揀！其他的鳥兒也開始揀，一顆一顆地揀，不停地揀！把所有的好種子揀到盤子裡，這次不到半個小時就揀完飛走了。

灰姑娘很高興，以為這下可以跟她們一起參加宴會了。但繼母卻說道：「你別再白費力氣了，你是不能去的。你沒有衣服，又不會跳舞，只會給我們丟臉。」說完便轉身與她兩個高傲的女兒急忙出發了。

pp. 98–99 現在，家裡的人都走光了，灰姑娘來到母親的墳前，在樹下哭著說：

「小樹啊，請搖一搖，為我抖落一套金銀禮服吧。」

於是小鳥為她拋下一套金銀製成的禮服，以及一雙絲與銀繡成的鞋子。灰姑娘急忙穿上禮服去參加宴會。她穿上金色禮服之後，看起來是如此的美麗，連她的繼母和姊妹們都認不出她，以為她是一位異國公主，壓根沒有想到會是灰姑娘，她們以為灰姑娘仍待在家中，揀灰燼裡的豆子呢。

王子向她走來，牽起她的手，跳起舞來。他不和其他的女孩跳舞，始終挽著灰姑娘的手不放。要是有人邀請灰姑娘跳舞，王子總回說：「這位女士是我的舞伴。」

灰姑娘一直跳舞跳到傍晚，才想起要回家。王子想知道這麼美麗的女孩是誰家姑娘，便說：「我送你回家去吧。」不過灰姑娘卻半路溜走，跳進了一間鴿舍裡。

王子在那裡等她父親回來，然後告訴他，那位不知名的女孩跳進鴿舍裡了。她父親心想：「會是灰姑娘嗎？」他們拿給他斧頭和鋤頭拆了鴿舍，不過裡面卻空無一人。

pp. 100–101 待大夥兒回到了家，灰姑娘已經穿上髒衣服躺在灰燼裡了，昏暗的小油燈還在架子上燃燒著。其實灰姑娘很快就從鴿舍後面跳了出來，跑到小樹前，脫下漂亮的禮服，將它們放在墳上，讓小鳥帶走，然後換上灰長衣坐回廚房的灰爐上。

第二天，舞會再度舉行，她的父親、繼母和兩個姐妹再次前去。灰姑娘來到墳前樹下說：「我的小樹啊，請你搖一搖，為我抖落金銀禮服吧。」

這次，小鳥為她拋下一件比昨天更美的禮服。當她穿著這套禮服來到宴會，所有人都為她的美驚訝不已。王子一直等著她來，她一來就牽住她的手，只跟她一個人跳舞。每當有人想邀她跳舞，王子總說：「這是我的舞伴。」

夜晚來臨時，她又要離開了，王子跟著她，想看她走進哪一幢房子。但她還是甩掉了他，跳進屋後的花園裡。花園裡有一棵漂亮的大梨樹，樹上結滿了香甜的梨子。灰姑娘像松鼠一樣，輕巧地攀在樹枝間，不讓王子知道她去哪裡。王子又一直等到她父親回來，對他說：「那個不知名的女孩溜走了，我猜她一定是跳上梨樹去了。」

pp. 102–103 父親暗想：「難道是灰姑娘嗎？」

於是他拿來一把斧子，把樹砍倒，但樹上根本沒人。等大家進到廚房時，灰姑娘又和平時一樣躺在灰爐裡了。原來她從樹的另一邊跳下來，脫下漂亮的禮服，讓墳前小樹上的小鳥帶回去，再穿上自己

的灰長衣。

第三天，父母和兩個姐妹離開之後，灰姑娘又來到母親的墳前，對著小樹說：「我的小樹啊，請你搖一搖，為我抖落一套金銀禮服吧。」

這次小鳥為她拋下一套比之前都還更要華麗動人的禮服，而且鞋子還是用金子做的。她穿著這身禮服來到舞會，大家都為她的美驚訝得說不出話。王子只肯與她跳舞，每當有其他人請她跳舞，王子總會說：「這是我的舞伴。」

夜晚來臨，灰姑娘要回家，王子急著要送她回去，但她又很快地甩開他，王子根本跟不上。但是王子想到一個點子，他下令把整個階梯抹上瀝青，當灰姑娘跑下階梯時，左腳的鞋子就給黏在階梯上了。

pp. 104–105 王子拾起鞋子，鞋子如此嬌小易碎，而且整隻都是用金子做的。次日早晨，王子拿著鞋子來到灰姑娘的父親面前，對他說：「誰的腳能剛好穿上這隻金鞋，誰就能成為我的妻子。」

灰姑娘的兩個姐妹非常高興，因為她們都有一雙漂亮的腳。大女兒把鞋子拿進房間裡試穿，母親陪在一旁看。可是鞋子太小了，她的大腳趾頭穿不進去。於是媽媽給了她一把刀，說道：「把大腳趾切了。等你當上皇后，還需要用腳走路嗎？」於是大女兒切掉腳趾頭，把腳硬塞進鞋子裡。

她忍著痛楚來到王子面前，王子便把她當成新娘抱上了馬，一同離開。

不過他們會經過墳墓，就在經過時，樹上的兩隻白鴿大喊著：「回頭瞧瞧！回頭瞧瞧！鞋子裡有鮮血，鞋太小，不是為她做的，真正的新娘還在等著你。」

王子看了她的腳，發現鮮血正從鞋裡滲出，他馬上回身將假新娘送回，說她不是真的新娘，於是就換她的妹妹試穿鞋子。妹妹把鞋子拿進房間，腳趾頭可以完全穿進鞋子，可是腳後跟卻太大了。

pp. 106–107 媽媽給了她一把刀子，說道：「把腳跟削掉一點，等你成了皇后，還犯得著用腳走路嗎？」女孩把腳跟削去一小截，把腳硬擠進鞋裡，忍著痛楚來到王子面前。

王子把她當做新娘抱上了馬，一起離開。當他們經過那棵樹時，樹上的兩隻白鴿又喊道：「回頭瞧瞧！回頭瞧瞧！鞋子裡有鮮血，鞋太小，不是為她做的，真正的新娘還在等著你。」

王子低頭一看，發現血正從鞋裡流出，連她的白色長襪也浸紅了，於是他就策馬回頭，把她送了回去。「也不是這一個，你還有別的女兒嗎？」

「沒了，」父親說：「只剩一個個頭嬌小的女傭，她是我前妻生前留下的女兒，她不可能是新娘的。」

王子命令

他把灰姑娘帶過來，可是這繼母卻回說：「噢，不行，她太髒了，見不得人的。」可是王子非常堅持，要求喚灰姑娘前來。

灰姑娘先把臉和手洗乾淨，走來對王子鞠了個躬。王子把金鞋拿給她穿，灰姑娘在凳子上坐下來，脫下笨重的木鞋，穿上鞋子，而鞋子穿在她腳上，簡直像是量身訂做的一樣。待灰姑娘起身，王子看著她的臉，認出這就是那位與他共舞的美麗女孩，喊道：「這才是我真正的新娘。」

pp. 108–109 繼母和她的兩個姐妹嚇了一跳，氣得臉都白了，而王子便抱著灰姑娘上馬，一同離開。

當他們經過樹邊時，兩隻白鴿叫道：「回頭瞧瞧吧！回頭瞧瞧吧！鞋子裡沒有血，鞋子剛剛好，與你共騎的正是你的新娘呀。」鴿子叫完後飛上前來，一左一右地停在灰姑娘的肩膀上。

在灰姑娘與王子的大喜之日時，兩位虛偽的姊妹跑來向灰姑娘示好，想分到一點好運。當這對準新人進了教堂，姊姊馬上跟在右邊，妹妹跟在左邊，可是鴿子卻分別啄瞎了她們的一顆眼睛。後來她們又跟了上來，這次姊姊站左邊，妹妹站右邊，結果鴿子又分別啄瞎她們的一顆眼睛。就這樣，姊妹倆因為虛偽又惡毒，受到了終生失明的懲罰。

Answers

1 Thumbling

(Answers will vary for open questions. 開放性問題，答案僅供參考。)

pp. 2–3

Stop & Think

- What is the peasant couple's wish?
  ➡ Their wish is to have a child.

- What did Thumbling want to do for his father?
  ➡ He wanted to bring the cart to him.

Check Up

1. **F**   2. **T**   3. **T**

pp. 4–5

Stop & Think

- How did Thumbling bring the cart to his father?
  ➡ He sat in the horse's ear and told him where to go.

- Why did the two strange men want to buy Thumbling?
  ➡ They wanted to exhibit him in a large town for money.

Check Up

1. **c**   2. **b**   3. **a**

pp. 6–7

Stop & Think

- Do you think it was right for the peasant to sell Thumbling?
  ➡ No, I don't think it was right for him to sell his son.
  ➡ Yes, I think it was right to sell Thumbling for a large sum of money.

- Did Thumbling really want to use the toilet?
  ➡ No, he didn't want to use the toilet.

Check Up

1. **slipped into**   2. **sum**
3. **frustration**

pp. 8–9

Stop & Think

- Look at "the rich pastor's silver and gold." Is a "pastor" a place, person, or thing?
  ➡ A pastor is a "person" because only a person can own silver and gold.

Check Up

1. **c**   2. **c**

Stop & Think

- Look at "went to the granary." Is a "granary" a place, person, or thing?
  ➡ A granary is a place because someone usually "goes to" a place.
- Did the maid find Thumbling in the barn?
  ➡ No, she didn't.

Check Up

1. **rascal**   2. **soundly**   3. **thieves**
4. **light**

Stop & Think

- Was Thumbling in a real room?
  ➡ No, he wasn't in a real room. He was in a cow's stomach.
- Why was the cow killed?
  ➡ The pastor thought that an evil spirit had gone into the cow.

Check Up

1. **F**   2. **F**   3. **T**

Stop & Think

- What did Thumbling say to make the wolf bring him home?
  ➡ He told the wolf that there was a magnificent feast at his father's house.
- Look at "in the pantry." Is a "pantry" a person, place, or thing?
  ➡ A pantry is a place because "ate . . . in the" is usually followed by the name of a place or a time of day, and it's not a time of day.

Check Up

2   3   1   4

Stop & Think

- Why did the peasant tell his wife to take away her scythe?
  ➡ He didn't want Thumbling to be hurt by the scythe.
- Did Thumbling's father regret selling Thumbling?
  ➡ Yes, he did, and so he went through sorrow for Thumbling's sake.

Check Up

1. **fetched**   2. **sorrow**   3. **spoiled**

2 Little Red Riding Hood

Stop & Think

- When did Little Red Riding Hood set out for her grandmother's house?
  ➡ She set out early in the morning before it got hot.
- What might the wolf do when he finds out where the grandmother lives?
  ➡ He might eat the grandmother.

Check Up

1. **d**   2. **c**   3. **a**   4. **b**

Stop & Think

- Why did the wolf want Little Red Riding Hood to look around?
  ➡ He wanted her to go off the path so he could run to her grandmother's house first.
- Did Little Red Riding Hood run off the path?
  ➡ Yes, she ran off the path.

Check Up

1. **T**   2. **F**   3. **F**

Stop & Think

- How did Little Red Riding Hood feel when she went into the room?
  ➡ She felt uncomfortable.
- What weird things did Little Red Riding Hood notice when she saw her grandmother?
  ➡ She noticed that her grandmother had big ears, big eyes, large hands, and a big mouth.

Check Up

1. **gathered**   2. **curtains**
3. **cottage**   4. **received**

Stop & Think

- Why didn't the hunter fire at the wolf?
  ➡ He realized that the wolf might have eaten the grandmother and that she might still be saved.
- What did Little Red Riding Hood learn after this terrible event?
  ➡ She learned never again to leave the path by herself and run into the woods.

Check Up

1. **b**   2. **a**

Stop & Think

- What did Little Red Riding Hood do when she met another wolf?
  ➡ She went straight forward on her way and told her grandmother that she had met the wolf.
- Where did the second wolf die?
  ➡ He died in a stone trough.

Check Up

3   4   2   1

3 The Golden Goose

pp. 28–29

Stop & Think

- How was Dummling treated on every occasion?
  ➡ He was despised, mocked, and sneered at.
- Why did the grey-haired old man punish the eldest and second sons?
  ➡ Because they didn't want to share their cake and wine with him. /
  Because they cared only about themselves.

Check Up

1. **F** 2. **F** 3. **T**

pp. 30–31

Stop & Think

- Did Dummling get the same cake and wine as his brothers had gotten?
  ➡ No, he didn't. /
  No, he got ash cake and a bottle of sour beer.
- Why did the old grey-haired man give Dummling the goose?
  ➡ Because Dummling had a good heart and was willing to share what he had.

Check Up

1. **b** 2. **c** 3. **a**

pp. 32–33

Stop & Think

- What happened when the eldest daughter grabbed the goose by the wing?
  ➡ Her fingers and hand remained stuck to the goose's wing.
- How many people were running after Dummling and his goose?
  ➡ Four people were running after them.

Check Up

1. **c** 2. **c**

pp. 34–35

Stop & Think

- How did the bell-ringer feel when he saw the five people running?
  ➡ He was shocked.
- Why did the princess finally laugh?
  ➡ Because she saw so many people running after Dummling and the goose.

Check Up

1. **workmen** 2. **son-in-law** 3. **set; free**

pp. 36–37

Stop & Think

- Do you think the little old grey-haired man helped Dummling?
  ➡ Yes, I think he helped him. /
  No, I think he caused problems for him.
- What must Dummling do to marry the princess this time?
  ➡ He must find a man who can eat a whole mountain of bread.

Check Up

1. **quench** 2. **cellar** 3. **furious** 4. **strap**

Stop & Think

- How long did it take the man to finish eating the huge mountain of bread?
  - ➡ It took him less than one day to eat it.
- Do you think Dummling was really a stupid man? Why or why not?
  - ➡ No, I don't think he was really a stupid man, because he knew how to get help when he faced problems. /
    Yes, I think he was really a stupid man, because he didn't worry about all the people who were stuck to his goose.

Check Up

4   3   2   1

4 Hansel and Gretel

Stop & Think

- Why couldn't the wood-cutter sleep at night?
  - ➡ Because he could no longer earn enough for himself and his family.
- What did the stepmother plan to do to Hansel and Gretel?
  - ➡ She planned to leave them alone in the forest.

Check Up

1. tossed   2. upset
3. unable   4. stepmother

Stop & Think

- What did Hansel put in his pocket?
  - ➡ He put white pebbles in his pocket.
- Why did Hansel keep throwing the white pebbles onto the road?
  - ➡ He was trying to mark the way home.

Check Up

1. T   2. F   3. F

Stop & Think

- Where did the children sit down and rest?
  - ➡ They sat down by the fire.
- When did Hansel take his little sister by the hand and follow the pebbles?
  - ➡ He did it when the moon had risen.

Check Up

1. F   2. T   3. F

Stop & Think

- How did the wood-cutter feel when he saw that the children had come back?
  - ➡ He rejoiced, for it had broken his heart to leave them behind alone.
- What did Hansel use to mark the way home this time?
  - ➡ He used crumbs.

Check Up

1. scolded   2. crumbled   3. guilty

Stop & Think

- Why did Hansel keep stopping and looking around?
  ➡ So that he could mark the way home with his crumbs.
- When did the children awake?
  ➡ They awoke at night.

Check Up

1. b   2. c

Stop & Think

- Look at "on the roof of which it settled." What does "it" refer to?
  ➡ It refers to a beautiful snow-white bird.
- What were the windows of the little house made of?
  ➡ They were made of clear sugar.

Check Up

1. exhausted   2. nibbled
3. settled   4. approached

Stop & Think

- How did Hansel and Gretel feel when they saw the ancient woman?
  ➡ They were terribly frightened.
- Why did the witch lure children to her house?
  ➡ So that she could kill and eat them.

Check Up

1. crutches   2. escape   3. harm

Stop & Think

- What sort of food did Gretel eat at the witch's house?
  ➡ She ate crab shells.
- What did Hansel do to make the witch think that he was still thin?
  ➡ He stuck out a little bone to her instead of his finger.

Check Up

1. c   2. d   3. b   4. a

Stop & Think

- What will Gretel probably do after the witch gets into the oven?
  ➡ She will probably close the oven door.
- What did the children find in the house?
  ➡ They found chests full of pearls and jewels.

Check Up

2   4   3   1

Stop & Think

- How did the children cross the stream?
  ➡ They rode on the back of a white duck.
- How did the father feel after he left his children in the forest?
  ➡ He felt very unhappy.

Check Up

1. c   2. a

5 Rumpelstiltskin

pp. 62–63

Stop & Think

- What special skill did the miller say his daughter had?
  ➡ He said that she could spin straw into gold.
- Did the miller lie to the king?
  ➡ Yes, he did, because his daughter had no idea how to spin straw into gold.

Check Up

1. **T**   2. **F**   3. **F**

pp. 64–65

Stop & Think

- What did the little man take from the miller's daughter the first time?
  ➡ He took her necklace.
- What will happen if the miller's daughter succeeds in spinning all of the straw into gold?
  ➡ The king will marry her.

Check Up

1. **b**   2. **b**

pp. 66–67

Stop & Think

- What did the little man want from the miller's daughter the third time?
  ➡ He wanted her first child if she became a queen.
- How could the queen stop the little man from taking her baby away?
  ➡ She had to find out his name within three days.

Check Up

1. **lament**   2. **pitied**   3. **messenger**

pp. 68–69

Stop & Think

- Where did the little man live?
  ➡ He lived by a high mountain at the end of the forest.
- How did Rumpelstiltskin feel when the queen told him his real name?
  ➡ He was in a rage.

Check Up

4   **2**   **3**   **1**

6 The Frog King

pp. 70–71

Stop & Think

- What did the youngest princess do when she was bored?
  ➡ She played with a golden ball.
- Why did the princess begin to cry?
  ➡ Because her golden ball had rolled into a well.

Check Up

1. F   2. T   3. F

pp. 72–73

Stop & Think

- What could the frog do to help the princess?
  ➡ He could bring her ball back to her.
- Did the princess take her promise seriously?
  ➡ No, she thought it was impossible for a frog to be a companion to a human being.

Check Up

1. c   2. a

pp. 74–75

Stop & Think

- How did the princess feel when she saw the frog outside the door?
  ➡ She was frightened.
- What did the king command the princess to do?
  ➡ He commanded her to open the door and let the frog in.

Check Up

1. d   2. c   3. b   4. a

pp. 76–77

Stop & Think

- Where did the frog want to sleep after the meal?
  ➡ He wanted to sleep on the princess's bed.
- What did the frog turn into after he fell down?
  ➡ He turned into a handsome prince.

Check Up

1. choke   2. satisfied
3. hesitated   4. willingly

pp. 78–79

Stop & Think

- Why did the prince become a frog?
  ➡ Because he was cursed by a wicked witch.
- When did Faithful Henry put iron bands on his heart?
  ➡ He did it when his master was a frog and was imprisoned in the well.

Check Up

1. cursed   2. salvation   3. imprisoned

7 Little Briar Rose

pp. 80–81

Stop & Think

- How many wise women did the king invite to the feast?
  - ➡ He invited twelve of them.
- Why did the thirteenth wise woman want revenge?
  - ➡ Because she hadn't been invited to the feast.

Check Up

1. **fulfilled**   2. **splendor**
3. **contain**   4. **revenge**

pp. 82–83

Stop & Think

- How did the twelfth wise woman prevent the princess from dying?
  - ➡ She changed the curse of death into a curse of sleep.
- Where did the princess find the old woman?
  - ➡ She found her in a little room in an old tower.

Check Up

1. **T**   2. **F**   3. **F**

pp. 84–85

Stop & Think

- What happened to everyone in the palace?
  - ➡ They all fell asleep.
- Why couldn't the princes get through the thorny hedge into the castle?
  - ➡ Because the thorns stuck fast together and the princes got caught in them.

Check Up

2   4   3   1

pp. 86–87

Stop & Think

- Why did the old man try his best to dissuade the prince from going to the castle?
  - ➡ Because many kings' sons had died in the thorny hedge when they tried to get through it.
- What did the thorny hedge turn into when the king's son came near it?
  - ➡ It turned into large and beautiful flowers.

Check Up

1. **b**   2. **a**

pp. 88–89

Stop & Think

- How did the princess awake?
  - ➡ She awoke when the prince kissed her.
- How was the marriage of the prince and princess celebrated?
  - ➡ It was celebrated with all splendor.

Check Up

1. **throne**   2. **wagged**   3. **contentedly**

8 Cinderella

pp. 90–91

Stop & Think

- What kind of people were Cinderella's two sisters?
  ➡ They were evil and cruel.

- Why did the two sisters call the girl Cinderella?
  ➡ Because she always looked dusty and dirty.

Check Up

1. **F**   2. **T**   3. **F**

pp. 92–93

Stop & Think

- What did Cinderella want from her father?
  ➡ She wanted the first branch which knocked against his hat on his way home.

- How many days would the festival last?
  ➡ It would last three days.

Check Up

1. **d**   2. **c**   3. **b**   4. **a**

pp. 94–95

Stop & Think

- Who did Cinderella ask to help her pick the lentils?
  ➡ She asked birds to help her.

- Where did the birds gather all the good grains?
  ➡ They gathered them into a dish.

Check Up

1. **c**   2. **b**

pp. 96–97

Stop & Think

- Do you think Cinderella will be able to go to the festival this time? Why or why not?
  ➡ Yes, she will, because the bird will help her pick the lentils out of the ashes. /
    No, she won't, because her stepmother doesn't want her to go.

- How long did the birds take to finish gathering all the good seeds this time?
  ➡ They took less than half an hour.

Check Up

1. **delighted**   2. **ashamed of**
3. **certainly**

pp. 98–99

Stop & Think

- What did the white bird give Cinderella?
  ➡ It gave her a gold and silver dress and slippers.

- How did the prince feel about Cinderella?
  ➡ He liked her so much that he would not dance with anyone else.

Check Up

1. **assumed**   2. **leapt**   3. **silk**

pp. 100–101

Stop & Think

- Why did Cinderella take off her beautiful clothes?
  - ➡ Because she didn't want anyone to know she had gone to the festival.
- What was special about the tall tree?
  - ➡ There were magnificent pears on it.

Check Up

1. F   2. T   3. F

pp. 102–103

Stop & Think

- What color were Cinderella's slippers this time?
  - ➡ They were golden.
- Why did Cinderella's left slipper remain stuck?
  - ➡ Because there was pitch on the staircase.

Check Up

4   2   1   3

pp. 104–105

Stop & Think

- What did the mother tell her eldest daughter to do?
  - ➡ She told her to cut her big toe off.
- What will the mother probably tell her other daughter to do to fit her foot into the shoe?
  - ➡ She will probably tell her to cut part of her heel off.

Check Up

1. peep   2. dripping
3. heel   4. delicate

pp. 106–107

Stop & Think

- What did the prince insist on?
  - ➡ He insisted on having Cinderella sent to him.

Check Up

1. b   2. b

pp. 108–109

Stop & Think

- Why did the two false sisters come to Cinderella's wedding?
  - ➡ Because they wanted to get into favor with Cinderella and share her good fortune.
- Will the two false sisters be able to see anymore?
  - ➡ No, they will not, because they have no eyes.

Check Up

1. d   2. c   3. b   4. a